Caitlin's Escape Route

Aideen Walsh

Copyright © 2024 Aideen Walsh

All rights reserved.

ISBN: 9798871645178

DEDICATION

To my husband, who never reads anything I write, but supports me in everything I do.

CONTENTS

DEDICATION iii

Contents v

ACKNOWLEDGMENTS i

Chapter One 1

Chapter Two 11

Chapter Three 21

Chapter Four 30

Chapter Five 36

Chapter Six 42

Chapter Seven 50

Chapter Eight 56

Chapter Nine 62

Chapter Ten 68

Chapter Eleven 73

Chapter Twelve 78

Chapter Thirteen 87

Chapter Fourteen 91

Chapter Fifteen 96

Chapter Sixteen 103

Chapter Seventeen 108

Chapter Eighteen 113

Chapter Nineteen 118

Chapter Twenty 124

Chapter Twenty-One 131

Chapter Twenty-Two 138

Chapter Twenty-Three 143

Chapter Twenty-Four 149

Chapter Twenty-Five 155

Chapter Twenty-Six 160

Chapter Twenty-Seven 164

Chapter Twenty-Eight 169

Chapter Twenty-Nine 175

Chapter Thirty 180

Chapter Thirty-One 184

Chapter Thirty-Two 189

Chapter Thirty-Three 193

Chapter Thirty-Four 200

Chapter Thirty-Five 204

ABOUT THE AUTHOR 209

ACKNOWLEDGMENTS

A big thank you to my sister for her constant support and editorial skills. My children who, like my husband, support me in everything I do. A special thank you to Jen and Pavi, my early beta readers and to my daughter-in-law, Rachael, an accomplished writer herself. Rachael and her book club were beta readers and supplied me with invaluable feedback.

CHAPTER ONE

The shrill scream almost caused Caitlin to drop the phone.

"Terri? Terri? What's going on?" she yelled.

There was no response. Caitlin could hear a man shouting, then some loud thumps.

"Terri?" she said again, shaking the phone as though that would somehow help.

More muffled noises followed by another scream. Silence for a few seconds, then a loud crash, and the line went dead.

Caitlin immediately hit redial. After three rings, her sister's voicemail picked up. She hung up and tried twice more. Each time, all she got was voicemail. And each time, it became more difficult to breathe. She felt as though her lungs could not function. The third time, she left a message asking Terri to call her back immediately.

What do I do now? She thought, her heart racing. She looked around the room as if for inspiration. It took her two attempts to stand up. She forced herself to take a couple of deep breaths.

Taking the narrow stairs two at a time, Caitlin bounded down the three flights from the attic flat, out the front door and down the stone steps to the basement flat. She hammered on the door until a slim man in his twenties opened it.

"Caitlin, what's up? Are you alright?"

"Oh Jim! I don't know what to do." Caitlin stood, holding her cell phone out to him, tears pouring down her face.

"My God, what's wrong?" he said, taking her arm and leading her into the kitchen. He handed her a tissue.

Caitlin wiped her face and took a deep breath.

"That's better. Sit down. I'll make some tea and you can tell me what the problem is." He put the kettle on and set a couple of mugs on the counter. Giving her time to regain her composure.

"I was on the phone with Terri. She called to tell me she was leaving Keith," Caitlin said, taking another deep breath. "Apparently, he became abusive almost as soon as they moved to California. She kept hoping it'd stop, but it got worse." Sipping the tea Jim had placed on the table in front of her, she continued. "She said he'd just left for a business trip, and she packed up and was about to leave for Seattle."

"Okay." Jim looked at her with his eyebrows raised. "And then?"

"Then I heard a scream. I could hear a man yelling. It sounded like the phone fell. I heard some more noises and a few more screams and then silence."

"I assume you tried calling her back?"

"Three times. It just went to voicemail. What can I do?"

"First, calm down, then call the police in—where're they living now?"

"San Mateo. You're right, I need to call the police!"

Caitlin grabbed at her phone, then looked up at him. "I need to find their number."

"Hang on, I'm searching," he said, looking up from his phone. "Okay, ready?"

As he called out the number, she tapped away, then listened to the series of clicks as technology took over and connected her cellphone to the number in California.

"My name is Caitlin Donnelly. I'm calling from Dublin, Ireland," she said, as soon as the call picked up.

She related exactly what had happened. Then followed a series of questions. Terri's husband Keith's full name. Their address, and her relationship with Terri.

"She's my twin sister and I'm her only living relative."

Finally, they said they'd check it out and call her back if they needed more information or if they had anything to report.

The call disconnected and Caitlin sat, staring dumbly at her phone. She felt there was a lead lump in her chest; it was pressing her against the chair. Once again, she couldn't breathe.

Just then, the door opened, and a tall man in a pilot's uniform came in.

"Oh, hey Caitlin, how are you doing?"

She took a deep breath and tried to think straight. "Hi Paddy. Not so good." She bit her lip, determined not to cry.

Paddy looked from her to Jim, who explained the problem to Paddy. He squatted down beside her.

"We never trusted that arsehole, Keith, and I know you didn't either. They're in The San Francisco Bay Area? Right?"

Caitlin nodded.

"I'm scheduled to fly to SFO first thing tomorrow morning. I'll make a couple of calls and see if we can't get you a seat on the flight. If there's a free seat, we can get you a buddy pass." Paddy stood up and pulled out his phone.

Caitlin jumped to her feet. "I need to pack a bag and make sure I have both my Irish and my US passports." She already felt better now that she could take action and do something.

As she hurried towards the front door, Jim chased after her with her phone.

"Don't forget this. The cops over there might call you back."

"Okay, you've got a seat on my flight," Paddy called out to her. "We leave here at six in the morning."

Caitlin rushed back into the kitchen and hugged both of the men before running back out again.

She climbed the stairs back up to her flat as fast as she had come down over an hour earlier. She packed a small roller bag with the minimum; a large bag would slow her down. She could buy anything she needed once she found Terri. Although it was almost eight pm, she wasn't hungry. She paced around the flat, wondering how on earth she would sleep tonight? *What had happened to Terri? Was she hurt?* A knock on the door interrupted her thoughts.

Paddy and Jim came in with fish and chips and a bottle of wine.

"You've got to eat something, and a glass of wine will help you relax. Just be sure to set your alarm," Jim said, as Paddy set the table.

"Thank you, guys." Caitlin blinked back tears. She had done enough crying. She hated crying. It wasn't something she did very often. "You've always been there for me."

As they were clearing off the table, Caitlin's phone rang. All three of them stood still and looked at it for a second before she made a grab for it.

"Hello—Yes, this is Caitlin Donnelly."

Jim and Paddy still hadn't moved as they watched Caitlin. Suddenly, she sat down on the nearest chair.

"Oh, my God! No! Is she okay—okay, thank you! I'll be there tomorrow evening."

"What?" both men said at the same time.

Caitlin swallowed hard. "Terri's in the hospital in San Francisco. The police sent someone to check on her after I called. I guess that was almost four hours ago now. The house was on fire. Someone had called 911." She shook her head. "They found her locked in an upstairs room, unconscious."

"Try to get some sleep, Cait. I'll be outside waiting for you at six in the morning," Paddy said. "I have to get to bed myself now." The two men left.

Next morning, Caitlin was standing on the graveled driveway at five thirty. As she stood waiting for Paddy, she stared across the street, watching the tide roll in. Thinking about her sister and what they had been through together.

Why does Terri always believe the best of everyone, and I believe the worst? Once again, she has been proved wrong. I told her Keith couldn't be trusted. Oh, I hope she is okay.

Paddy came out of the basement flat, interrupting her thoughts.

"Good morning, Caitlin. Have you have been standing here all night?"

"Not exactly, but I got very little sleep. Hopefully, I'll sleep on the plane."

"I'm sure you will. It is a direct flight, Dublin to San Francisco."

As soon as they got to the airport, Paddy organized her tickets for her and left her at the check-in counter.

"See you on board," he said as he headed off with the rest of the flight crew.

Two hours later, with the long line at security, passport and US immigration, and then a second security check behind her, Caitlin finally arrived at the gate. She heard her name being called to report to the counter. There, she was told that Paddy had requested they put her on the wait list for an upgrade. There was a seat available for her in first class. She decided this was a good omen.

As they got ready to take off, she heard Paddy's voice on the intercom, welcoming the passengers and advising them they would be in San Francisco in approximately ten and a half hours.

Thank God for Paddy and Jim. They have always been there for me.

Before closing her eyes, she asked the flight attendant to wake her when they were serving meals. She got about five hours of reasonable sleep, somewhat broken. By the time they landed, she was ready to get off the plane and find Terri. Paddy stood at the door to the cockpit, smiling and thanking the passengers as they left. When she passed him, he told her to wait at the arrival gate for him and they could go into the city together. She found a seat as she exited the gangway and waited. There was a short gap between the last of the passengers and the flight crew. Paddy spotted her and came over.

"I'm going to get a taxi to my hotel. We'll get it to drop you off at the hospital on the way. You said she is at Stanford Medical Center?"

"Yes. But isn't that out of your way?"

"My hotel is in San Carlos; Palo Alto isn't that much further."

"Great, thanks."

Because she hadn't checked in any bags, they went straight to the exit since all the immigration and customs had been taken care of before departure.

Less than thirty minutes later, Caitlin climbed out of the taxi and the driver lifted her bag out of the trunk and placed it on the sidewalk in front of the main entrance to the hospital. Paddy gave her a hug and wished her good luck.

"Where're you going to stay tonight?"

"I don't know, probably here at the hospital with Terri, or I'll find a hotel nearby. That's the least of my worries."

"Okay. Call me if you need anything at all. Give our love to Terri."

He got back in the cab as Caitlin hurried into the hospital.

At reception they directed her to the ICU where she found Terri, bruised, and battered but sitting up in a hospital bed. A nurse was removing the IV from her arm as Caitlin walked in. She stood there speechless, trying to recognize her sister behind the swollen, bruised face. Her honey blonde hair was tied back in a messy ponytail and her brown eyes were bloodshot, one of them almost closed, surrounded by purple bruises.

Dear God, I want to kill that bastard, Keith! She thought, fighting back the urge to punch the wall.

Caitlin's Escape Route

"Caitlin!" Terri cried out. "I'm so glad you're here!"

"Did...did he do this to you?" She almost whispered. She swallowed hard. "What happened?"

"As I was talking to you, Keith came back. He'd forgotten something. Of course, he assumed I was going to meet some imaginary lover. Not that it would have made much difference. When I told him I was leaving him, he lost it." Terri paused and took a sip of water before continuing. "He hit me so hard I slammed into the wall and fell to the ground. He kicked me—I don't know how many times. I lost consciousness. The next thing I know I was being loaded into an ambulance. He set fire to the house, Cait! I could have died!"

The nurse finished up, putting the drip away. "We're moving her out of ICU and into a ward now. There's a waiting room just past the nurses' station. I'll come get you once she's settled." She nodded to an orderly who had just come in and was standing by the end of the bed.

Caitlin understood there was no point in arguing. She watched as they pushed her sister's bed out of the ICU and down the hall to the elevators. She found the room the nurse had directed her to and waited. Thankfully, the room was empty. It was the first time she had felt able to think since she heard that scream on the phone. *Was that just yesterday?* It seemed longer, so much had happened.

At least Terri's alive. But this should never have happened.

Of course, she knew it happened. She, too, had been a victim of this sort of violence. She had become a nurse to help people.

Fat lot of help I was to Terri. It's not enough to heal their wounds; we need to do something to stop it happening in the first place.

The nurse's return interrupted her thoughts. She gave her the room number, and her directions. She found Terri sitting up in bed, waiting for her.

"Where is Keith now?" she said as she perched on the side of the bed, studying her sister's battered face.

Terri sighed, "I don't know. My boss said that he had called the office trying to find out where I was. Of course, they didn't give him any information."

"So, clearly he knows you escaped the fire."

"The police are looking for him. I mean, obviously he's wanted for questioning. I can testify that he beat me up. Presumably he set fire to the house as well, and they had to break down the door to get me out." She paused. "The police are fairly confident they can charge him, but it's just my word against his if they ever find him—unless they can find any witnesses to him setting the fire."

"Didn't he grow up around here? Does he still have family in the area?"

Terri nodded. "Yes, he lived in Northern Cal until he was twelve, but no longer has family here. His parents died in a car wreck. He had to go live with his uncle in Ireland. That was the only family he had."

"So, he's on his own."

"Yes, but apparently he cleaned out our bank account, so he has plenty of cash."

Caitlin stood up and walked over to the window. It looked out over the parking lot to the back of the hospital. She watched cars pulling up and people hurrying into the hospital. Visiting time was in progress.

Keith won't let Terri go. He'll come after her, either to try to reconcile or to finish her. Caitlin knew Keith had tried to get them to break their trust fund. *Thank goodness we didn't, but he probably won't let the opportunity for a share go so easily!* She looked out beyond the parking lot, to Palo Alto. The city where they were born and now she was finally home. *But we can't stay here now. We have to get away.*

Terri watched her, saying nothing. She was nodding off when Caitlin finally turned around and came to stand beside the bed.

"We need to get you out of here, and we need to leave California. We can't be sure that Keith won't try to find you. There's no guarantee that the police will catch up with him. If they do, we can't rely on the law when it comes to domestic violence—especially when there were no other witnesses."

"So, what do you suggest?" Terri asked.

"You remember Angela, from my Aikido club? She moved to Texas last month. We can head there, at least to start off with. I know we can stay with her until we decide what to do next. According to Angela, there are lots of high-tech jobs in Austin where she's living. You could easily get another job there—if you want to."

"But you have been waiting to return to the Bay Area since you were nine years old, Cait. It's all you ever talked about. Now you are finally here."

"It's safer. At least till they catch him. We can always come back then."

Terri just nodded and waited for her sister to continue.

"I'll go rent a car and get you some clothes. We should head off this evening." Caitlin waited for Terri to say something.

"You mean we don't wait for them to discharge me?"

"Correct. We can't afford to waste time. If you're out of the ICU, you're out of danger. Besides, I'm a nurse, you'll have undivided care. The longer we hang around now, the more chance there is that Keith will come looking for you. Besides that, we don't want to leave any information with the hospital that might help him track you down. We can worry about settling any bill when we're out of state. You can call your office once we're on the road; they won't be expecting you back anytime soon."

Caitlin gathered her things and left, telling Terri she would be back before the end of visiting time.

It didn't take as long as she expected. Although Terri had lost everything in the fire, she just bought the minimum to get them to Texas. Before leaving the mall, she found the information desk; they directed her to a car dealership down a side street. Next to the service area was a car rental. Less than an hour later, she drove into the hospital parking lot in a mid-sized Ford.

Terri got dressed with help from Caitlin and they merged with the groups of visitors, heading to the elevators. A ball cap and sunglasses mostly covered Terri's injuries, and she kept her head down. They got to the car without incident and headed towards the Dumbarton Bridge. Terri dozed off almost immediately, and Caitlin concentrated on the road. Although she had been back to the US a few times on vacation and had experience driving on the right-hand side of the road, she had never done it immediately after a long transatlantic flight, and a gut-wrenching shock, like that when she saw Terri's injuries. Although Terri was sleeping, she was clearly not relaxing. It seemed that she opened her eyes and sat up every twenty minutes, looking around with wide eyes, before sighing and closing them again.

Less than two hours later, they pulled into a motel just outside Los Banos, where they got a room. They had something to eat in a Denny's next door. Once back in the motel room, Caitlin pulled a bottle of wine out of her backpack. She opened it and filled up two of the small plastic cups from the bathroom.

"Here's what I think we should do, Terri. I have been thinking about this for a while, not just on the way here."

"Go to Texas, I know, you said."

"Yes, but when we get there." Caitlin paused. "You remember that incident with Mack after the Christmas party when he got rough?"

"I remember, that was when Jim and Paddy rescued you and you swore off men."

"Well, ever since that night I've wondered what it must be like to be tied to a man like that—I hesitate to say you're lucky, but at least you're free of Keith now. Imagine what it would be like if you were stuck with him? And if Jim and Paddy hadn't been there—who knows what Mack would have done to me? Since then, I've seen a few victims of domestic violence when I was working in the emergency room. It was awful!" Caitlin paused and studied her sister's injuries. "Some were even worse injuries than yours. One woman lost an eye. I wanted to prevent it. I've been working on a plan to start an escape route for victims of domestic violence; that was part of the reason I did my master's in psychology. Nurses can help the physical wounds to heal. There's so much damage done psychologically that needs to be fixed too. Something needs to be done to stop it from happening. We can afford to go wherever we want, and we have each other; we need to help victims who are less fortunate."

"I think that's a terrific idea, Cait. But how can we do that?"

"Working with the shelters for battered women could be a good starting point. We can talk about it as we drive."

Next morning, they were up early, filled up the tank and after a quick breakfast at the same Denny's, they headed for I-5, turning towards Bakersfield and I-40. They drove through Albuquerque, New Mexico, and then headed south. By the time they reached Austin, Texas, three days after leaving California, they had formed a plan and were excited to put it into action.

***

Keith left the store and crossed to the parking lot. Putting on his helmet, he climbed on the Yamaha and headed over the bridge and out of Seattle. He wondered if they had found his car.

I doubt it. That gorge was deep and by the time it hit bottom, I couldn't see it through the trees.

He didn't want to dump it, but they would surely have found him if he hadn't.

Luckily, we had enough in the bank to keep me going, and I was smart enough to clean it out before they started looking for me.

He had bought a used motorbike for cash to replace the car. Getting the job at the computer repair shop was a no brainer. He didn't need to tell them he was a computer programmer, just to show that he knew enough about computers and mobile devices to do the job. Of course, it was way below his pay grade, but it was work and it was also unlikely anyone would think to look for him there. He pulled around to the back of the motel and locked up his bike, out of sight from the road.

His plan was to get himself an apartment and then figure out his next steps. He was pretty sure that Terri had come to Seattle. After all, the company she worked for had offices there. That is where he would start.

He was so sure that returning to California was the right thing to do—for both of them. They were both born here, and both had similar experiences; being moved to Ireland as kids, both beaten by people who should have been protecting them. Terri by her father. His uncle was as bad, or worse. He was always drunk and always violent. He remembered when he finally was big enough to fight back.

I got so much satisfaction from beating the shit out of him. Keith thought, remembering leaving his tormentor in a bloody heap on the kitchen floor. That was the last time he saw him.

It just didn't work out the way he had hoped. If only Terri had got a job at the same company as he had, then she wouldn't have made friends with people he didn't know. He had to track her down and talk some sense into her.

Damn whoever called 911. If they hadn't arrived so quickly, I might have gotten away with it. At least they didn't see me. And damn Terri. I just know she was flirting with those guys she works with. This whole thing is her fault.

CHAPTER TWO

Caitlin and Terri pulled into the long driveway that curled in a circle around a large pecan tree in front of Aunt May's home. As Angela said, it was a big house. They climbed out of the car and stretched.

"I can't believe how hot it is! Lucky, we bought little in the way of clothes before we left California. They'd surely have been too warm for here," Caitlin said.

"What the hell is that noise? It seems to be all around us, in the air!" Terri said, pressing the doorbell. Angela opened the door and hugged her friends. She was almost as short as Caitlin, with curly brown hair and gray eyes.

"Sorry about the hug, Caitlin. You'll have to get used to it. Everyone hugs you here," she said.

I will never get used to that. Caitlin shuddered. She didn't enjoy getting that close to anyone except her sister, and maybe Jim and Paddy.

"Hey Angela, what's that noise?" Terri said again.

Angela laughed. "Cicadas, you'd think they were huge from the noise, wouldn't you? They're big—for insects, but that loud continuous buzzing and whining is part of living in central Texas. You'll get used to it. Come in. Aunt May is looking forward to meeting you." She led them into a large, open space. The kitchen and dining area were at the back, with a vast living space at the front of the house.

As they entered the living room, a gray-haired lady looked up from her book. She was sitting in a comfortable leather recliner with a small, adjustable table to one side and a pair of crutches resting against the other.

"What a lovely space. The house looks too old to have such an open living area," Terri said.

"My uncle had walls removed when they bought the house. This is Aunt May," Angela said.

"Welcome my dears! Come on in and sit down. Angela has told me so much about you both." She looked closely at Terri, "Your injuries are healing nicely. How are you feeling—inside?"

Terri looked from Angela to Caitlin. "You know all about what happened?" Aunt May nodded.

"To be honest, I feel stupid—and ashamed," she said.

"That's very normal, my dear," Aunt May said. "It'll pass too." Terri and Caitlin said nothing.

Angela said, "Aunt May has had similar experiences. I thought it might be helpful for you to hear her story."

"Experiences?" Caitlin said.

"Yes. Angela told me what you girls plan to do and I support you. If there is any way I can help, let me know—" Aunt May paused, "my father was very violent. He had a bad temper and he and my mother didn't get along. If she annoyed him, he would beat me. I never knew if it was because he was afraid to touch my mother, or because he thought it would hurt her more to see me being beaten. Either way, I was his victim."

"You said experiences, plural?" Terri said.

Aunt May nodded. "When I first came to the US—I'm from Ireland, you know? When I first came here, I took up with a boy. It soon became clear that he had a lot of problems." She paused as her memories took over, then continued, "He had a manic, aggressive cadence."

"You could see it coming?" Caitlin said.

"Yes, at first, I tried to deflect it. Distract him if you will. I soon realized I couldn't. Funny thing is, when I first met him, he seemed able to contain his aggression, then we moved out of state and that is when it got much worse. He hit me on the back of the head with a bottle once. I suppose I was lucky that it didn't break—that neither broke. My head or the bottle." She raised her hand to the back of her head. "Even so, it split my scalp. Yes, I can still feel the scar. It bled so much it actually frightened him out of his mood that time. You see, I think once he had moved me away from my support network, he felt empowered."

"But you left him, right?" Angela said.

"Eventually, I did. I stayed with him for almost two years. At first because I thought I could fix him. Then afterwards because I was afraid. He said he would kill me if I tried to leave."

"And what happened to make you leave?" Caitlin said.

Aunt May looked at her for a few seconds before replying. "A colleague noticed bruises and told me to call him if I ever needed help. The next time it happened, I left and went into work—of course, the office was empty because it was late in the evening. I just didn't know what to do. I considered sleeping on the floor there, then I remembered what my friend had said and called him. He and his boyfriend came and got me, and I stayed with them until I got myself sorted out."

"Ah," said Caitlin. "Gay men to the rescue." She nodded her head, looking at Terri.

"Anyway, enough about the past," Aunt May said. "You ladies have a lot to do. You're going to have a busy few days ahead looking for accommodation and getting set up." She turned to Terri. "And you, my dear, you need to allow yourself to heal—not just physically, but emotionally. Just because we can't see those wounds doesn't mean we should ignore them."

"Yes, I realize that I'm going to have to work on that," Terri almost whispered.

"Angela will show you to your rooms and then how about we have something to eat?"

"There are five bedrooms, four up here, and one downstairs. Naturally, Aunt May has the one downstairs. It is a master suite with its own bathroom. I'm down the end of the hall. There is a bathroom beside my room," Angela said as they climbed the stairs. She opened the doors into two bedrooms. "You are here, on either side of this bathroom."

"This is luxury. Thank you so much, Angela," Caitlin said.

Terri nodded in agreement as they put their bags in the bedrooms and followed Angela back downstairs.

After dinner, Aunt May disappeared into her bedroom as Caitlin and Terri helped Angela to clear the table and load the dishwasher.

"I've some work to do, and I'm sure you are both exhausted," Angela said.

The sisters agreed and headed upstairs.

"I could really do with a shower," Caitlin said.

"Me too, but I think I'm going to wait until the morning. I just want to sit and think about what Aunt May said."

"Want to chat about it?"

Terri nodded, and they both went into Terri's room.

"You know, Terri, I never thought about how traumatized you must be. After all, the man you loved and married tried to kill you! That's awful. But when you think about it, we never really talked about what Dad did to us."

Terri studied her hands for a moment before responding. "I'll be honest. I didn't want to even think about how I felt about that. He was our father, we'd just lost our mother and instead of protecting and caring for us, he wallowed in his own misery and took it out on us. As if it was somehow our fault! We were only nine years old. It was wrong, but I excused him. When we finally fought back and he said he was sorry, I just wanted things to be back the way they were before Mom died. Like it never happened. I forgave him because I needed to. You, on the other hand…"

"I never forgave him. I never really believed that he would not do it again. I was always waiting for the next time."

"And now you don't trust any man, and I—even after Keith—I want to trust. I want to fall in love and live happily ever after. I want the fairy tale. I still believe it exists."

"Well, I believe I'm safer not trusting. If only we could take a little from each other."

"But remember, Cait, Dad did stop. He never hit us again after that."

"He also sent us to boarding school and started traveling to every war-torn part of the world, writing about the horrors he saw. He was rarely close enough to hit us."

"Yeah, but we loved boarding school. To be fair to him, he provided for us financially, if not emotionally. Not only did he stash all the money he made from his writing in a trust for us, but he also left that huge insurance settlement. I often thought he had a death wish. He didn't want to live without Mom and that was why he took such risks."

"We'll never know. But at least we can do something to help other victims. Perhaps that'll act as some sort of catharsis? It is also a type of justice that we can use Dad's money to help people who have been abused. Like he is paying for it."

The sisters were silent for a few minutes, then Caitlin stood up.

"Anyway, I'm heading to bed. Goodnight Terri."

"Night Cait, sleep well."

The following day Terri, Caitlin and Angela sat down at the kitchen table with a pile of rental printouts that Angela had gathered for them. Everything from apartments to mansions, to start their hunt for somewhere to live.

Three weeks later, weeks spent visiting one rental after another, the sisters stared out over the lake from the back patio of the house they were viewing. They looked at each other and nodded. They were getting tired of house hunting, but this place made it worth the trouble, even if it was some distance from the city.

"This'll work," Terri said.

"We'll take it." Caitlin told the agent.

The house had two bedrooms, each with their own bathroom, upstairs. A living room, dining room and kitchen downstairs plus a half bath and an attached garage. Best of all, it was part of a small, gated community set back behind a hillside. The homes in the community all had large, tree filled lots. It was private and out of sight except from the lake. The backyard comprised a long stretch of grassy hill leading down to the rocky shoreline.

They'd been staying with Angela for almost a month while searching for a place to rent. This was perfect. It was on the outskirts of a small town about 20 miles North-West of Austin on the North shore of the lake, a bonus they had not expected. Within a week, they had furnished it and moved in. Terri set up her computer. She had a desk set into a small alcove off the main living room; it overlooked the lake.

"Let's discuss our next step towards setting up the ER," Caitlin said.

"ER?" Terri frowned at her sister. "What ER?"

Caitlin grinned. "Escape Route—ER—appropriate given I'm a nurse, don't you think? If I'm going to front this network, I think I should be based in Austin. At least until we are certain they have caught Keith. He is unlikely to find you tucked away here, and he would expect us to be together. So, best to have the operation well away from where you're located."

"How on earth would Keith find us here? He'd have no reason to think we're in Texas. That's why we came here."

Caitlin shook her head. "We can't take any chances. He's no fool."

"I think you're being a little bit paranoid, Cait."

"Humor me. I just want to be sure that he never gets near you again."

"Okay. So, what do you suggest?"

"How about I rent a place in Austin, close to where Angela lives? She's offered to help when she can. I can stay there and maybe just come out here from time to time."

"I guess that makes sense; after all, we are a bit off the beaten track here and we may need to be in a position to move faster than this location would allow." Terri nodded.

"And Terri? Let's get a boat. See the dock?" Caitlin pointed to the small, covered slip at the shoreline. "If we pick a marina on the other side of the lake, we can keep a boat there. When I'm coming here, I can drive to that marina—see here on the map." Caitlin pulled out her phone and brought up a map of the lake.

On the opposite side of the lake, which was fairly narrow and winding around a bend, was a large marina.

"By road from that marina, it would take over an hour—maybe two—to drive here. If I get a place near Angela, that would be about half-way by road, between that marina and here. Driving to the marina and then taking the boat across to that dock," she pointed again, "would be easy and, most of all, very difficult for anyone to follow me."

"Did I mention you are paranoid?" Terri said, smiling at her sister, "but I have to admit it makes sense. Better safe than sorry, I suppose."

"You know the saying, 'It's not being paranoid if they're out to get you' and I'm quite sure that Keith is out to get you," Caitlin said.

Caitlin and Angela spent some time searching for a small rental, eventually settling on a duplex about a mile from where Angela lived.

"This will work. Not exactly luxury, and no lake," Caitlin said.

The night before Caitlin moved into her new location, she was having dinner with Angela and Aunt May. She told them she had decided to rent a small apartment separate from the duplex as an official office.

"Why have a separate office?" Angela asked. "I thought that was the purpose of the duplex."

"I decided if I'm going to be actually living at the duplex, it might be safer to meet victims in person, somewhere totally faceless. I found a small efficiency in a large complex. Multiple blocks all looking exactly the same. I'm hopeful that will make it more difficult to locate, should someone follow a victim, or their abusers somehow find the address."

She told them she had also bought a pay-as-you-go cell phone specifically for what she was now referring to as the ER. She ordered stickers with the cell number and "Caitlin's Nails" printed on them.

"Nails?" Angela said when she saw the stickers.

"It is better than 'Domestic Violence Escape Route'," Caitlin said. "I mean, it's benign. I know I might be going way overboard on this, but I want to stay safe and keep our clients as safe as possible, too. Most men are suspicious and want to know your every move. At least, most men who beat up women, and from my experience, that is most men, period. Any man seeing that in your purse would not even give it another look."

"It's true that some men are like that, my dear. My first husband was very suspicious." Aunt May paused.

By now, Caitlin had become familiar with the fact that she was revisiting her memories and would continue in her own time, so she waited quietly.

"He wasn't always that way though, come to think of it. When we first got married, he was quite normal. Hard working. Then it became obvious to me that he was 'fooling around', as they used to call it. He often went out with a crowd of his single colleagues until the early morning, coming home drunk and disheveled—he called it work. He never realized that I was smarter than he was." Aunt May chuckled to herself before continuing. "After that, he became more and more suspicious of me. I suppose he felt if he could do it, then I probably did too. He went through my purse every night after I went to bed. If I brought work home, he would go through that too. He made sure that I didn't have access to his bank account, my salary went into that also, there was no joint anything. I never knew how much he was earning. I discovered by accident that his company was actually very profitable. I think the term they use for what he tried to do to me is gas lighting." She looked at Caitlin. "So, you see, dear, there are many different kinds of abuse. Now, tell me all about your new home?"

Caitlin told her it was very basic, that the lake house where Terri was living would be the actual home.

"Well, you be sure and come back and visit me from time to time, dear. After all, you will be just around the corner, really, won't you?"

Caitlin promised she would do that.

***

Terri sat on the balcony with her coffee. Her laptop was open on the small table beside her. Mesmerized, she watched the lake until the screensaver drew her attention back to her job search. She had called her boss in California and explained her situation to him and followed up with an email, officially giving notice. Although she was still on sick leave because of her injuries and could probably have continued working for the same company remotely. She and Caitlin had agreed it was safer to cut all ties to minimize the chances of Keith finding her.

Her gaze returned to the lake as she thought about Keith. Looking back, she could see now the signs were there all along. How controlling he was. It wasn't so obvious when they were together, in the same classes, working on projects, and then he moved into their apartment. They were almost never apart. But on the few occasions when she spent time with Caitlin, he had pouted like a child. When he moved in, they drove to classes together, and she no longer cycled to and from college. Caitlin still did, but her schedule differed from theirs.

Perhaps Cait's right. Maybe I do trust too much. Maybe I'm too much of a romantic.

Terri turned back to her laptop and tried to focus on her job search. By lunchtime, she had a short list of possibilities. Top of the list was an opportunity to work from home. In fact, the company didn't maintain an office in Austin and hired programmers from all over the United States.

She had a quick lunch and started working through her list. By the end of the afternoon, she had scheduled an on-line interview for the following day. Angela was right, there was so much opportunity for software engineers here.

As she prepared dinner and set the table, her mind wandered back to Keith. She had been so excited when they first arrived in the Bay Area. The Menlo Park house was perfect; it was a convenient drive to their jobs and close to the house in Palo Alto, where she had lived as a child.

Before Mom died and everything changed.

How odd, it was in the Bay Area the two biggest, life-changing events had occurred. Of course, when she married Keith, she thought that was the biggest event in her life.

The biggest mistake, more like. She sighed. *Someday I'll find the right man and live happily ever after.*

She found it amusing to think about what Caitlin would say if she voiced that wish to her. Caitlin had trusted no man since she was nine years old, and her experience with Mack just made it worse.

Terri poured herself a glass of wine and sat on the balcony watching for her sister. She had only taken one sip when she saw their boat appear around the bend, heading up the lake. She smiled when she thought about the complicated plan to avoid Keith finding her. Of course, it was a good idea. Most of Caitlin's ideas were good, but it was still amusing because it was so typical of her sister. She watched as the boat pulled into the slip and as the tent dropped over it; she went back into the kitchen to serve dinner.

***

Keith looked around the tiny apartment. At least he was out of that lousy motel. The apartment might not be much, but it was cheap and there was no lease. He didn't expect to be there very long. He knew that as long as he was employed, it would just be a matter of time before the police caught up with him. Once he figured out where Terri was, he would move on.

When he tried calling Terri's company on the pretense that he wanted to make an appointment to see her. He was told there was no one of that name based in the Seattle office, but they refused to give any other information. He was fairly sure she had left the Bay Area, but so far, he had been unlucky tracking her down. Probably a good idea for him not to stay too long in the same place, anyway.

He set up his laptop on the table, then went into the kitchen and got a plate and knife and fork. He emptied the burger and fries onto the plate and sat down to eat. Before returning to the computer, he washed the grease and ketchup off his hands and caught sight of himself in the mirror over the bathroom sink. He almost didn't recognize himself. The beard was coming in well and his hair was getting long and shaggy. He nodded in approval and went back to the laptop.

I'm certain Terri'll buy herself a new place. With all the money she has, it'll be no problem for her. And when she does, I'll find her.

He started working on his plan, spending the rest of the evening searching the Internet to find the data he needed.

CHAPTER THREE

Caitlin moved into her new accommodation with the minimum of furniture. She didn't need much. A bed and a kitchen table and a couple of chairs. TV was not her thing. She had her laptop, and she could use the kitchen table as a desk. She certainly wasn't planning to entertain, and she could go out to the lake for downtime.

A bonus was a strip mall just around the corner. With a gym and Karate club, it was within walking distance. She was looking forward to getting back to her regular workout routine.

Caitlin's first task was to visit the local police station. She wanted to be certain that the police were aware of what she was doing in case she needed a quick response from them.

I might be paranoid, and I hope I am, but that doesn't mean Keith won't try to find us.

As soon as she approached the front desk at the police station, a cop came over to her. He was tall and good looking in a rugged way. He had jet black hair and dark brown eyes. Caitlin guessed he must be over six-foot-tall, but his muscular frame made him look much bigger.

"Hi, my name is Caitlin Donnelly." She offered her hand, and he shook hands with her.

"I'm George Little," he said. "What can I do for you today?"

"I've just moved into the area and wanted to make you aware of our presence. We plan to work with shelters to assist victims of domestic violence to escape their situation and start a new life."

George didn't say anything, he just stared at her.

Caitlin's Escape Route

"I wanted to be sure you guys were aware of us. I mean, you might need our help if you got called out to a DV. And we might need your help someday, too." Caitlin took a deep breath before continuing. "You see, my sister's husband is wanted for attempting to murder her—in California—and there's always the possibility that he might turn up here, in which case I thought it'd be a good precaution to ensure that you knew."

George nodded. "Okay. Good point." He pulled out a keyboard and looked at her with his hands hovering, ready to type. "Can you give me his name, and your sister's name? Your contact information too, please?"

He typed as she gave him the information. She also handed him a photo of Keith.

"I guess you must be Irish, with a name like that and your red hair?"

"My hair is auburn, not red. And I'm half Irish. I was born in the Bay Area." Caitlin was sure if she were a dog, the hair on the back of her neck, her auburn hair, would be standing up straight.

Red hair! Dad had red hair. My hair is auburn!

"Sorry! Of course, auburn." The man's face reddened as he avoided looking at her.

"Could you give me any information on shelters for victims of domestic violence?" Caitlin asked, attempting to keep her voice even, afraid it might come out like a growl.

He pulled out some leaflets and handed them to her.

"Great! Thanks!" she said.

"You are welcome. DV's a big problem, and the shelters are always crowded. Your service will be very useful to help with a bad situation."

As she turned to leave, Caitlin had a thought. She pulled a wad of stickers out of her purse and handed them to the officer.

"Perhaps you can give these to any victims you encounter? Let them know it is not really a nail salon, but it is how they can contact me if they want to leave their abuser."

"Good idea. Thank you." He put the stickers in his wallet.

As Caitlin opened the door, she glanced back and locked eyes with Officer Little. He hadn't moved and was watching her leave. Feeling her face flush, she looked away and hurried out.

***

Brian, his colleague, looked up. "What was that about?"

"She's running some sort of escape system for DV victims. Helping them to get away from their abusers and start a new life."

"The shelters can use all the help they can get. Strange mission for such a pretty lady."

"Yeah, apparently someone beat her sister and left her for dead in her home in California. I think it's what got them on that path. You might just make a note of her details in case she calls for help. The suspect, the sister's husband, has an APB out for his arrest. Out of California. Here, take some of her stickers. And I agree, she sure is a pretty lady."

"Caitlin's Nails?" Brian said. "Are you serious?"

"I know, it seems a bit cloak and dagger, but she wanted to be sure that an abuser wouldn't take any notice if they saw it."

"I guess that is a good idea when you think about it." Brian tucked the stickers into his wallet. "Still, I better warn my wife about them. Don't want her getting suspicious! Or calling to get her nails done." The two men laughed at that idea.

George turned to the computer and spent some time reading up on the APB for Keith.

***

Caitlin spent the next week visiting the three shelters closest to her. She introduced herself to the women running the shelters and explained what she was doing. She also spent some time talking with the victims who were staying there, handing out her stickers.

The last place she visited was the nearest to where Angela lived. It was a large house, set back off the road, very similar to Aunt May's house. It had seen better days and was probably once a stately home. Perfect for its current purpose; there was enough space to house many people and still have separate office areas.

The manager introduced herself as Peggy, and invited Caitlin into her office, where she sat down behind a large, somewhat battered wooden desk. She sat in an ancient wooden chair with wheels that squeaked as she moved. The desk was littered with folders and stacks of papers. On the wall beside her was a large digital clock. It displayed the time and date in black against a light gray background. There were two chairs in front of the desk, one with cream leather padding and a high back, like an old dining room chair. The other looked like a folding chair from a school assembly room. Caitlin chose to sit on the dining room chair. It looked a little more comfortable.

Peggy was an older woman, possibly in her early sixties. Tall, but then everyone was tall to Caitlin, who was only five feet. Her iron gray hair was probably quite long because it was in a braid that was twisted around her head. Her casual outfit included dark blue jeans and a light blue denim shirt. She told Caitlin that she had a PhD in psychology and had been a victim herself many years ago.

"How do you plan to do this?" Peggy asked.

"Our plan is to identify victims who want to escape from their situation and set up a new life for themselves. We'll help them do that. In turn, we hope that some of them will join our network and help us move our 'escapees' to new areas, find them accommodation and work and they'll be available to help others, eventually. Until we cover the entire country."

"That's quite an undertaking," Peggy said. "I'll help you in any way I can. Our shelter, and the other shelters in the Austin area, are not only full, but have a waiting list. You could start by moving the women in the shelters to safer locations. Help them find accommodation and work. That would assist us. It would allow us to concentrate on the more troublesome cases. Those women with children. They can't leave the state and have long legal battles to fight. Count me in on your network!"

Caitlin wanted to hug the woman, but she didn't. The only person she could remember willingly hugging since her mother died was her sister, and of course Paddy and Jim, but that was different. There was the hug Angela orchestrated, but that was not willing, despite how much she liked Angela.

"By the way," Peggy added, "I assume you know you can probably apply for a grant to support your efforts?"

"That never occurred to me. Thanks for mentioning it." Caitlin made a mental note to have Terri follow up on this possibility.

"Let me get Robby to give you some information about that. He handles all the business side of things for me." Peggy left the room and was back in a few minutes with a post-it note. She handed it to Caitlin. "These are a couple of URLs that should give you the information you need. Also, Robby suggested you should consider speaking with a lawyer, to make sure you're operating within the regulations. Why don't I set up an appointment for you to meet with Alex—he's usually here one day a week."

Caitlin thanked her and put the note in her purse. When she got home, she called her sister and gave her a summary of her week.

"Peggy has offered us a small room in the shelter where we can talk to the women. That way, we can establish who wants to move on and who we feel we can help."

"Great, I don't start work for another two weeks, so that should work well. And as I'll be working from home full time, and with flexitime, it'll be no problem."

"That would definitely fit in with our plans for sure! Though you know you really don't have to work?"

"I know, but coding is something you have to keep working on or you not only lose your skills, but you also get left behind by changes in technology. Besides, I love it," Terri said.

"One thing, Peggy said. She told me we could probably get a grant for what we're doing. Could you follow up on that?" Caitlin gave Terri the URLs.

"Sure. I'll look into it. We might have to be a lot more formal, though. I'm sure they don't give money to just anyone. I'll find out."

"Thanks. Meanwhile, I'll pick you up tomorrow morning and we can move forward with that."

"Okay, see you then, Cait."

Terri and Caitlin set up in the small office at the shelter, in the room Peggy had assigned to them. To start off, they spent a few hours each day talking to the women. Once they had completed their initial review of all the women, Caitlin planned to spend at least one day a week there. Making herself available and getting to better understand these women and their different situations. Terri referred to it as interviewing them. Caitlin preferred to be a little less businesslike.

"After all, Terri, these poor women have not only lost everything, but they have also suffered major trauma," she said to her sister. She looked at her sister. "I don't really need to tell you that, sorry."

Terri smiled. "I know what you mean. I'll chat with them, instead of interviewing them. But we need to establish the most likely candidates to be successfully relocated. We want them to not only rebuild their lives but help us with other victims."

At the end of two weeks, they had identified six women who were eager to move out of Texas. They were also very willing to be available to help any other victims along the same route. One particular young woman, Pat, said that she wanted to stay in Texas and help them in any way she could. She was a little taller than Caitlin, with wavy ash blonde hair and dark brown eyes.

"Why do you want to do that?" Caitlin asked her.

"My parents are still living in the area and my ex-husband is no longer in Texas. And I've a job here—I used to have before all this happened. I'm a special needs teacher; I'm sure I can get another position once I've got a home," Pat said. She stared out the window for a few minutes before continuing. "He beat me regularly, but the last time, when I served him with divorce papers, he nearly killed me. I was in the hospital for two weeks." She looked up at Caitlin. "They locked him up for a few weeks after that. During that time, he agreed not to contest the divorce and as soon as he finally made bail, he took off. I believe I'm safer here because I know he'll never come back. Like most abusers, he's a coward." She finished with a satisfied smile. "It took me a long time to learn to admit to all of that. I used to pretend everything was fine and normal."

"Good for you," Caitlin said, smiling, then she continued, "why didn't you move in with your parents?"

"They don't have the space. Besides, I didn't want to draw his attention to them."

Terri looked at her in silence for a full minute. "We could really use the help. Thank you!" Caitlin nodded in agreement.

"We'll be in touch with you next week to put this in motion. We'll need to find a place for you to live and operate out of. Where do your parents live? Perhaps we can find somewhere close to them," Caitlin said.

"They live in Temple, just about twenty-five miles north of Austin."

"Great, we should find a place there. It'll be convenient, as any route out of Texas is going to be a long one."

Pat thanked them and left with a smile. She was their last appointment of the day.

"Let's head to the Lake, Caitlin. We've a lot to talk about and even more to do."

Not only had they bought a boat and rented a slip at the marina, but they had also rented a lockup garage in the storage unit next to it. Caitlin parked the car in the garage. From there, they took the boat and crossed the lake to their own dock, just a mile out of sight, around a series of bends through the canyon. There were no convenient bridges in that section of the lake. If anyone followed them to the marina, they could not easily get a boat to follow on the water; if they managed to, they would be very conspicuous. They reached the lake house just as the sun was setting.

"Quick Terri, let's grab a glass of wine and catch the last of this beautiful sunset."

Terry smiled at her sister. "You and your sunsets." She teased, but she got two glasses of wine, and they sat in silence relaxing and enjoying the view.

"The sunset over the water will always remind me of when we were kids back in Ireland. Watching the sunset over the Atlantic from the garage roof. It was our safe haven," Caitlin said.

"I know. You always loved that."

"I used to watch the sun go down, knowing that the same sun was shining on California and another sunset would follow there. It made me feel connected to home. Now it does the same in reverse. That same sun was setting over the Atlantic about five or six hours ago, back in Ireland. It is a connection."

Terri smiled at her sister. "I admit I loved our evenings on the garage roof, too."

The sisters sat quietly as the sun slowly disappeared.

"Okay, it is almost dark. Let's get something to eat and make plans," Terri said, leading the way inside.

Caitlin closed the door, and they were soon sitting at the table eating and discussing next steps.

Terri got on her computer and located several rental properties in the Temple area. They agreed Caitlin would drive up to Temple with Pat and see if any would work; she texted Pat to let her know she would pick her up the next day.

By midday, Pat and Caitlin sat in the real estate office and went through Terri's list. They came up with four likely properties and set off to view these. The first place they visited was not promising. It was so rundown that they didn't bother going inside. The second, however, was ideal. It was an apartment within walking distance of where Pat's parents lived and had two bedrooms and two bathrooms. Ideal for when Pat had victims staying with her, which they both agreed might happen from time to time.

Their plan was for Pat to drive to Austin whenever a victim needed to be moved into the ER. From there, she could drive them to the other side of Dallas and drop them off with another helper. There would definitely be times when it would not be possible to make the drive from Austin to Dallas in one trip. When that happened, they could stay overnight in Temple. Heading on to Dallas the following day. Occasionally, the Dallas helper might come to Temple to do a pickup from there.

Once they had signed for the apartment, Caitlin drove Pat to a used car dealership and purchased a car. Pat looked at her in amazement.

"This is for me?" she said, "I can't believe this. It's like a dream, my own home—close to my parents, and a car!"

"Well, how else would you get from here to Austin, and up to Dallas? Plus, you can sign up with a rideshare company and make extra money that way," Caitlin replied.

She waved as Pat drove off in her new, somewhat used, vehicle. She was going to sleep on her parents' couch for the few days it would take before she could move into the apartment.

Well satisfied with the day's work, Caitlin drove home.

It feels so good to do something positive to stop the abuse. And to help the victims.

As she pulled up outside the house, her ER phone rang. *Another victim.*

"Hello, Caitlin's Nails. How can I help you?" She was training herself to respond this way just in case it was a suspicious abuser checking the number.

"Hi. My name's Maria, and a friend recommended you. She gave me one of your stickers and said you could help me."

"How can I help you?" Caitlin repeated.

"My friend said you work with domestic violence issues, and I wonder if we could meet and talk about it."

"Do you believe you're a victim?" Caitlin asked.

"I think so." Maria did not sound very sure.

"Okay Maria, I can meet you in about an hour if that suits you, alternatively, first thing tomorrow morning."

"Tomorrow morning would be better for me."

Caitlin was relieved. All she wanted to do was put her feet up and relax. It had been a busy day. She gave Maria directions, and they agreed to meet at ten the following morning.

Caitlin's Escape Route

Caitlin arrived at her office at nine-thirty the next morning. It was in an enormous apartment complex. There were at least twenty buildings, all identical. Caitlin's unit was in the center. All the ground floor apartments had a small garage. She pulled into the garage and lowered the door. There was an entrance from there into the apartment.

She got out her laptop and spent thirty minutes catching up on email, which, as usual, mainly entailed deleting spam. At ten, she started watching out for Maria in case she couldn't locate the apartment.

At eleven, Caitlin decided to wait outside. She walked up and down the parking lot in front of the building, stopping frequently to check the ER phone in case she had missed a call from Maria. She waited another fifteen minutes before heading home.

For another twenty minutes, she sat in her car just in case. Finally, she drove off, thinking, *I hope that poor woman is safe.*

CHAPTER FOUR

Terri sat at her computer while Caitlin perched on a stool at the kitchen counter as they went through a review of their progress so far.

"We now have six helpers in our network. All from Peggy's shelter. Pat in Temple, Nancy, who's now settled in Georgia, Bridget in New Mexico—"

"Hang on, Cait, slow down," Terri said, tapping away on her keyboard. "Okay, continue."

"Emma and Heather are both in Kansas." Caitlin counted on her fingers. "Who am I missing?"

Terri stopped typing to consult an open notebook beside her.

"You missed Stephanie. She's heading to Ohio and will contact us once she gets there." She returned to her typing. "Okay, got it. I've entered their new addresses and phone numbers. Currently, they're all doing rideshare work, but I expect that to change as they get settled. I know that Emma and Heather hope to start a childcare center, and of course, Pat wants to get back into teaching."

"That's our network so far. I'm thinking I should start writing up a report following any conversation with a victim—client. I think it's important to keep track of them. We will, of course, if they become part of the network. But if they don't, we want to be sure we've a written report. You know? A record of our conversation. I think it'll help us learn as we go."

"That's a good idea, Cait. You can send a report to me after each meeting, and I'll store it along with our network information."

For the next two weeks, Caitlin was kept busy with calls from victims looking for advice and information, and a couple of meetings at her office. Only one of these contacts resulted in the victim deciding to take the next step. She carefully documented each contact, even if it didn't result in a meeting.

Caitlin made a point of trying to avoid influencing her clients in any direction. These decisions were too big. Too life changing to be made by anyone but the victim. If they were not fully committed to their decision, the results could be catastrophic. She also had a couple of calls from people looking to get their nails done. After the first one, she decided any further calls like that she'd tell them the salon was closed. She didn't hear from the client Maria, who had missed her appointment and eventually forgot about her.

When Brenda called her, it was clear she had made up her mind.

"Hello, is this Caitlin?" A woman's voice said as she answered the call on her ER phone.

"That's me. What can I do for you?"

"Hi. My name's Brenda, and I'm married to a monster." The statement sounded like an opening to an Alcoholics Anonymous meeting.

"Okay." Caitlin paused. "Would you like to meet, and we can talk about your options?"

"Yes please. I'm free today. My children are spending the day with their grandparents."

Caitlin's heart sank. *Children. It was always so complicated and heartbreaking when children were involved.*

"I can meet you—" She looked at the clock on the stove, "say one hour? Let me give you the address and directions."

An hour later, she opened the door to Brenda. She was a tall, chubby woman in her thirties with short brown hair with a distinctive gray, almost white streak on one side. Despite the Texas heat, Caitlin noticed she wore a silk scarf around her neck.

"Come in." Caitlin led her into the office.

Brenda looked around before sitting in the chair Caitlin indicated.

"Tell me your situation, and what I can do to help."

Brenda removed the scarf and sat there in silence, watching Caitlin's reaction. Her neck was covered in bruises at various stages. Some were almost gone; some were bright purple and every shade in between. Most looked like fingers and thumbs had caused them, but there was also what looked like a rope mark circling her neck.

"Your husband did this?" she said.

Brenda nodded. "He's a complete control freak, and he gets off on choking me, to where I almost lose consciousness, then he lets go. If I don't do exactly what he says, or the kids don't do exactly what he says, he does it. He does it if he doesn't like something I say, or even something I cook. He does it in front of the kids." She recited this as though she had been practicing it. Her stoic demeanor crumbled, and tears poured down her cheeks. "If he goes out at night, he ties me to the bed and puts a noose around my neck. I'm so worried because if the kids need something or there's an emergency, I can't do anything about it."

"Okay Brenda. Where children are involved, you can't leave the state at least, not without their father's permission." Brenda opened her mouth and Caitlin put up her hand before she could say anything. "I know, I know, but being a monster doesn't nullify the fact that he's also their father. Right or wrong, the law respects that. If you leave the state with the children, without his consent, that's kidnapping."

Brenda's eyes widened. "Well, I won't leave without them. But doesn't the law care about the damage he's doing to them?"

Caitlin shook her head. "There are legal avenues to pursue to get that one sorted."

"So, what can I do? Is there nothing I can do?" Caitlin could see the desperation in the woman's eyes and hear the defeat in her voice.

"Yes, there's something you can do, and we'll help you. If you agree, I'll take you—and your children—to a shelter for victims of domestic violence. We have a relationship with many in the area. They'll take you and the kids in and help you get legal advice and start working towards a solution; hopefully you can get a restraining order against him for a start. Can you bring the children here tomorrow? Say they have a dental appointment or something?"

Brenda nodded and wiped her eyes. "Yes, I can do that. What time?"

"Say—ten in the morning?"

"That should be easy to do. I'll see you here tomorrow." Brenda stood up.

"And Brenda—before you go, one more thing. Bring nothing you wouldn't bring to the dentist. That is, don't pack any clothes for any of you. You might get away with it, but if he notices, you'll never make it here. Also, let me take a few photos of your bruises. They'll be very useful when you need to prove violence after the fact."

As soon as Caitlin was satisfied that she had all the photos she needed, she showed Brenda out and said goodbye.

"See you in the morning." She closed the door and went back to get her things. Before she left, she called Peggy at the shelter and let her know she would bring Brenda and her kids the next day.

"Thanks Caitlin. I'll make sure we have accommodation and services ready for them. I appreciate the heads up."

Next morning, Caitlin drove to the shelter and Brenda followed in her own car, her three children sitting wide eyed in the back. Peggy came out to greet them. She looked at the car Brenda was driving.

"First question, who owns this car?" she asked Brenda.

"I do. My dad bought it for me."

"That's good." Peggy smiled. "Hi there kids, come on in. We have snacks!"

The kids climbed out of the car and Brenda locked it up and followed them inside with Caitlin.

After showing the kids and Brenda their quarters; introducing them to a few of the other residents. They were as settled as they could be under the circumstances. Caitlin drew Peggy to one side.

She held up a USB key. "I took some photos of Brenda's injuries yesterday. Should I give this to you?"

Peggy shook her head. "Good idea, but no. I'll introduce you to our lawyer, Joe. You can give them to him. You need to talk to him, anyway. He is here today, and he'll be speaking with Brenda later. Follow me." She led the way to her office at the back of the house. As she entered, a tall slim man in his late thirties rose from the desk. He had a shaved head and bright blue eyes.

"Joe, this is Caitlin. I was telling you about the work she and her sister are doing helping with our residents." Peggy turned to Caitlin. "This is Joe, our lawyer."

"Nice to meet you, Caitlin. We appreciate all the help we can get." They shook hands.

"Caitlin just brought us the mother and her three children I told you about. She has several photos she took of the mother's injuries."

Caitlin handed over the key to Joe. "Very astute of you to think of that, Caitlin. That'll be extremely useful."

Caitlin continued. "Peggy suggested that my sister and I should talk to you about our operation. It'd be useful to get some legal advice before we get in too deep. You might also be able to help us with some other issues. Could we set up an appointment?"

"Absolutely. I'd be happy to help in any way I can. Here's my card. Give my office a call and make an appointment. You'll need to talk to my junior partner, Alex. He'd normally be here today, but he has a few days off and I'm standing in."

"I'll do that, thank you!"

Once Caitlin was back in her car, before driving off, she called Terri.

"Hey. I just met Peggy's lawyer, well, the lawyer for the shelter. It occurred to me that we should get legal advice to make sure we are staying within the law. I also thought he might help with your divorce—at least if he can't, he can recommend someone who will."

"That's a good idea. When do we see him?"

"I'll call his office as soon as I get home and make an appointment. I'll let you know when it is."

"Great. See you soon."

Two days later, Terri and Caitlin arrived at the offices of Trainor & Walsh. The receptionist showed them into Joe's office immediately.

"Thanks for seeing us so quickly, Joe." Caitlin shook hands with him. "This is my sister Terri."

Terri stepped forward, and they shook hands.

"Good to meet you, Terri. This is my partner, Alex," Joe said as a younger man stood up and shook hands with them. "He handles all of our domestic violence cases. Please ladies, sit down."

Almost an hour later, the sisters left.

"Well, that was very useful," Terri said. "And Joe seems to be a really nice guy."

"Yes. Good to know that so far, we are doing things right, and it'll be great to be able to call him or Alex, if in doubt."

"Best of all, he's going to put me in touch with his partner, who can advise me on my divorce." Terri looked at the card Joe had given her. "I'll call him tomorrow to find out what my options are." She tucked the card away in her purse. "Let's head back to the lake. I bet you could do with a bit of relaxation."

Caitlin nodded. "You would win that bet."

The sisters were having coffee the following morning when the ER phone rang. They looked at each other as Caitlin picked up.

"Caitlin's Nails."

"Hi Caitlin. This is Maria. I'm so sorry I didn't turn up for our appointment. My husband decided to stay home, and I couldn't call you because he'd have been suspicious."

"Hi Maria, I'm glad you are alright. I was worried about you. Do you want to make another appointment?"

"Yes please. Would you be available this afternoon?"

"How about two-thirty? Would that work for you?"

"That'd be perfect. I've got the address and directions. See you then."

Caitlin hung up.

"That was the woman I told you about, the one who didn't turn up a few weeks ago."

"Hope she doesn't let you down today. But at least she's safe," Terri said.

Terri sat down at her computer and called the lawyer's office. As soon as she gave her name, the girl on the other end of the line said that Joe had told her to expect the call. Phil had found time in his calendar for her tomorrow morning, if that would suit.

"That'd be great. I certainly didn't expect him to see me so soon," Terri said.

"Joe told him it was urgent, and he made the time, actually he's off tomorrow. He's coming in specially to see you."

Terri made a note of the appointment in the calendar on her laptop and hung up.

"Tomorrow?" Caitlin said.

"Yes. It'll be good to get things moving. I better get some work done if I'm going to be out tomorrow."

Caitlin gathered her things, and they said goodbye. By two-thirty, she was once again sitting in her office waiting for Maria. She spent an hour working on her laptop, glancing at her phone every few minutes, looking for a message from Maria. At three-thirty, she started to pack up. Before leaving, she called Maria to check on her. The call went directly to voice mail. She added a quick note to her report and headed home.

Looks like I'll need another hour at the gym. I don't know whether to be irritated or worried.

CHAPTER FIVE

Terri studied her image in the rear-view mirror, patted down her hair, though it looked fine; she took a deep breath, glanced at her watch and got out of the car and headed towards the entrance of Trainor & Walsh Lawyers. Halfway to the door, she turned back and checked that she'd locked her car. She looked at her watch again before going into the building. She walked up and down, watching the three elevators. As soon as she heard the ping, she stood waiting for the door to open. Stepping in, she pressed the button for the third floor and let out a deep breath as the door closed. She hadn't realized she was holding her breath. And she wasn't sure why.

The doors opened to reveal a young woman behind a large glass table, busily tapping away on a computer.

"Good morning…" Terri glanced at the nameplate on the desk, "Lucy. I've an appointment with Phil Walsh."

"Terri Donnelly?"

Terri nodded.

"I'll tell him you're here. Please take a seat." Lucy waved toward a low glass table with leather upholstered chairs around it.

"Thank you." Terri sat down on the nearest chair and glanced at the magazines on the table, but didn't have time to pick one up.

"Phil will see you now. This way, please."

Phil was a balding man in his fifties. He was dressed like every lawyer in every TV series. Gray suit, white shirt, blue tie with a pocket handkerchief. He stood up and came around his desk to shake hands with Terri.

"Please sit down. Joe told me what you and your sister are doing. Great work. I know Peggy appreciates it."

Terri smiled and nodded.

"By the way," he added, "Peggy is my sister."

"Oh, really?" She wasn't sure what to say.

"Okay, to business. I understand you want advice on filing for divorce?"

"Yes, I do." Terri took a deep breath before continuing in a rush. "My husband beat me, locked me in an upstairs bedroom and set fire to the house." Terri sat forward slightly, watching for Phil's reaction.

"Was he arrested?" Phil said, apparently unmoved.

She relaxed into the chair. "The police are looking for him, but so far as I know, they haven't found him. I think they'll let me know when he's arrested—I hope so."

"Absolutely they will. You're a witness and the victim. I assume you're the only witness?"

Terri nodded.

After an hour of questions, answers and explanations, Phil rose and said, "I'll go ahead and file a Motion to Serve by Publication. As he's wanted for attempted murder and arson, I see no problem having the divorce granted, even if he's not found. The fact that you have no children and no shared assets, considering he allegedly set fire to the house, and he already cleaned out your bank account. That actually leaves no grounds for contest, anyway."

As Terri stood up to shake hands with him, there was a knock on the office door and Joe stuck his head around.

"Hi Joe, we are just finishing up here," Phil said.

"Hi Terri, I thought we could grab an early lunch if you have time?" Joe said.

"Thank you, Phil," Terri said. She turned to Joe. "Lunch sounds good. Thank you."

Joe held the door open for Terri. As they walked into the restaurant, a man came forward with a stack of menus in one hand.

"Hi Joe, table or booth?"

"A booth please Leo."

They followed Leo to a booth, where he placed two menus on the table.

"Your server will take your order. Enjoy your lunch."

Terri smiled at Joe. "I see you're a regular here."

"They've a great menu and it is very convenient for the office," he replied, picking up the menu.

Over lunch, they chatted first about the divorce, then about their escape network.

"Tell me about yourself, Terri." As they were waiting for the check.

"Oh, I think you know way more about me than I know about you, Joe; your turn to share."

"There's not much to tell, really. I was actually born in Germany—an army brat. We moved around a lot until my father ended up as an instructor in West Point. I was lucky enough to get into Harvard Law School. And here I am."

"Are you married? I probably should have asked you that before I agreed to have lunch with you."

Joe grinned. "I wouldn't have asked you to lunch if I were married. The answer's no. I was married a long time ago, but we were too young, and we divorced after two years. No children—before you ask." He glanced at his watch. "I'm afraid I've got to go; I don't know where the time went. I have to get back to the office."

As he walked Terri back to her car, he said, "I'd love to see you again. Perhaps we can do dinner sometime?"

"I'd really like that, but it might be better to wait until my divorce is final, or maybe when they catch Keith. Hopefully that's soon. I don't want to put you in danger."

He looked at her and frowned slightly. "I don't think I can wait that long. I'm prepared to risk it—if you are?"

Terri smiled up at him. "If you're sure?"

"Never been so sure of anything in my life." He glanced at his watch again. "You've got my card, email me your phone number—I know it's in Phil's file, but I don't want to cross the lines here."

Terri nodded as she got into her car and pulled out her phone and his card from her purse. "I'll do that right now. And thank you for lunch. I really enjoyed it."

As he turned and hurried towards his office, Terri sent the email and then she hugged herself before starting the engine and driving towards the lake.

I can't wait to tell Caitlin.

As soon as Terri got back to the lake house, she called Caitlin.

"Well, how did it go?" Caitlin said.

"Great. We had lunch, and he wants to meet me again. I think he likes me!"

"Wait—what—who? Your divorce lawyer? I don't think that is a good idea."

"No sorry, not Phil—he is the divorce lawyer—Joe. I had lunch with Joe, and we agreed to meet again and have dinner sometime. He asked for my phone number…"

"Terri! You can't be serious! That's so not a good idea. When will you learn that you just can't trust men?"

"Never. I will not allow Keith or Mack, or anyone else—before you say Dad—destroy my belief in humanity."

Caitlin sighed. "Okay, okay, so how did it go with Phil?"

"He thinks that the divorce will go through with no problem, even if we never find Keith. Keith literally burned his bridges when he set fire to the house and emptied the bank account. We have no shared assets to argue over and as my money—yours and mine—was all neatly tied up in a trust fund before I ever met him. He has no right to that."

"That is an enormous relief. How long does he think it'll take?"

"I didn't ask him. But he seemed to think it was going to be straightforward. Thank goodness we didn't have kids."

"Amen to that, sister! Oh, and Terri—" Caitlin paused, "Maria was a no-show again."

"Oh, for heaven's sake. That's so frustrating because you just don't know if she's hurt or just flaky."

"That's exactly the way I feel."

They chatted for a few more minutes before hanging up.

Terri poured herself a glass of wine and sat down on the balcony, her phone pinged. She checked her email and opened the one at the top of the list.

Hi Terri - thanks for a very enjoyable lunch and for sending me your contact information. I'll call you later and we can arrange to meet for dinner. Meanwhile, this email was sent from my personal email address and my personal phone number is at the bottom. Looking forward to seeing you again soon, real soon. Joe.

Terri sat back and smiled at the lake for a few minutes before moving inside and sitting down to work at her computer.

***

Caitlin's Escape Route

Caitlin looked at the phone and slowly shook her head.

I just hope Joe is to be trusted. Terri has had enough to deal with as it is.

Caitlin paced up and down her kitchen and into the hall. She was worried about her sister getting involved with yet another man. Then she did what she always did when she felt under stress. She headed to the gym and spent an hour taking it out on the kicking bag.

Having relieved some of the stress, she showered and then decided to walk down the street to the local restaurant and have dinner. She didn't feel like cooking or cleaning.

As she paid for her meal, Caitlin watched the young couple at the corner table. She had spotted them shortly after she had been served and had been watching them while she was eating, pretending to study her phone.

The young woman was a pretty blonde, her long hair tied back in a loose ponytail. Her green silk blouse made her eyes look a deep shade of green. Her companion was a well-groomed, clean shaved, young man with short, dark hair. He wore a navy-blue business suit and a crisp white shirt open at the neck. Caitlin was fairly sure he had a necktie rolled up in one of his pockets. He just looked like that type. And it was obvious that they were having a disagreement.

That was not what had caught her attention; lots of couples have disagreements, it was the way the man reacted that was disturbing. At one point, he'd taken his fork and pressed it into the woman's thumb as her hand rested on the table. Neither of them spoke as he glared into her eyes. He pressed a little harder before lifting the fork and continuing to eat. A few moments later, the woman stood up and headed towards the ladies' bathroom. She was tall and slender. It was difficult to tell if her faded, torn jeans were because she kept up with the latest fashion, or if they were just old.

Caitlin followed her into the restroom and as they stood side by side in front of the mirror, she noticed the woman was holding her hand under the cold water. Her thumb was swelling. Fortunately, it looked like the fork had not broken the skin.

"You know you don't have to tolerate that sort of treatment?" Caitlin said.

The woman looked at her and replied, "You don't understand."

"I understand. I know what it's like. You don't deserve to be treated like that." She paused. "I know you think you have no choice, but I'm going to give you one." Caitlin handed her one of her stickers. "If you decide to leave him, I can help you."

"Caitlin's Nail Salon?" She looked from the sticker to Caitlin.

"Keep that in your purse. If he sees it, he won't consider it to be threatening. Call me if you need help. I'll help you; it is what I do. You can get out of this situation safely if you want to. We operate an escape route for victims of domestic violence."

The woman stared at Caitlin with her eyebrows raised, her mouth opened and closed, but she made no sound. After a moment's hesitation, she put the sticker in her purse and she walked out of the restroom.

CHAPTER SIX

Caitlin had only just fallen asleep when she sat up in bed, wide awake and sweating. "That nightmare again!" She muttered to herself. She rested back against her pillow, wondering when the nightmares would stop, if ever.

Perhaps when Keith is locked up. Though she knew better. She closed her eyes; During the years her father beat her, she had nightmares almost every night, until he died. To her horror, they began again after that incident with Mack.

She was just dozing off when a loud banging from downstairs woke her again. Sitting up again, she listened intently and realized someone was knocking on the back door. She slipped out of bed and hurried downstairs, putting on her robe as she went. She peered at the doorstep, through a gap in the curtains on the bay window. Before opening the door, she disabled the alarm system. The young woman from the diner staggered into the kitchen. Caitlin almost didn't recognize her. Her face was covered in bruises, and she was bleeding from an open wound under one eye.

"Help me, please!"

Caitlin guided her to a chair and turned on the lights.

"He did this to you?"

"Yes, my boyfriend Malcolm."

"What's your name?"

"Sally."

"Hi Sally, I'm a nurse and I need to make sure you don't have any serious injuries, other than what we can see."

Once Caitlin had established that she had no broken bones, and no apparent internal damage, she asked Sally if she wanted to go to the hospital to get checked out.

"No! Malcolm warned me to never go near the hospital. I don't want to and I don't need to."

"In that case, I would like to take some photos of your injuries before I dress them. Is that alright with you?"

Sally nodded; the movement caused her to wince.

Caitlin took photos of Sally's face from several angles and then asked if she had any other injuries. Sally pulled at the neck of her once beautiful green shirt and exposed more bruising. Caitlin took some more photos and then got out her first aid kit. She cleaned and dressed the wounds in silence. When she finished, she put the kettle on and made some tea. She handed a cup to Sally.

"I need to ask you a few of questions, Sally, and I want you to be completely honest, OK?"

Sally nodded.

"First, why did you come to my door?"

"You gave me one of your stickers at the diner. I live just around the corner, and I saw you going into your house when we were driving past."

"Did he see you come here?" Caitlin asked, frowning.

"No, he went out, probably to the bar. He usually goes there and gets drunk after he hits me."

"Do you have any children?" Caitlin assumed she didn't, as she would have had to leave them alone to come to her house, but she had to be sure.

"No," Sally responded.

Caitlin established Sally was a native of Austin, but no longer had any family there. She had family in Cambridge, Massachusetts.

"This question is very important, Sally. Are you prepared to leave him and everything you own? If you are, I can arrange that immediately. We can get you to Cambridge. If not, your only option is to go to the police. But I'm sure you don't need me to tell you that might just make matters worse." She paused. "Will you leave him and your life now?"

Sally didn't hesitate. "Yes, I want nothing more to do with him. I want to go as far away as possible and never see him again. But why are you doing this for me?"

"Let me get dressed and we'll go. I'll explain on the way."

A few minutes later, Caitlin came back downstairs. Grabbed her purse and car keys and took Sally by the elbow and led her out of the kitchen, down the hall, setting the alarm before opening the door into the garage.

Caitlin would not normally start the car before opening the garage door, but she was still worried that Sally's boyfriend might be out looking for her. She didn't open the door until they were both strapped in, and the engine was running. As soon as the door was up sufficiently, she drove out and closed the garage door as she turned out onto the road and headed north.

"I usually meet my clients at my office. That's where we are going. I don't give out my home address just in case."

"Sorry for coming to your home. I didn't know where else to go," Sally said.

"Don't worry, Sally. You did the right thing. I can help you. I promise." Caitlin had already made good on this promise more than once and expected there would be many more times in the future. As she drove, she explained to Sally what to expect.

Caitlin pulled into her office garage and led Sally into the apartment.

"I use this location because it has no personality. It's difficult to find anything here, as every building looks the same. And I can keep the car out of sight. I can pretty much stay out of sight myself."

As soon as they sat down at the table, she said. "We're building a network of people who are volunteers. Most of them are women who were themselves the victims of domestic violence. I called Pat while I was getting dressed and she'll be here in about an hour to collect you. She'll bring you to her home where you can stay tonight. In the morning, she'll supply you with the essentials, a change of clothes, toiletries, etc. Then either she'll drive you on to the next stage or someone else will collect you and move you along the escape route as far as Ohio. Stephanie will take care of you from there and make sure you get to your family in Cambridge."

"I don't know how to thank you," Sally said. "You've saved my life!"

"Just take advantage of all we're offering you and stay safe. That's all the thanks I need. This is not witness protection. You will not get a new identity, so I recommend you're very careful who you contact over the next few months. Most batterers will move on to another victim within six months and lose interest if there are no children in the relationship."

When Pat arrived and drove off with Sally. Caitlin locked up and headed back to her home. She could still get a few hours' sleep before daylight. That would not happen.

As she climbed the stairs, there was a hammering on her back door. *What now?* She was about to go back downstairs to see who was at the door when she heard shouting.

"Sally, Sally! I know you're in there. Don't make me come in and get you!" a man's voice.

Oh my God! No!

Caitlin ran up to the top of the stairs, pulled out her phone, called 911 and reported that someone was attempting to break into her home. She was glad that she had already established a good relationship with the local police. They would react quickly when they saw her name on the report. She moved closer to the wall at the top of the stairs and listened. Then suddenly, all hell broke loose. There was a loud crash from the kitchen, followed by the urgent screech of the alarm. Caitlin moved to the top of the stairs as the man from the diner came from the kitchen and looked up at her.

"Where's Sally?" He yelled at her as he came up the stairs two at a time.

Caitlin stood calmly until he was almost on top of her. Then she snapped her leg out, perfectly connecting the ball of her foot with his throat, sending him backwards down the stairs. He landed in a heap at the bottom of the stairs. It was very obvious from the angle of his leg the fall had done some damage. It was not the first time she was thankful for Paddy and Jim suggesting Karate—and for saving her from Mack. She could not only defend herself, but fight back if necessary.

"Oh, thank you, George!" Caitlin said as the large police officer came into the hallway from the kitchen.

"Are you alright?"

"Yes, thank you. He'd only just broken in when you got here."

George looked down at the man, prone at the bottom of the stairs.

"What happened to him?" Squatting beside him, he felt for a pulse. He pushed a button on his radio and called for an ambulance.

"He charged up the stairs and attempted to grab me. I tried to fight him off and next thing I knew, he fell down the stairs."

"If he gets out of hospital, he'll get locked up tonight. But I can't guarantee he'll stay locked up. If he makes bail, he could be out pretty quickly." George looked at Caitlin with concern. "Is this related to your work with the DV victims?"

"Yes. I'm afraid so. His girlfriend came to the house this evening. She was badly beaten. He must have found out she came here because he was yelling her name when he started banging on the back door."

"You'll need to come down to the station and give a statement. This was obviously breaking and entering, and Texas law allows you to defend yourself and your home from intruders, so don't worry about that part of it."

George helped Caitlin to nail the back door shut and made sure it was secure. As soon as the police left, she went to bed. Despite how tired she was, it took her a while to get to sleep.

Next morning, she called the landlord to report the break-in and the damaged door. Then she went to the police station where George took her statement.

"Malcolm, the guy who fell down your stairs last night? He's in the hospital, but he's not in critical condition. He should be fit to appear in court in a few days."

"I hope they don't grant him bail," Caitlin said.

"Probably they will, unfortunately—if he can pay the bail."

"He looked pretty well heeled. No doubt he can," Caitlin said with a sigh.

"Yeah, I'm afraid so. You were lucky last night, though."

"We make our own luck."

George nodded. "Very true. You know, my mother was a victim of DV. My stepfather beat her regularly when I was a kid. Eventually it got too much for me and I attacked him with my baseball bat."

Caitlin's eyes widened. "What happened?"

"He beat me senseless. I was in the hospital for a week."

"Oh no! That is awful! Hopefully, you were alright. No lasting damage, except I suppose emotionally."

"I was better than alright. He was charged and actually went to prison for six months because he resisted arrest. But the best part was that my mother left him, and we never looked back."

"That is almost funny," Caitlin said. "I had a similar experience, not

Caitlin's Escape Route

as bad as yours. My father used to beat me and my sister—he never put us in hospital, but we were always covered in bruises. One night we fought back, and I hit him on the back of the head with a hurley stick. He never did it again after that."

"Hurley stick? What on earth is a hurley stick?"

Caitlin grinned. "Hurley is an Irish game. Played with a stick a bit like a hockey stick. It's a cross between field hockey and lacrosse, sort of." She laughed out loud. "I still remember the look on his face. It was priceless."

"You have beautiful blue eyes; you should smile more often," George said.

"If we are done with the statement, I need to go." Caitlin grabbed her purse and almost ran out of the station.

Damn it! Why did I open up to him? Will I never learn?

She had to force herself to stick to the speed limit. She just wanted to get home.

***

George watched her go, slowly shook his head, and trudged back to his desk. He sat down at the desk and started working on his report. He was reading Caitlin's statement when Brian stopped by his desk.

"Was that Caitlin I saw rushing out of here? What did you do to frighten her off?" Brian laughed.

George nodded with a half-smile. "Opened my big mouth without thinking. I guess she thought I was being fresh."

"What on earth did you say to her?"

"She laughed. It was the first time I even saw her crack a smile. I told her she had beautiful eyes. She does. They are deep blue and when she laughed, they sparkled." He shook his head. "Guess I should have kept that thought to myself. She definitely wasn't comfortable with it."

"Women," Brian said. "You never know what's going to set them off."

George turned back to his report.

***

A few hours later, Caitlin let herself in the back door of the lake house and dumped her keys and her bag on the table, in the hallway leading to the stairs.

She found Terri in the kitchen preparing dinner.

"Hey Caitlin! I'm so happy you were able to get here this weekend."

"Hi Terri, that smells good!"

Caitlin poured herself a glass of wine and took a sip before continuing.

"I nearly didn't make it this time. We need to talk. We need a better escape plan for us."

"Why? What happened?" Terri rested the spoon she was using on a saucer before picking up her glass and studying Caitlin with concern on her face.

"Our most recent escapee turned up at the house. She lived in the neighborhood and spotted me going in."

"Oh, no!"

"Yeah. And after I got her into the pipeline, her boyfriend turned up and actually broke in."

"Are you OK?" Terri studied her sister.

"I'm fine, just a little worried, well actually, a lot worried. I kicked him down the stairs just before the police turned up."

Terri burst out laughing. "I know it isn't funny, but I can't help laughing. I bet he got a shock."

Caitlin smiled. "It's funny now. It wasn't at the time."

The two women served themselves and sat down at the table with their plates and glasses.

"So," Terri said. "I know you already have a plan. Let's hear it?"

"My suggestion is, we look for a duplex, or better yet, a fourplex to buy. We can put in our own escape route, perhaps across the roof space of all four units. If some angry batterer turns up looking for revenge, it should be possible, and relatively simple, to slip away without being seen."

Terri said nothing for a few minutes. She took a sip of her wine and nodded thoughtfully. "That could work really well. We could rent out the other units, too."

Caitlin couldn't help smiling. Terri was the one with the head for business. Renting out the empty units would bring some extra income as well as looking less obvious. Empty units might look suspicious.

They cleared off the table, refilled their glasses, and sat down to watch the sunset over the lake. *Just like when we were children back in Ireland.* Caitlin thought. It surprised her that she actually felt nostalgic about Ireland, having once been so unhappy to be moving there.

As the sun disappeared, Terri sat down at her computer and started searching real estate websites. She was looking for a suitable location for the next episode of their mission. Getting out a notepad, she jotted down phone numbers and addresses of properties that looked likely.

For two weeks, they spent most of their time viewing and eliminating buildings from their list. Finally, they made an offer on a large, old fourplex in Northwest Austin, just about a mile from Caitlin's current location. It needed some serious renovation. Their offer was accepted immediately.

"Thank goodness the housing market is in a bit of a slump right now," Terri said.

"Yeah, now we need to find a contractor who'll take care of the renovation and our escape route, then I can give notice at the current place," Caitlin replied.

Terri was silent for a few minutes before she said, "I'll talk to Joe about it. He can probably give us some good contacts."

"Good idea!" Caitlin said.

***

Keith had been working on his code most of the night. Every time he thought it was ready, he ran it just to find another bug. Now, he believed it was done. He had gathered several documents from web sites listing properties sold and stored them in a directory on his computer. He had designed and written a program to open and search these documents for Terri Donnelly's name. It also checked for Terri and Caitlin Donnelly, and finally for Caitlin Donnelly.

He was convinced that they would eventually buy a place either separately or together and when they did, he would track them down.

This time his program worked flawlessly, in so far as it opened all the documents and reported 'Unfound' without error. Next, he edited one of the documents, adding the sisters' names in various formats. He ran the program again.

Success! The program ran without error. When it completed, the word 'Found' flashed on the screen, and a copy of the document in question was saved to another folder on his computer.

Now for the difficult piece. *Just a few more tweaks to this code and I'll be able to locate the bitch.*

CHAPTER SEVEN

When Terri called Joe, he said he would be happy to help, and he could put them in touch with a friend of his who was an architect.

"I'll call him today and perhaps we can talk about it over dinner tonight."

"That would be lovely. How about I cook dinner? Say seven-thirty?"

"It's a date! See you then."

As soon as Joe hung up, Terri called Caitlin.

"Hey, I just spoke to Joe, and he has a friend who is an architect in Austin and he's going to talk to him."

"That's good news. Glad you thought of it," Caitlin said.

"Oh…and another thing, Cait, just in case you were planning to come here this evening…don't."

"Why? What's up?" Caitlin said.

"Joe's coming over for dinner. You don't mind staying away, do you?"

Caitlin sighed. "No, I don't mind. Of course, I worry about you, but he seems like a nice guy. Just be careful. And Terri…"

"What?"

"Have fun. You deserve it."

***

Caitlin hung up and sat for a few minutes thinking about Terri...and Joe.

I know Terri thinks I should be more trusting. I just can't. Sometimes I wish I could. Too much has happened to convince me that it's foolish to trust. The weird thing is that Terri has experienced worse, and she trusts everyone!

She let her mind wander back to the day she and Terri finally stood up to their father. They were nine years old. Their elderly neighbor, Dan Egan, noticed bruises on Caitlin's legs and assumed they were caused by fighting with other children. He told them that the only way to deal with bullies was to stand up to them. They assumed this also applied to their father, who was the bully responsible for the bruises. One evening, they decided it was time to stand up to him. They made a plan and a lot of noise; that was what usually set him off.

Sure enough, their father came rushing out of his study with clenched fists and a red face, nostrils flared like a bull. He was faced with Terri, who was holding a stool in front of her, with the legs pointing towards her father and a frightened but determined look on her face. He charged at her and bending down; grabbing the legs of the stool, he tried to pull it out of her hands. Terri clung on as she was being pulled forward. Suddenly their father let out a yelp, sounding like a surprised dog; he let go of the stool, causing Terri to almost lose her balance. He swung around to see Caitlin standing behind him with a hurley stick raised over her head, ready to strike again. He tried to grab the stick away from her, but Terri rushed forward, ramming him as hard as she could with the stool, held like a battering ram, driving him against the wall. She screamed at him, "Why are you doing this? Why do you hate us? If Mom were here, you would never hurt us like this! She wouldn't let you—she loved us!" He slid to the floor with his hands over his face and started crying uncontrollably. Terri dropped the stool and went over to him. She put a hand on his arm.

"Dad?"

He gathered her into his arms and kept crying and muttering that he was sorry. Caitlin stood out of his reach and watched, ready to run if necessary.

Even back then, Terri was prepared to forgive and trust, while Caitlin never trusted her father again. Perhaps it was just part of their genetic makeup.

I wonder if we'll ever be able to figure it out.

Caitlin's Escape Route

She shook her head, as though to get rid of the memories, and looked around the kitchen, trying to decide what she would do for dinner herself. Then she grabbed her gym bag and headed out the door.

Two hours later, she was back in the kitchen preparing dinner for one. She had spent an hour at the gym and picked up some groceries on her way home.

She sat down to eat, allowing her thoughts once again to stray back to her childhood in Ireland. *I just wish I could talk to Dad about what he did to us.* The thought jerked her back to reality. Or maybe it was the fact that her ER phone was ringing. She glanced at the caller ID before picking up. *Maria again!*

"Hi Maria, what happened to you? Are you okay? I do hope you're alright?"

"Hi Caitlin. I'm so sorry about the last time. My husband broke my phone so, not only could I not call you, the directions were on it. I just got a new one. Could we make another appointment, and can you tell me how to get there again?"

Caitlin gave her the address and directions and said, "I can see you at ten in the morning, but if you can't make it this time, at least call me. We can't keep doing this."

"I promise I'll be there at ten tomorrow. Thank you."

***

Terri was clearing up after breakfast when her phone pinged. She read the text from Caitlin.

Call me when you get a chance and let me know how things went last night.

Terri smiled as she waited for Caitlin to answer the phone. She answered on the second ring.

"Well?" Caitlin said.

"It was wonderful, Cait. We talked for hours; Joe is so easy to talk to. By the way, his architect friend, Steven, is going to contact you to discuss the work we want done on the fourplex."

"Great, I do want to get moving on that as quickly as possible. I'm glad your evening went well—and glad you're safe."

"Oh Cait. When are you going to relax and believe there are more good people out there than bad? And, just so you know, Joe stayed here last night. He just left." Terri waited for a response, not knowing

52

what to expect.

"Thank you for letting me know that. Still glad you're safe. And Terri…" Caitlin paused for just a brief second, trying to find the right words. "I think I'm working on my trust issues. Last night I had such a strange thought."

"What?"

"I wished that I could talk to Dad about the beatings—to try to figure out what was going on in his head. Pointless, I know, but I think that might be progress?"

Terri took a deep breath. "I do believe it is! Well done you! I'm proud of you."

"Yeah, well—we'll see. Oh, and by the way, I'm at the office waiting for Maria. She called again."

"Again! Oh, for heaven's sake. I hope she turns up this time. What time is she supposed to be there?"

"Any minute now. I'll let you know how it goes."

***

As she hung up, Caitlin heard a tapping on the front door and jumped up to answer it.

"Hi, Maria?" Caitlin said as she opened the door. "Please come in."

"Thank you for seeing me after all the trouble I must have caused you." Maria stepped inside, looking around.

She was a skinny little girl. She looked little more than a teenager.

"Do you live here?" Maria asked, looking at the living room with just a table and two chairs in the middle of the room.

"No, this is just my office." Caitlin smiled. "Have a seat and tell me what is going on with you."

Maria sat down and fiddled with her phone before putting it in her purse. She put the purse on the floor beside her and took a deep breath.

"I'm not really sure. My friend, the one who gave me your sticker, said that my husband is abusing me, and I should speak to you."

Caitlin remained quiet and sat still, waiting.

"But he told me it's my own fault. He said I'm forcing him by deliberately pushing his buttons. I don't know how to stop pushing his buttons. Can you tell me how?"

"Maria," Caitlin paused and slowly shook her head, "people do not have buttons. And no one should deliberately hurt another person, particularly not someone they claim to love. It's not acceptable."

"He does love me."

"Do you have children, Maria?"

"No. Chris says I would be a terrible mother, so he doesn't want any kids." Maria wiped away a tear.

"Has he ever hit you? Or been rough in any way?"

"No, sometimes he looks like he wants to, but he never hurt me."

"And what happened to your phone? You said it broke?"

Caitlin could see Maria's face slowly redden and she glanced down at her hands as she pulled at the hem of her T-shirt. "He threw it on the ground and stomped on it."

"Why?"

"Because I was looking at Facebook and he said I wasn't paying attention to what he was saying."

"You don't think that was abusive?"

Maria shook her head and said nothing.

"Do you want to leave him? I can help you if you do. If you don't, there's nothing I can do."

"No! I don't want to leave him. I want to know how to stop pushing his buttons."

Caitlin stood up. "In that case, Maria, I recommend you find a good therapist. That's not what I do. However, if you decide you want to leave him by all means, call me."

Maria stood up and picked up her purse off the floor. "How do I find a therapist?"

"You should ask your doctor to recommend one. If you can talk Chris into going to couples' therapy, that would be the very best solution. Do you think he would consider that?"

"No. Oh no. I couldn't suggest that. None of this is his fault. He said so."

Caitlin walked towards the front door. Maria shrugged and followed her.

"Goodbye Maria. I hope you can sort this out. Please be safe and do call me if you change your mind." Caitlin sighed heavily as she closed the door. *I can only help those who want to be helped.* The thought made her feel even more unhappy. She sat down and typed up her report and sent it to Terri before heading home.

Caitlin's Escape Route

A few days later, Caitlin met with Steven at the fourplex and showed him exactly what she envisioned as an escape route. He also went over all four units and made a list of suggestions for improvements.

"It'll cost a bit, but if you want to rent these units out, these changes will ensure not only that you get good tenants but also a good rental income," Steven said.

The renovation included a new roof across all four units. Steven suggested skylights at intervals to help light the escape route, which was to run through the attic area. The paint on the outside stucco wall was a dirty yellow. All the windows were rotting wood with peeling cream paint. They would transform it with white painted walls and new vinyl windows in a matte black. The units on either end were slightly bigger than the two center units, and each had a bay window in the front and another at the back. New fiberglass front doors with a mahogany-grain finish would replace the existing warped wooden doors.

Caitlin's next task was to call into the police station to let them know she would be moving. George was on desk duty again, and he got to his feet and came over to greet her as soon as she entered. She explained she was going to be moving and gave him the new address.

"It won't be for at least two months. There's a lot of renovation to do. I'll let you know the date for moving as soon as I know it."

He made a note of the address. As she left, she could feel his eyes on her. She avoided turning to look and hurried out.

CHAPTER EIGHT

Caitlin continued to live at the old duplex while the new location was being renovated. Her feeling of security had not returned even with the installation of a new, stronger steel door. She took extra care, double checking that she had locked everything, and the alarm was on at all times. She couldn't wait to move into the new unit with the escape route. Meanwhile, she continued to visit the shelter at least one day per week and also see clients at the efficiency. As she was leaving the shelter to meet Steven at the fourplex, her phone pinged.

"Caitlin's Nails. How can I help you?"

"Hi Caitlin. My name is Margo, and I got your details from a friend. I wonder if I could make an appointment?"

"Sure, Margo. I'm free tomorrow. What time would suit you?"

"Any time in the morning?"

"Okay, let's say ten-thirty? Let me give you directions."

After Margo had repeated the address and directions, Caitlin hung up.

Next morning, as Caitlin sat waiting for Margo, she allowed her thoughts to wander over the past few months. They had achieved a lot in a short time, and she was feeling more confident about their efforts to help victims. She had learned so much from Peggy, Joe, and Alex. A knocking on the door brought her back to the task at hand and she went to open it.

"Margo? Come…" Caitlin stared at the couple on the doorstep.

"Hi Caitlin, this is Roger, my husband."

The woman was in her fifties, beautifully dressed. She had blueish gray hair, carefully arranged and sprayed into place. The man with her was about the same age and equally well dressed. He removed his hat, exposing a bald head, which he nodded at her. They both walked in, almost knocking Caitlin to one side as she quickly stepped aside and closed the door behind them.

"You are Margo, right?" Caitlin said as they continued into the office.

"That's right, you said ten-thirty. Here we are, right on time."

Caitlin sat down behind her desk and stared at the couple, not sure what to say. As she studied the woman's face, she noticed that her heavy makeup was barely disguising a black eye. She turned to look at the man. He had a scab beginning to form under his chin.

Were they both victims? If so, who was the abuser, and how do I deal with it?

"Please explain to me what you are doing here, Margo."

"Well, like I told you, my friend gave me your contact information. She said you help people involved in domestic violence."

"Margo, I help victims. Yes, are you saying that you are both victims?"

"Exactly!" Roger said.

Caitlin took a deep breath. "Okay, can one of you please explain it to me? Who is abusing you?"

"We abuse each other. We keep fighting, and it almost always comes to blows, so we would like you to help us stop," Margo said.

"Wait a minute—you mean, you are a couple and you hit each other? No third party involved?"

"That's it," Roger said, sitting back and nodding.

"I'm sorry. I think your friend misled you, Margo. I'm not a couple's therapist. I can't fix your situation. If you both genuinely want to do that, you need to go to family counseling." Caitlin stood up and headed towards the door, hoping they would follow.

"Well! That was a total waste of time, Margo. Why didn't you get your facts straight?" Roger said, jabbing his finger at his wife.

"Don't you talk to me like that! I'm the one trying to find a solution. I don't see you being any help there," Margo yelled at him.

Oh, my God. They are going to start fighting in front of me! I can't believe this.

"Please leave now," Caitlin said, holding the front door open and holding her breath. As they both hurried out, still shouting at each other, Caitlin closed the door and leaned against it, forcing herself to take slow, deep breaths. Once her heart had returned from somewhere near her throat and stopped beating so fast, she went back to sit down at her desk.

I need a drink. That was just nuts!

It didn't take long to type up the report, and she added a note at the bottom.

'*We need to start compiling a list of therapists to recommend to clients.*'

Gathering up her things, she looked out the window to make sure the couple had gone. She was in time to see them drive off, clearly still arguing. She locked up and headed home.

At least I move into the new place tomorrow.

Caitlin and Terri met at the fourplex the following day. The renovation had taken almost three months, but it was worth it.

The two middle units were ready to be let out, and they had kept the fourth unit empty as its attached garage was the escape route exit. Although they did not expect it to be occupied, they furnished it and set up timers to switch lights on and off at appropriate times to make sure it looked occupied.

As they unpacked Caitlin's suitcases and put her things away, she told Terri about Margo and Roger.

"Oh, for heaven's sake, Cait! That is totally crazy. What made them think you were a family counselor, or therapist, or magician?"

"I have no idea. Apparently, Margo's friend told her I worked with victims of domestic violence. I guess she just assumed—"

Suddenly, they both saw the funny side of it and burst out laughing.

"Still, we should be able to help people like them—and Maria, which is why I want to start compiling a list of therapists to recommend."

"I'll start doing some research into that, and perhaps ask Peggy," Terri said.

An hour later, everything was done. Caitlin looked around and nodded.

"This is going to be so much safer and more comfortable."

"I assume you'll continue to live here most of the time?" Terri asked as they put the final touches to the kitchen.

"Yes, I will," Caitlin replied. She looked around. "It isn't bad. The kitchen has everything I need, and I've no use for a dining room. The new couch in the living room is lovely, and the bedroom is comfortable. Plus, I've a bathroom upstairs and a half bath down here.

That's way more than I need. I doubt I'll ever even go into the second bedroom, but I might think about setting it up as an office at some stage. Besides which, as long as Keith is still free out there, we need to keep your location separate from the ER tunnel. I'll come out to the lake for the weekends when I can."

Terri nodded and sighed. "I do wish we could be free of him."

"The police are still looking and I'm sure he won't be able to stop himself from victimizing some other poor woman. I'm positive they'll catch him." Caitlin tried to sound confident, though they both knew that too many batterers got away with it over and over again. They frightened their victims into silence.

"Do you really think he would be able to find us...me?" Terri said.

"I know it sounds unlikely. It's a long way from San Francisco to Austin and he has no reason to believe we would be here. I mean, we never had any ties to Texas." Caitlin looked at her sister. "We just can't afford to take any chances. After all, you're the only witness and he tried to kill you. Locking you in the house and setting fire to it that's attempted murder. It also shows just how vicious he really is."

"I know you're right," Terri agreed. "But..." Her voice trailed off as Caitlin gave her a hug.

"Let's go back to the lake. I'll stay there tonight and come back tomorrow and make sure we've a light at the end of the tunnel. That's what I'm calling this location—The Tunnel." They smiled at each other.

As they locked up, a car pulled up in front of the unit.

"Hi George," Caitlin said. *What on earth is he doing here?* "Terri, this is George, the cop I was telling you about. George, this is Terri, my sister."

"Thank you for watching out for my sister, George. Nice to meet you." Terri shook hands with him.

"I'm fairly sure she can take care of herself," George replied, smiling at Caitlin, who was fidgeting with her keys and looking uncomfortable.

"You've certainly improved the place. The new paint job was sorely needed. I was just passing by and stopped to see what you had done with it." He nodded towards the building.

"We're just leaving," Caitlin said, turning towards her car.

"Well, take care and don't forget to call if you need anything at all," George said as he got back into his vehicle and drove off.

"Oh my. Looks like you have an admirer, Cait."

"What? Don't be silly."

"I'm not being silly. It's obvious from the way he looks at you that he's smitten. We should invite him to dinner some evening. Or maybe we could double-date?"

"Don't you dare Terri Donnelly!"

Terri laughed. "Surely you can trust a policeman? He won't hurt you."

"I'm not ready to do that yet. I'm working on it."

"I know you are Cait." Terri hugged her sister.

***

Keith sat down in front of his computer and signed in. He was curious to see how the latest version of his program had performed. This version was designed to go out into cyberspace and find all public data on home sales. Download it and, to make it more generic, search for anyone or a combination of the names Terri, Caitlin and Donnelly, and to do this for every state. He inspected the logs and was relatively satisfied. The program had run to completion with almost no errors, and none that were of any consequence. He was pretty sure he could speed it up, but for now, it was doing what he wanted. He did notice that he was getting several false positives, a few people called Donnelly, but none were Caitlin or Terri. A few instances of their first names alone as well. He made a small change to his code to add extra checking for these and eliminate them.

So far, he had only searched through one week of data and for this to work, he would need to go back a lot further. He calculated his wife would have been in a position to relocate and possibly purchase a house any time during the past six months.

He spent some time tweaking the code for extra logging and setting up the configuration to search from a specified date, watching as it started up. When he was sure it was running and doing what he wanted, he went to the fridge and got himself a beer.

He sat down and turned on the TV. *I'll make her pay for this*. He couldn't remember when things started to get sour between them. Everything was fine while they were in Dublin. She changed when they got to California. At first it was just little things. She kept asking him about work and what friends he had made there. He had made none; they were all busy trying to prove they were better than everyone else.

But she wouldn't let it go. Then she started talking about all the friends she was making at her job. Going out to lunch with them, almost all of them were men. When he started questioning her about the men, she got defensive and accused him of not trusting her.

She just didn't understand how difficult it was for him, starting a new job in a new city.

Next morning the program had completed. He checked the output and stared in amazement. A hit! He opened up the log and searched through it. There it was! *Austin Texas. That is a place I would never have guessed they would go to.*

The following day, he stuffed what few clothes he had into the saddlebags, tied his backpack, a small tent and sleeping bag on the back of his bike, and headed south. He hadn't bothered to give notice at the Computer Store. Planning to stay away from hotels, motels, or any populated places. He was going to pitch his tent in isolated locations on the way to Texas. He figured he could make it in three days if he could ride for ten hours each day.

CHAPTER NINE

Almost as soon as it was available, they let the first center unit, number two, which was next to Caitlin's. They had decided that they would let both fully furnished, that way they could use them for either short term or long term.

Rosie called within hours of the unit being advertised and arranged to view it immediately. She was a schoolteacher and had just moved into the area from Wisconsin to take up a job at the elementary school a few blocks away from their location. She was a slim girl in her early twenties, with long, light brown hair, gray eyes, and a bubbly personality. Rosie told Caitlin that she had been staying in a motel since arriving in Austin the previous week. A fully furnished apartment was exactly what she was looking for. It saved her from having to buy everything from scratch. Caitlin showed her around the unit.

"It's quite small." She warned her as she unlocked the front door.

There were two bedrooms and a bathroom upstairs and a kitchen, living room and half bath downstairs. The half bath was an addition that they had put in as part of the renovations. They had installed it under the stairs.

"I love it," Rosie said. "I'll be living here on my own, so it's plenty big enough for me."

Caitlin called the property agent Steven had recommended and directed Rosie to his offices to complete the lease paperwork.

Three days later, Caitlin was coming out of the second of the two center units—number three—when she saw Rosie at the door of number two with a large suitcase.

"Hi Rosie!" She called out. "Welcome home."

Rosie looked up, smiled and waved. "Hi Caitlin, thank you. I'm delighted to be home."

"I'm just waiting for someone to come view this unit. With luck, that will be occupied soon too," Caitlin said.

"Good luck," Rosie said, as she hauled her suitcase in.

As Rosie closed the door, a car drove up and parked. Two young men climbed out.

"Caitlin?" One of them said with his hand out towards her. "I'm Jeremy and this is Pete." They all shook hands and Caitlin let them into the unit.

A couple of hours later, back in her own unit, Caitlin sat at the kitchen table with a mug of coffee and her laptop. She picked up her phone and called Terri.

"Hey Terri," she said as her sister picked up. "I'm happy to report that both units are now rented out. Rosie just moved into number two and two guys, Jeremy and Peter, are heading towards the property agent's office as we speak, to sign up."

"That's good news!" Terri said. "It was quick too. I was a bit worried it would be hard to get a long term let with them being fully furnished. I'm glad you decided to take responsibility for showing the units, rather than letting the property agent do it. I'm happier knowing you have met the tenants before they become neighbors."

"Well, apparently not. There are a lot of people moving into Austin. Most of the younger ones haven't accumulated furniture, at least as Jeremy put it, nothing that was worth transporting across the country. And I agree, I feel more comfortable meeting the potential tenants myself. After all, they are going to be my neighbors."

The following week, Caitlin was returning from the gym when Rosie came out of number two and waved to her.

"Hi Caitlin, do you have a minute?"

"Sure, what's up, Rosie?" Rosie blushed and looked around awkwardly. "Come on in," Caitlin said, holding the front door open.

Rosie stepped in and Caitlin led her to the kitchen.

"I'm just going to make some coffee; would you like a cup?" Rosie nodded but said nothing. "How are you settling in?" Caitlin said, hoping to prompt Rosie to say whatever was on her mind. She really

Caitlin's Escape Route

wanted to take a shower.

"Great thanks. I love it," Rosie finally said. "I—actually—I met this guy at work, and we have been out a few times. I wanted to know if it would be okay if he stayed over sometimes?" She paused and then said in a rush, before Caitlin had time to answer. "You see, he lives way down South Austin. He shares a house with a bunch of guys, so it would be easier for him to stay over—sometimes?"

"Sure thing." Caitlin smiled at the obviously embarrassed girl. "As long as you pay the rent, you can have who you like to stay. You don't need my permission. Unless he's going to move in?"

"Oh, thank you. I wasn't sure, so I thought I would ask. And no, he isn't moving in."

The two women finished up their coffee and Rosie hurried out. Caitlin shook her head slowly and headed for her delayed shower.

The next evening Caitlin noticed a car pulling up outside number two and Rosie got out and went into the unit followed by a young man, about her own age. He had a scruffy dark brown beard, and his hair was long and tied back in a ponytail. He was wearing dirty jeans and a t-shirt that had seen better days.

I guess the boyfriend isn't a teacher at the school, by the looks of him. Caitlin thought to herself.

Now that both center units were furnished and let, Caitlin spent some time getting familiar with the built-in escape route. She wanted to be certain that she could quickly slip away if an angry attacker ever turned up again. There was always the worry that Keith would locate them, though she was beginning to think that was unlikely at this stage. If he had any sense, he would have left the country, perhaps gone back to Ireland.

It soon became obvious to Caitlin that Rosie's boyfriend had become a permanent resident next door. They drove off in the morning together and returned together in the late afternoon. One afternoon, they arrived home just as Caitlin was leaving to meet another victim.

"Hi Rosie," Caitlin said, standing expectantly, looking from her to her boyfriend.

Rosie just nodded and stood there looking uncomfortable. Caitlin stuck her hand out and introduced herself to the boyfriend, who shook hands with her and said his name was Brad. Rosie continued to say nothing and studied the ground.

Caitlin walked to her car, feeling uncomfortable. She started the engine and took one last look at the two as they walked in the front door.

Something doesn't feel right. But Terri would probably just call me paranoid, still I don't like the look of that guy and Rosie was definitely not her usual bubbly self.

As Caitlin pulled into the garage at her office, she noticed a young woman approaching the front door.

"Ruth?" she called to her as she got out of her car.

"Hi, Caitlin?" the woman replied. "Sorry, I'm a little early."

"No problem, come on in." Caitlin opened the door and led the way into her office area.

She sat down and indicated to the chair opposite her. "Have a seat."

Ruth had long, dark hair and beautiful, dark brown eyes. She wore neat blue jeans and a navy blue T-shirt. Sitting down, she looked around her, saying nothing.

"What can I do for you?" Caitlin said, after a long pause.

"I'm really not sure if you can do anything for me. I just need to talk to someone to find out if I'm losing my mind." Ruth sighed.

"Let's start with how you got my name and why you set up this appointment."

"Okay—" Ruth paused again, then continued, "a friend gave me a sticker with your name and number on. She explained it was not really a nail salon, that it was a help line for victims of domestic violence. She seemed to think that I was experiencing domestic abuse, and she told me it would do no harm to contact you—" She paused again, studying Caitlin's face.

Caitlin just nodded.

"Carol—that's my friend who gave me the sticker—she told me she considered the way my boyfriend is treating me to be abusive." She paused, shaking her head before continuing. "But he has never hit me, or been violent, so I'm not so sure."

"Tell me what he does that makes Carol believe he is abusive?" Caitlin prompted.

"He says things like—'even though you are not pretty, I still love you'—and he often accuses me of things I really didn't do. Like—he might say I promised to phone him and I just know I didn't, but sometimes it is easier to just apologize than argue because he just keeps

Caitlin's Escape Route

insisting. Whenever we go out together, he accuses me of making eyes at other men, and questions me about how I know them. But I don't. I really don't. I'm afraid to look at anyone because he'll assume I'm having an affair with them. Then he goes on and on at me, to just admit it and he'll forgive me—it never ends." Ruth sighed and looked down at her hands.

"Anything else?" Caitlin asked.

"He empties out my purse every evening and goes through it. He says he is looking for proof. And he goes through my phone too and then accuses me of deleting texts so he can't see them."

"As a matter of interest, Ruth, why are you still with him? That sounds like a really horrible way to live. It's emotional abuse. Carol is correct."

"Really? Abuse? But sometimes he's so good to me, and he says that he loves me—he says that no one else could love me as much as he does."

"Absolutely, it's abuse. It's a means to control you and it's not acceptable behavior. Abuse doesn't have to be physical. In fact, sometimes emotional abuse can be every bit as damaging as physical abuse, but no one can see the scars."

"So, how do I make him stop? How do I convince him I'm not seeing other men?"

"You won't be able to do that, not ever."

"So, what do I do?" Ruth sounded miserable as a tear slid down her cheek.

"My advice is to walk out of the relationship and don't look back. I also recommend finding a good therapist to help repair the damage he has already done to you. Do you have somewhere you can go? Family in the area?" Caitlin handed her a tissue.

Ruth shook her head, wiping away the tears. "My family is in Dallas. I was living there when I met Mark. Then we moved here for his job."

"And what about your job?"

"I gave up my job in Dallas to move here with him. I'm still looking for work here."

"What about Carol? Could you stay with her?"

"No. She lives in Dallas too. She was just visiting us last week. She's gone back now."

"Do you have a car?" Caitlin asked.

Again, Ruth shook her head. "No, Mark told me to sell it before we came here. He said it would be more economical to just have one car. I was able to use it to come here because he's attending a conference in San Antonio today and tomorrow and he went with a colleague in his car."

"So, he won't be home tonight?"

"No, he'll be back tomorrow evening."

"And Ruth, are you ready to leave him—no regrets?"

"Oh, I'll have regrets. I regret already that he was not the man he pretended to be, but I can see now, you're right, that he won't ever change. Probably he'll continue to get worse. I have to go."

"Okay. Let's go. I'll follow you back to your place and stay while you pack your things. Then I'll have someone drive you to your parents' home in Dallas."

"Should I not wait to explain to him that I'm leaving?"

"No, you should not give him the opportunity to even try to talk you out of it. And you know he will try. You need to get away and recover your self-confidence before you even think about talking to him again—and I recommend you never do."

The two women stood up. Caitlin headed to the garage after letting Ruth out the front door and locking it behind her. On the drive, she called Pat and asked her to be ready to transport Ruth to Dallas.

Two hours later, Pat met them at Caitlin's unit. As the two women drove off towards Dallas, she waved goodbye to them, having repeated her warning for Ruth to avoid speaking to Mark again. She said that he would try to make her feel guilty and sorry for him and not to even pick up the phone or read any texts. She also told her to block him on all social media. Ruth promised she would do that, and she agreed to find a therapist in Dallas.

CHAPTER TEN

Over the following month, apart from a couple of days spent at the lake catching up with Terri, Caitlin was kept busy. She met up with three women at her apartment location. Two of them agreed to think about the escape network being offered, and one accepted the opportunity to escape. That was about average. So many battered women were still emotionally tied to their batterer, or believed they could somehow fix them, yet more were too afraid of them.

She was returning from one of those meetings, as she turned onto the road leading to the house, when she noticed someone disappearing around the back of her unit. Deciding to err on the side of caution. Instead of pulling into her own garage, she drove to the end unit and pulled into that garage, quickly pushing the button to close the door behind her. She sat in the car for a few minutes trying to figure out her next move, and wondering who was creeping around the unit.

Finally, she decided the best thing to do was go upstairs and see if she could identify him; she assumed it was a man but couldn't be certain. As she peered out the window of the upstairs back bedroom, she could make out the head and shoulders of a man. He was going to each of the back windows and attempting to look into the unit. She knew he could see nothing as she kept the windows covered at all times with heavy shades. The only way she would be able to get a good look at the man was if she were to open the window and lean out. Not a good idea, as she would surely draw attention to herself if she did that. As she watched, the man backed away and looked up at the upper-story windows. Caitlin pulled back in case he glanced in her direction, though she was fairly sure he wouldn't be able to see her from down there. Better safe than sorry.

Slowly, the man turned and walked back around the corner of the unit towards the front. Caitlin hurried to the front bedroom and watched him go to the front door again and knock on it a few times. Again, he stepped back and looked at the upstairs windows, still all she could see was the top of his ball cap. He started to walk away towards the road, then he changed direction, went up to Rosie's unit and knocked on that door.

She waited while he appeared to be talking to whoever answered the door. A few minutes later, he turned away and climbed on a motorbike that he had parked around the side of the unit. As he disappeared down the road, Caitlin hurried down the stairs and out the front door. She knocked on her neighbor's door and waited.

"Hi Rosie, sorry to disturb you."

"Hi Caitlin, what's up?"

"I noticed some guy looking at the house. Did he talk to you? I just wondered if he was looking to rent a unit?"

"I don't think so. He wanted to know if a Terri Donnelly lived here. I told him I never heard of her."

"Oh, Okay, thanks."

As Caitlin turned to go, Rosie added, "I gave him the name of the management company. If he wants to rent, he can go to them."

"Thanks again." Caitlin walked quickly to her door and fumbled with the key in her hurry to get inside.

As she locked the door behind her, Caitlin pulled her phone out of her purse and dialed George's number. He answered on the second ring.

"Hello Caitlin, is everything alright?"

"Hi George, yeah no immediate problem, just wondering if that guy Malcolm, the one who—fell down my stairs, is still in hospital or jail—or out?"

"Let me check."

Caitlin walked up and down the hall with the phone clutched to her ear, listening to the tapping of a keyboard.

"Looks like he is out on bail pending a court date. Why?"

"Oh, nothing serious. Some guy was prowling around here just now, but I didn't get a good look at him. Obviously, I didn't want to confront him if it was Malcolm—or any other disgruntled batterer."

"Very sensible."

"Mind you, my neighbor said he was asking if Terri lived here. Malcolm wouldn't know Terri." *But Keith would!*

"That is not good, just the same. Do you want me to come over?"

"No. No. That won't be necessary! Thanks for your help. Bye." Caitlin hung up quickly. *The last thing I want is George coming over here. I do not need that complication!* Her phone rang.

'Sorry, Caitlin, one more thing." She heard George say as she picked up. "A guy called Ted might be contacting you. I gave him one of your stickers yesterday."

"A guy? Why would you give my sticker to a guy? They are for victims of domestic violence."

"Right. We were called out to a DV last night. The wife slashed this poor guy with a carving knife. He refused to press charges, unfortunately that is fairly normal too. But it wasn't the first time and I'm sure it won't be the last if he doesn't get out."

"A guy?" Caitlin repeated, shaking her head slowly, "but most men are stronger than most women."

"Why? Do you think that being bigger, stronger—and, or male—automatically means violent?" George snapped, then more gently continued, "Caitlin, not all men are violent and there are some women who are extremely violent." He sighed heavily. "It's just a lot harder for men to admit that they're being battered by a small female. Also, most people don't believe a man if he says his wife or girlfriend attacked him. And if he fights back, they'll automatically assume him to be the aggressor." He paused. "Caitlin? Are you still there?"

"Yes, I'm here. I'll take care of Ted if he calls me. Thanks George and—sorry." She hung up and sat down at the kitchen table, staring at the phone for a long time, thinking.

Finally, she made a decision and headed out to the lake to talk to Terri about setting up surveillance at the tunnel.

Terri looked up from her computer as Caitlin let herself in the back door.

"Hi Cait. I got your text and I have just finished ordering all the equipment we need for both the tunnel and here."

"When will we get it? And more important, when can we get it set up and working?"

"I've ordered it in two separate lots. One to be delivered to you at the tunnel and one here. Paid extra to overnight it."

"Great. That'll be a relief. You can't imagine how frustrating it was to not be able to see anything but the top of that guy's ball cap and his dirty jeans."

"I can imagine! Did you even catch what color his hair was?"

"Nope. Apart from the ball cap, he had a jacket with the collar pulled up around his ears, no hair showing, though I think he had a beard. I can't say for sure." Caitlin sighed and shook her head. "What's your plan for setting it all up?"

"I'll do the tunnel first. That's more likely to need it. If you stay here tonight, we can head back early in the morning and as soon as it arrives, I'll get working on it."

"What about your delivery here? Don't you need to be here to receive that?"

"No. I have 'In Garage' delivery." Terri grinned at her sister. "I think we should set up the control center in the empty fourth unit. Best to put it in the escape tunnel. Put cameras all around the perimeter of the building, a video doorbell on your unit, along with audio recording. Might be a good idea to put audio in the fourth unit too, as that is where the actual tunnel exits. What do you think?"

"I agree, whatever you say. This is definitely your domain," Caitlin said.

Early the following morning, they took the boat across the lake, tied it up at the marina, and drove to the tunnel.

It took Terri most of the day to get everything set up. Caitlin helped where she could, holding the ladder as Terri climbed up to fix the cameras in place; luckily, they were all Wi-Fi and solar powered, so they didn't need to run wires anywhere.

Finally, Terri set up the monitor inside the escape tunnel at the fourth unit. It was accessible from either end units, and hidden from sight.

It was mid-afternoon before they had completed and tested the system. Everything worked perfectly. Sitting in front of the monitor inside the escape tunnel, Caitlin could clearly see Terri waving at each of the cameras. Although the system saved the video to the cloud, she could zoom in and take screen shots. They tidied up and headed back to the lake.

Terri checked the garage and everything she needed to repeat the installation at the lake was sitting there waiting for her.

"Let's take care of that in the morning," Caitlin said. "I'll stay and help you with it. In theory, it should be faster as there's less house, and we have had more practice."

Terri grinned at her sister. "Let's hope so!"

Next morning, they got started early. Two hours into their efforts, Caitlin's ER cell phone rang.

"Hello? Caitlin here," She answered.

"Hi Caitlin, my name's Ted. George gave me your number. I don't need my nails done, but I'd like to talk to you sometime today if you're free." His laugh sounded a little forced.

"Absolutely Ted. George told me to expect your call. What time's good for you? I can meet you at my office any time between—" She checked her watch, did a quick calculation and continued, "—say midday and three?"

"Midday would suit me. Thank you."

"No problem. Do you have a pen handy to write the address?"

"Ready."

Caitlin gave him the address of the apartment she referred to as her office and hung up. She looked at her sister.

"Sorry Terri—"

"I know, you gotta go. Not a problem because all the difficult stuff is done. I can finish it up on my own and have it tested before you even get to your meeting. Besides, I've a date tonight myself—I'm meeting Joe for dinner."

Caitlin looked at her sister in silence, shaking her head. Then she sighed and said, "please be careful…and have fun. Talk to you later." Caitlin hurried down to the dock and set off back to Austin.

CHAPTER ELEVEN

Caitlin pulled her car into the garage at the apartment complex—her office—fifteen minutes before twelve. She had given Ted precise directions but was fairly sure he would have difficulty finding it. That was the whole point of this location, so she sat at the front window watching for someone looking lost. She spotted him ten minutes later and went to the door to call him.

"Ted?"

"Ah. There you are, sorry, but these buildings all look the same!" She stood back to let him in, closing and locking the door behind him.

"This way." She led him into the only room in the apartment other than the bathroom.

He was average height, approaching forty, she guessed, with a slight paunch and a raw-looking scar across his cheek. She could see where the stitches had only recently been removed.

"Sit down and tell me your situation."

Ted sat in the chair she indicated, took a deep breath and then exhaled; he looked at her for a few minutes saying nothing.

"George told me a little about you. He said your wife had cut you with a kitchen knife?" She pointed to his cheek. "There?"

"My girlfriend, but yes. Correct. She sometimes gets into a sudden frenzy and starts screaming and throwing things…mostly." He paused as his eyes seemed to glaze over. Then he blinked a few times and pointed to his face. "This wasn't the first time she cut me, but it was the worst. The first time was across my hand when I tried to take the knife away from her. That time I didn't go to the hospital…I should have, but I didn't want to answer their questions."

Caitlin nodded, remaining quiet. She had learned that it was best to not interrupt victims; it was hard enough for them to talk about their experiences. They all expressed shame and deep embarrassment that they had allowed themselves to get into such a situation and had stayed in it.

"This time I told her I was leaving her, and that is when she slashed my face. I don't think she intended to cut me," he blurted. "I think she got as much of a fright as I did. There was so much blood...." He shook his head slowly. "Then she yelled at me for bleeding on the kitchen floor."

"I had to go to the hospital this time. I couldn't stop the bleeding and the cut was almost all the way through into my mouth." He sat there silently, looking at Caitlin.

"Did George explain to you what we do?" she asked him quietly.

"Yes, he did."

"Are you prepared to leave now, right now?"

"Yes. Absolutely."

"Last question—do you have any children? Because that complicates matters."

"No. I don't. My girlfriend has a son—Bobby—he's not mine, but I look after him when he's not at school. I drive for rideshare companies, so my hours are very flexible."

"Where's the child now?" Caitlin asked with a frown.

"He's at school and I have arranged for one of the mothers to pick him up and keep him till his mom gets home from work. I had to go to the hospital to get my stitches out this morning. I told her it was later today so she wouldn't expect me to pick him up."

"At work? Why is she not in custody?"

"I didn't call the police, Bobby did—I told them it was an accident, and I wouldn't press charges."

"And you never gave her any reason to do this to you? Never got rough with her?" Caitlin asked.

"No. Never."

"Not even after she did this to you?"

"No. Never," Ted repeated quietly. "I didn't want to hurt her or traumatize Bobby any more than he already was. I didn't want him to think it was okay for men to be rough. I couldn't do anything about the impression he had of his mother or what that'll do to him. Besides all that, she'd have blamed me and if she had any marks at all, I'd have ended up going to jail. No one believes that a man could be the victim of domestic violence. Everyone blames the man."

Caitlin looked at him, blinked hard a few times and said, "I'm so sorry, Ted. We'll help you."

"Great. I packed a small suitcase before I left the house, so I'm ready to go."

After she explained to him how they operated, she said, "We've never had a male escapee before, but that won't be a problem. In fact, when you get settled, it'll be very useful if you would be prepared to volunteer to help other male victims in the future. Many of our ladies are now working as rideshare drivers, so you have a head start there. It's something you can do anywhere, and it's very anonymous, though I doubt she would go looking for you."

Ted smiled for the first time since arriving and let out an enormous sigh. "I'd love to be of help in any way I can. And…thank you so very much. Please thank George for me."

Caitlin made a few calls, and within the hour, Ted was on his way to a new life. This time he was driving himself, but she'd supplied him with names and addresses where he could stay overnight on his way to Philly.

By the time Caitlin got home to The Tunnel, the afternoon was almost over. It had been a very busy two days, but they had achieved a lot in that time. Surveillance systems were operating at both houses. And yet another victim was free to start over.

She had promised Ted she would thank George for him and let him know he was 'saved', as he put it. She poured herself a well-earned glass of wine and called George.

"Caitlin, everything okay?" he said as soon as he picked up.

"Yes, all good, George, thanks. I'm just calling to let you know Ted is on the move to a better life and he wanted me to thank you."

"That's great news. Thank you, Caitlin." There was a pause. He added, "I don't suppose you would care to have dinner with me?"

"Actually, I would love to," she replied.

"Really? Tonight? Now?"

"Yes, please. I'm shattered and hungry. That would be great."

"Terrific! Pick you up at…is six-thirty too early?"

"Six-thirty would be perfect. See you then." Caitlin couldn't help

Caitlin's Escape Route

smiling. George sounded almost like an excited child.

As she showered, Caitlin thought about the day. A male victim, that was something she had never considered. *I have got to admit that he definitely convinced me that he was not the aggressor. Poor guy was very beaten down.* She dried off and picked out an outfit that was comfortable, stylish but not too over the top. A brown skirt and a mustard yellow, long-sleeved blouse. She didn't want George to get any ideas. *Yes, I agreed to have dinner with him, but that was all. To be honest, I'm still not sure if it is a good idea.*

Thirty minutes before he was due to pick her up, she decided to change. She thought she looked a bit too drab. She picked out a deep red sleeveless dress with shoulder straps. Then she called Terri to bring her up to date. As she sat at the kitchen table and hit speed dial, she noticed the glass of wine she had poured earlier. As she was taking a sip, Terri picked up.

"Hey Cait. How did it go with Ted?"

"Very interesting. He really is a victim. Poor guy had a nasty scar on his face. I'm still processing it all."

"Processing what? That a man could be a victim and not an aggressor?"

"Yeah. Given me a lot to think about. Did you get the system set up at the lake house?"

"Yes, all working. When you're out here next, I'll show you how to switch between monitoring both houses. Probably be a good idea to do that tomorrow if you're free?"

"I'll be out there first thing in the morning! Oh, there's the doorbell. Gotta go, I'm having dinner with George."

"What? Dinner with George? What did you say?" Terri shouted. "Caitlin!? Hello?"

Caitlin didn't hear her and hung up.

George pulled into a parking spot close to the restaurant.

"I hope you like Tex-Mex food?" he said. "I should've asked you. We can go somewhere else if you would prefer?"

"No, this is perfect, thanks. I love Tex-Mex." Caitlin smiled at him.

He sat looking at her without saying anything until she said, "are you okay? Should we go in?"

"Oh. Sorry. I'm so pleased you agreed to have dinner with me. I'm not sure what to do or say for fear of chasing you off. Let's go in."

He climbed out of the car and came around to open the passenger door for her. She was already out and heading to the entrance. He stood there for a second, staring after her, then quickly caught up with her and held the door open.

Over dinner, Caitlin asked George about his experiences with DV.

"I just never considered that women would be the aggressor. Have you come across that before?"

"A few times, yes. Obviously not as often as men, but I sometimes wonder if that's because men would be too ashamed to admit that a woman had that sort of control."

Caitlin considered that for a few seconds as she built another taco from the fajita plate they were sharing.

"You know, I think I'll get some stickers made for a barber shop." She paused. "Something male anyway."

"That's a good idea."

When they pulled up outside The Tunnel sometime later, Caitlin opened the door, then turned to George.

"Thank you, George. That was a lovely meal. We should definitely do that again. I had fun and—"

"Look Caitlin, I understand your misgivings and I promise I would never harm you. I'd love to do this again and I won't ever impose myself on you. We'll do this on your terms."

Caitlin could feel the tears filling her eyes as she turned to get out. She didn't want him to see her cry.

"Thank you. I appreciate that more than you know. Good night, George."

"Good night, Caitlin, take care. I look forward to doing this again soon."

Caitlin closed the door of the car quietly.

He watched her until she had opened the front door and she turned and waved to him, watching him drive off with a smile on his face.

CHAPTER TWELVE

Next morning Caitlin headed to the lake. She stopped at the local coffee shop and picked up a large latte and a couple of blueberry muffins before heading to the marina. As the boat engine fired up, the noise didn't quite drown out the sound of a motorbike pulling into the parking lot by the marina. Caitlin glanced up but could see nothing.

The sisters spent some time going through the monitoring system. Terri made sure that Caitlin was completely familiar with the system before having her download the app for her phone. Over coffee and the muffins Caitlin brought with her, Terri explained how the app worked with the system.

"Okay," she said, "this app will allow you to monitor both systems. I've set the system up with two admin accounts, one for you and one for me. Now! Tell me about your date with George!!"

Caitlin blushed and shrugged her shoulders. "Nothing much to tell, really. We went to a Tex-Mex restaurant—it was really good—had a nice dinner, and he dropped me home."

"That's it? You didn't invite him in."

"No! Of course not."

Terri sighed and shook her head. "I suppose that's progress. What made you change your mind?"

"It was Ted. Do you know he never fought back? Because he didn't want to hurt her! But I think what struck me most was that he didn't want to give her son a bad example. That was what really convinced me that he was basically a good man and an unwitting victim, just as all the other victims we've encountered, who just happened to be female."

Terri wiped a tear away and hugged her sister. "I'm so glad that's a tremendous breakthrough and I'm happy you're giving George a chance. I sense he's a good guy, and it's obvious he thinks the world of you."

Caitlin nodded, "I know. He seems to understand and is giving me the space to come to terms with this 'breakthrough', as you call it. Plus, he's not afraid to talk about it. That helps a lot." Caitlin paused. "I don't mind telling you, I'm nervous. I mean, I do like him—a lot—but—I can't explain—"

"Just try to take it a day at a time. Your experiences, since you were nine years old, have convinced you that all men are potential danger. And Mack just cemented that conviction. That doesn't change overnight. You can do this."

They headed to the kitchen and sat looking at the lake as they ate lunch.

"I love how quiet the lake is during the week," Caitlin said.

"Yeah, the only activity is the occasional worker barge. I did see a jet ski go up the lake just after you arrived. But that's pretty rare during the week," Terri said.

Caitlin looked at her phone. "Look at the time! Better get going if I'm to avoid the rush hour traffic."

As soon as Caitlin got home, she headed to the escape tunnel entrance on the ground floor; there were two entrances. The upstairs was in the main bedroom, the walk-in closet had been reduced in size to accommodate a ladder leading up into the roof space. A pressure point on the floor in one corner of the closet caused the wall, including a set of shelves at the back, to slide open to give access to the ladder.

The entrance downstairs was beside the garage door. A similar pressure point on the wall operated this, covered by a framed movie poster. Caitlin moved the poster to one side and applied pressure on the spot. A section of wall beside the entrance to the garage slid silently to reveal another ladder. She stepped into the space beside the ladder and pressed on a lever on the floor. The wall slid back into place as she climbed up through a trapdoor and into the roof space. Large sheets of thick plywood had insulated and covered the entire roof space across all four units. Spongy rubber sheets, like thick yoga mats, covered this. When it had been first completed, Caitlin ran and jumped on the flooring while Terri stood in the room below. She could hear nothing.

Just the same, Caitlin walked carefully and quietly towards the end unit. The command center, she called it. This was where Terri had set up the monitoring for the surveillance system—a small table and stool tucked into a corner with a computer, monitor and headset.

Caitlin sat down at the computer and spent an hour making sure that she could repeat all that Terri had shown her at the lake. It amused her to be able to see Terri, in real time, putting out the trash. When she switched to the app on her phone, she could see exactly the same view.

The system worked perfectly, and she was confident that she would have no problem operating it, should it be necessary. She almost hoped that she would get an opportunity to use it for real—almost. She hoped that she would never need it. While doing a final scan of the outside of her home, it surprised her to see George approaching her front door. She quickly made her way to the ladder and down into the house as the doorbell rang.

As she opened the door, he smiled and said, "I was going to bring you some flowers but thought that might be a bit too forward?"

She smiled up at him, nodded and said, "you're probably right. What's up?"

"Nothing much. I just came off duty and wondered if you'd like to grab something to eat?"

"I was just about to head out to get something myself, so sure. What do you have in mind?"

"Oh. Good! Nothing fancy. How about the Italian place by the gym?"

"That works for me. I've been there a few times. It's good. I would need to change if it were anything fancy." She looked down at the worn jeans she had put on that morning.

This time, when they pulled up outside the restaurant, Caitlin waited in the passenger seat while George came around and opened the door for her. As she climbed out, she felt his hand on the small of her back. It somehow made her feel cared for instead of threatened. She paused for a second, confused by her own reaction.

"Everything okay? Did you forget something?" George said.

She shook her head and smiled. "No. All good thanks."

Over dinner, she told him she'd heard from Ted.

"How's he doing?"

"Great. He told me he's settled in Philly and is doing the rideshare driving he was doing here. He has also offered to be part of the network. So now we have a presence on the East Coast!"

"It's sad that your service is so necessary and kept so busy," George said.

"I agree, but I'm glad we can do it."

When George dropped her home, he turned to say goodnight.

She noticed his hands tightly gripping the steering wheel, and she smiled to herself. *He's being so careful not to invade my space.*

"Do you have time to come in for a few minutes? I'd like to show you what Terri and I have set up."

George's eyes widened, and he nodded. "Sure, I'd be interested to see what you have been up to."

They both climbed out of the car and once inside, Caitlin immediately walked up to the poster on the wall. She moved it, showing George where the pressure point was.

"Press right there. You can feel it's a little softer than the rest of the wall."

George pressed the spot she pointed to and took a step back as the wall slid away to reveal the ladder.

"There is a similar entrance in the back of the closet in the bedroom," she said as she climbed the ladder.

"Press the foot lever in the far corner before you mount the ladder."

When they reached the roof space, George stopped and looked around.

"Gee! This is incredible," he said. "You ladies have really figured this out. I'm impressed."

Caitlin showed him the surveillance system and explained how it worked, and that it monitored both homes.

"I really can't believe all this. But I'm glad you showed me. I feel a lot better about your safety now."

"Well, I'm glad I showed you then, but the main reason I did was I thought if I ever have to use it and I call you for help, you'll know exactly where to find me."

Finally, she showed him where the exit into the fourth unit was. It was a trapdoor with an accordion type ladder. As soon as the trapdoor opened, the ladder unwound down to the floor of the garage.

George opened and closed the trapdoor a few times, watching the ladder fold and unfold itself.

Caitlin's Escape Route

"That's way cool," he said.

They climbed down and Caitlin pressed a button by the door; the ladder folded back up, and the trapdoor closed over it. She led the way through the unoccupied fourth unit, out the front door, and they walked back to George's car.

When they reached the car, he stood awkwardly, fiddling with his keys for a few moments.

"Okay—well, thanks for the tour, Caitlin."

"Good night."

"Good night, George." She watched him drive away before going inside and locking the door.

Early the following morning, Caitlin had just finished dressing when she heard a loud banging on the front door. She grabbed her phone and opened up the app Terri had installed. She stared at the figure outside her front door. He was standing a few steps back, looking at the upstairs windows. *Malcolm! How the hell did he find me here?*

She almost ran into her closet, opened the exit to the tunnel and stepped inside, closing it behind her. She climbed the ladder as quickly as she could and made her way to the monitor. Once she sat down and had the front door view on the screen, she called George.

"George! Malcolm's outside banging on the door!" She whispered as soon as he picked up.

"I can't hear you; did you say Malcolm?"

"Yes. At my front door—wait, he's going around to the back now—I thought there was a restraining order?"

"There is. It was a condition of his bail. I'll be there as quickly as I can. Are you okay?"

"Yes, I'm in the tunnel space I showed you."

"Good! Hold tight, I'm on my way."

Caitlin tracked Malcolm as he walked around to the back door and started hammering on that.

"I just want to know where Sally is! I won't hurt you," He shouted. "I will not leave until you tell me where she is."

Good, you just stay there.

Caitlin continued to watch him until George and two other cops came around to the back of the house and led him to the squad car parked out front. Caitlin came down the ladder to the ground floor and opened the front door. The squad car was driving off with Malcolm in the back. George stepped inside and put his arms around her.

"Thank goodness you're safe," he said, holding her close.

"How did he know where I moved to?" Caitlin said, her voice slightly muffled as her face pressed against George's chest.

"Apparently, you shared the same landlord, and he's also a customer at the bank where Malcolm works. He told him he lost track of you while he was in hospital and the landlord gave him your new address."

"Damn it!"

"The good thing is he'll go back to jail now and because he violated the restraining order, they'll revoke his bail."

"But...if the landlord told Malcolm, then he could also possibly tell Keith," Caitlin said.

"I'll talk to him," George said. "Hopefully Keith has not located you, besides Keith is a stranger to him. I doubt he would tell a stranger."

Caitlin nodded silently.

"If you're sure you're okay, I need to get to the station. Dinner tonight?"

"I'm fine, thanks George. And yes, dinner would be lovely." She smiled at him.

"I'll pick you up at seven-thirty if that works for you?"

"That works. See you then."

George turned and got in his car. He waved to her and drove off.

Caitlin closed the door and went into the kitchen to make some coffee and call Terri.

"Hi Terri, just wanted to let you know that Malcolm called by just now."

"Malcolm?" Terri said.

"Yeah, the guy I kicked down the stairs, remember?"

"Oh no, him! Are you okay?"

"I'm perfectly fine, just wanted you to know the surveillance and escape tunnel worked perfectly. Oh, and I'm having dinner with George again tonight."

"We'll have to think about double-dating!"

"Okay, I guess we could try that again." They both laughed. "I'll suggest it to George, and you can see how Joe feels about it."

Over dinner, Caitlin asked George if he would be interested in having dinner with Terri and Joe.

"Sure. What does Joe do?"

"He's a lawyer; he works with one of the shelters; His partner is helping Terri with her divorce."

"See if you can set something up for next weekend. I've got the entire weekend off, so Friday or Saturday works for me."

"Great! I'll let Terri know."

***

Terri was sitting at her computer when her phone pinged. She finished up what she was working on before looking at it. A text from Caitlin, confirming that George was on for a double date next weekend. She sat back and stared out the window at the lake. Her feelings were mixed between being happy that Caitlin had finally met someone and let her guard down, and worried that she would get hurt.

Whoa! She thought to herself. *How strange she would be worried now that Caitlin was doing exactly what she had been telling her to do. Trust that not all men are bad. Perhaps working with victims of domestic violence actually altered Caitlin's conviction that all men were abusers. But is it doing the opposite to me? Didn't we agree we needed to learn from each other?*

She turned back to her computer; it was already late, and she had put in more than enough hours on work. Instead, she opened up the folder containing all the reports Caitlin had sent her so far. As she started reading them, she set to work on compiling them into one document. Caitlin had been meticulous about putting a date and time against each one. As she read through each report, she could see how it would influence Caitlin's thinking. It also definitely put a tarnish on her own idea of happily ever after.

Perhaps you can't trust everyone; clearly you can't if you look at these reports. But you have to trust yourself and learn as you go. Life may not be the fairy tale I want it to be, but it's what we make of it ourselves. I'll believe I can be happy some day and I'll trust that Joe is a good man.

The following weekend, the four of them met outside a restaurant built on the side of a hill overlooking the lake. Introductions done, they went in and followed the host, who led them to a table on the outdoor deck.

"How long have you been on the police force, George?" Joe said.

"Seven years now. Too long. I joined when I graduated from UT in

San Antonio. First job I could get."

"What's your degree?"

"I majored in Criminal Justice, and since then I completed my masters. And you? I understand you're a lawyer? What kind of law do you practice?"

"Criminal defense. I guess that puts us on opposite sides of the room?" They both laughed.

"And you work for the shelters?" George said.

"That is a voluntary thing. Peggy runs the shelter. She is my partner's sister. We do what we can to help her and the victims. When we started, we added a junior partner Alex, he specializes in domestic violence, and he handles the shelter work. I was just lucky that he was off for a few days, and I was there when Caitlin came in, so I got to know these two ladies."

They continued chatting over dinner and waited to watch the sun go down over the lake before leaving.

Terri and Caitlin hugged. The men shook hands.

"If you ever consider leaving the force, George, call me. We could do with someone with your expertise."

"I will definitely call you Joe. That sounds very interesting. I'm actually looking to make a change."

"Great! Glad I thought to mention it."

***

As Malcolm was being detained. Keith was working on his own monitoring. He was sitting in yet another sleazy motel room. This time on the outskirts of Austin; he had managed to get a job there as night cover on the front desk. It didn't pay much, but at least the room was free.

He studied a map of the lake and the north shoreline on his laptop. Zooming in, he pinpointed all the possible locations Caitlin might have been heading. He calculated she would likely want to keep the boat trip to less than thirty minutes.

The house is somewhere in this area. That is the direction she took.

She would need somewhere to dock the boat, and it would have to be close to at least one house or apartment.

Those stupid bitches think they can outsmart me.

Later that day, he headed out on his motorbike towards the North

Shore. After two hours of winding hilly roads, he came within sight of the lake multiple times but could not get close enough to see which houses had docks. Too many gated communities and private parks blocked him. He realized the only way to do that was to approach from the lake. It was already getting dark, and he needed to get back to his job at the motel. He headed that way, cursing to himself. *Stupid bitches! I need to figure a way to be able to follow Caitlin.*

He decided that the most likely time she would go to the lake was on a Friday afternoon. It was a Friday that he followed her to the marina the last time. He would rent a jet ski the following Friday and take it out on the lake and wait for her there. And he would do that every Friday if necessary until he figured out where Terri was living.

CHAPTER THIRTEEN

Caitlin's phone pinged. She looked at the caller ID. *Pat. I wonder what she wants.*

Pat told Caitlin that her father had died, and she had found a retirement home in Austin for her mother. As a result, she was hoping to move back to be close to her mother.

"I'm so sorry to hear about your father. Of course, move back. We'll give up the rental you're in up there in Temple and, at least for the moment, you can move into number four, the end unit here."

"Thank you. That's a great relief. My mom's not doing well, so I want to stay close to her, but I don't want to let you down, either."

"Of course, you need to be close to your mother. And to be honest, our network is growing. You would probably be more useful here in Austin."

Pat said she would give notice to the apartment that she was leaving. It would take a few weeks to move her mother to Austin.

When she hung up from Pat, Caitlin called Terri to let her know Pat was coming back.

"I didn't check with you first, I'm afraid, but I told her she could move into number four, at least till we sort out something for her."

"Actually, Cait, I think that's a great idea. You could give her your ER cell phone and let her begin to take over that side of things. You could move into a more supervisory role."

Caitlin thought about that for a few seconds.

"Cait—Cait, are you still there?"

"Yeah, sorry, I was just thinking about what you said. It makes a lot of sense. I'd like to free up some time to give more attention to the shelters. I know Peggy could do with the help. In fact, we might get Pat involved there too. She's a special needs teacher, after all. She could really help the kids at the shelter."

"Good thinking! I bet that'd help a lot. And I think she'd still have time to help with victims. In fact, she could hold sessions for new victims coming into the shelter, to help them adjust and, where possible, move them through the ER too."

They chatted for a few more minutes. Caitlin promised to let her know how Peggy reacted to the idea.

Caitlin was at her office; she had just finished up a meeting with another victim. An older woman. She hadn't given up on the idea of "fixing" her violent husband. They had spent some time talking around in circles. Finally, the woman left, promising to call if she changed her mind. Caitlin sighed, gathered up her things and was about to leave when her ER phone rang.

"Caitlin's Nails." Realizing her voice sounded a bit low energy, she said with more enthusiasm, "how can I help you?"

"Hi Caitlin, this is Margo again."

Caitlin sat down and managed to stifle a gasp.

"Hello?"

"Yes, sorry Margo, I'm surprised to hear from you."

"I realize you must be, and I'm sorry. We didn't even thank you for seeing us. I've been thinking about what you said, and I'd really appreciate an opportunity to talk things over with you—just me. Would you mind?"

"Well—I'm not sure if I can be of any help, but I'd be happy to do whatever I can. I'm free right now if you want to come to the office. You remember where it is?"

"Yes, and I'm only about fifteen minutes away. I'll be there shortly. Thank you."

Fifteen minutes later, Margo arrived. She carefully balanced a cardboard tray containing two takeout coffee cups, which she placed on the desk.

"I brought a peace offering. I hope you like latte. There's also some sugar in case you prefer yours sweetened." Margo studied Caitlin's face, her eyebrows drawn together, biting on her lower lip.

Caitlin couldn't help smiling. "Thank you, Margo, I do like latte, and I don't need sugar. That was a very kind thought. I could do with it right now."

The two women sat and sipped on their coffees in silence, studying each other.

"I see your black eye has healed up nicely."

Margo nodded. "I spent a lot of time thinking about what you said. And I really did misunderstand the service you offer." She took another sip of coffee before continuing. "What's more, you helped a lot. After we calmed down, we did some research and found a therapist who does couples counseling and we've seen him a few times. He also recommended us to an anger management group."

"And how is all that working for you?"

"Well, it hasn't been very long, but so far, it seems to be really helping. It also helps that we're both going together. As soon as one of us sees tempers flaring, we can talk each other down."

"Yes, I can see that would be useful. You're lucky that you're both prepared to admit your issues and do something about it. Well done!" Caitlin waited, still not sure why Margo wanted to see her.

"Although we came to you by accident, your advice did help us—"

"I'm so sorry, Margo, that I couldn't be of more help to you at that time. What it made me realize is that I needed to compile a list of therapists and couples counseling for future clients, should they need them."

"Exactly. That was what I was thinking. Also, knowing what you do for people who have no one else to turn to, well—it started me thinking that I would like to do something to help. So—" Caitlin waited expectantly as Margo drained her coffee cup before continuing. "I've started making a list of therapists. I've been collecting names and recommendations from the people I meet at our anger management sessions." Margo pulled out an envelope and handed it to Caitlin. "They're all there, each with a few words to describe why they're being recommended. I do hope that'll be useful to you?"

"That's amazing, Margo! That's exactly what I've been trying to do. Your list will be invaluable."

"Oh, I'm so glad." Margo got up to leave, gathering up the empty coffee mugs.

"Don't worry about that. I'll take care of clearing up. And thank you for the coffee."

As they walked toward the door, Margo said, "if there's anything I can do to help you in the future, please don't hesitate to ask. My contact details are in there, too." She nodded towards the envelope Caitlin was still holding.

"I just might take you up on that, Margo. Thanks again and the very best of luck."

As soon as she closed the door, Caitlin hurried back to her desk and opened up the envelope. There were three pages of names and addresses of therapists with comments beside each one. Some highlighting to show those that specialized in couples and anger management. She opened up her laptop and typed up a report on Margo's visit. Then she added all the information she had given her to the list she and Terri had already started compiling. Next, she called Terri to let her know to expect it.

"My God Cait, that's amazing! And we laughed at them!"

"I know. That's what I kept thinking. We've a lot to learn."

CHAPTER FOURTEEN

Caitlin arrived at the office with time to spare. She had an eleven o'clock appointment with Victor. He was only the second male victim, and she was interested in hearing what his story was.

She sat down at her makeshift desk and set up her laptop. She had just finished going through her email when the doorbell rang. The young man on the doorstep was tall and slim with short blond hair. He wore what looked like designer jeans, though Caitlin didn't know much about designer clothes. She thought he was stylishly dressed, in a carefully casual manner. He introduced himself as Victor, and she invited him in.

As he took a seat at her desk and looked around dubiously at the sparsely furnished mini apartment. She gave her usual explanation as to why she used this location rather than a more obvious office space.

"Well, that sounds very sensible," he said, eyeing her with an approving nod.

"What can I do for you, Victor? I assume you got my sticker from someone?"

"Yes, actually a cop gave it to me."

"Why? Were the police called to a domestic dispute?" Caitlin asked.

"Yes. Sort of. What happened was—" Victor paused and took a deep breath before continuing. "We were in our car, parked at the mall, having an argument about something. I don't even remember what, when my boyfriend suddenly lost his temper and started yelling and then he slapped me across the face. Apparently, someone in the parking lot noticed and called the cops. Well, this cop came up and tapped on the window of the car on Fred's side. He asked him what was going on while another cop came to my window and asked me to get out of the car to talk to her."

"Okay, and then what?" Caitlin said when he paused and seemed to be lost in thought.

"Then what? Oh, right. Then I told her it was just a lover's disagreement, but she saw the red mark on my face. She gave me your sticker and said she recommended I call. I told her I already had a good manicurist. That's when she explained it was a cover for helping victims of domestic violence." He looked at Caitlin, his head turned slightly to the side, his eyebrows raised. "Is that true?"

Caitlin smiled and nodded. She explained to him exactly what they did, then said, "was this the first time he had hit you? Or is there a history of this sort of thing?"

"We met on the Internet and have been dating for about a year and only recently moved in together, well—I moved in with him. Before that it was a long-distance thing, we only got together a few times in that year, the rest was on-line. Almost as soon as I moved in with him, I realized it was a mistake. I quit my job to move here." He shook his head slowly. The look on his face revealing his feelings. "I can't believe I was so stupid."

"What happened?" Caitlin prompted him.

"He owns lots of guns and he thinks it's funny to play around with them. He's also very controlling. If something doesn't go his way, he either threatens to shoot me, or more often, to shoot himself and make it look like I did it. To be honest, I'm not sure what to do. I'm afraid if I leave, he'll do exactly that—frame me—can you help me?"

"Absolutely, I can help. First, we'll set up an appointment for you to speak to a lawyer. He can advise you on the best way to protect yourself from that unlikely event. In my experience, this sort of threat is used to control, but they rarely follow through with it. However, talking to my lawyer is a good idea because I'm definitely not an expert."

Victor nodded, relaxing into the chair and unclenching his hands.

"My recommendation is that once you've spoken to Joe—the lawyer—you leave town and return to Florida. Don't contact Fred again and don't respond to any attempt on his part to contact you." She paused. "The other alternative is to move somewhere totally different and start a new life where, hopefully, he wouldn't think of looking for you. However, that's probably unnecessary. Your relationship is very new, and my belief is he'll just get back on the Internet and search for another victim. Sadly, that's a lot more difficult to stop."

Victor sat quietly, nodding his head and stroking his chin with his right hand.

"So, would you like me to call Joe and go down that route?"

"Yes, please. That sounds like a good plan."

Caitlin picked up her phone and called Joe's office.

"Hey Lucy, is Joe available? I'd like to speak to him on an urgent matter—okay, I'll hold—" She turned to Victor and was about to say something when she spoke into the phone again, "Oh, hi Joe, sorry to disturb you but I've a complicated issue with a client and I was hoping you could advise us—him—Really, now? That's terrific. We can be there in about fifteen minutes."

"Wow Victor, you're in luck," she said as she hung up. "Joe's free now. Let's head over there immediately."

As they left the apartment, Caitlin said that she'd drive and after the meeting with Joe, she'd drop him back at his car.

"Thank you so much for seeing us on such short notice, Joe," Caitlin said as Lucy showed them into Joe's office.

After the introductions were done, Caitlin and Victor sat down. Joe asked if it was okay to record the meeting. They agreed and Victor explained his problem. Joe listened without interrupting until Victor finished.

"My advice is that I have Lucy transcribe this statement. You can sign it and then I recommend you do as Caitlin suggested and head home."

Victor nodded his agreement, and Joe took the recorder out to Lucy.

"Fred's out of town this week at a conference in Vegas. He wanted me to go, but I had a couple of job interviews lined up. I can go home, pack my bags and be back in Florida before he even knows I'm gone."

Joe and Caitlin exchanged looks, remembering what happened to Terri when she thought she had time to pack her bags.

"I'll get George to send a couple of police officers to meet you at your apartment and stay while you pack. Just in case."

Victor nodded. "I'd appreciate that. Thank you."

A few minutes later, Lucy came in and handed Joe a couple of sheets of paper.

"Here you go Victor, read over this carefully and if you are happy that it's exactly what you said, sign it and Caitlin and I will witness it."

Victor read over the two pages carefully, slowly nodding his head as he did so.

"Yes. This is exactly how it happened and what I said to you."

He initialed both pages and signed the document. Joe and Caitlin also signed and dated it, and they all shook hands.

"That's it, Victor. Best of luck," Joe said.

Caitlin and Victor thanked him for his time and drove back to the office. Once there, Caitlin called George and explained what she wanted.

"No problem, darling. I'll get two of the guys to meet him. When?"

"Thanks George, he says it'll take him about thirty minutes to get there."

She hung up and told Victor he was good to go.

"Thank you so much, Caitlin," Victor said as they shook hands. "I'll be in touch to give you my contact details. If I can help in any way, in your efforts, please let me know."

"That'd be great. We don't have a contact in Florida yet." Caitlin smiled at him and waved as he drove off.

This operation's teaching me a number of lessons. Straight or gay, male or female. Not all men are bad, not all women are good. I really do need to listen and learn the lessons, no matter how hard it is.

Caitlin was about to leave the office when her phone rang again.

"Caitlin's Nails." She managed to sound cheerful. "How can I help you?"

"Hi Caitlin. My name is Susan and I've a friend who's in a terrible relationship—I understand you help victims of domestic violence?"

"Hi Susan, yes, that's correct."

"Great. Could I possibly bring her to you?"

"Where are you located?"

"Well, we live in San Antonio, but we're in Austin right now. She came to my house this morning after they had a fight. I got one of your stickers last week and decided it was time to do something, so I just put her in my car, and we drove here."

"Okay. Let me give you my address. I'll be here for the next hour." Caitlin gave her directions to the office.

"Great! Thank you so much. I'm looking at it on my GPS and we're really close. See you soon." Thirty minutes later, Susan and Grace arrived. Caitlin had no difficulty identifying which one was Grace. She had bruises on her face and her arm was in a sling.

"Have you been to the hospital?" she said, pointing to the injured arm.

"Yes," Susan said. "We did that before heading to Austin."

As they sat down in the office, Caitlin asked Grace the usual set of questions. She established she had no children and was determined to leave her boyfriend. They were not married. She had family in Bangor, Maine.

"I just want to go home," She said in a small voice, wiping the tears away awkwardly using just one hand.

Caitlin outlined how the ER worked and what to expect.

"That sounds amazing," Susan said. "I would love to be of any help I can if you need someone in San Antonio."

"We need all the help we can get. Thank you! For now, we need to get Grace to Temple, where Pat can start moving her through the pipeline—"

"I'll take her to Temple," Susan said before Caitlin could finish. "Just tell me where."

Caitlin called Pat and within twenty minutes, Susan and Grace were gone and she locked up and headed home.

CHAPTER FIFTEEN

Caitlin woke with a jolt. She thought she heard a scream. She sat up in the dark and listened. Total silence. *I guess it was that nightmare again, but it doesn't normally come with screams. After all, Terri and I never cried or screamed when Dad hit us. We were determined to never give him that satisfaction.*

She lay down and as she drifted back to sleep, she heard a dog howling in the distance. *That must have been what woke me up.*

Next morning, as soon as she had her coffee, she went outside and as she dragged the trash can to the curb, Rosie came out of the next-door unit with the same chore. They passed in the driveway, going in opposite directions.

"Good morning, Rosie."

"Good morning." A slightly muffled reply, as Rosie turned her head away.

Caitlin checked to see what Rosie was looking at. There was nothing of interest to see.

"Hey Rosie, did you hear screaming last night? I woke up from a nightmare and was afraid that I'd screamed out loud. I hope I didn't disturb you."

Rosie glanced at her and said, "no, I heard nothing."

"Was your boyfriend there last night? Did he hear anything?"

"He was here, but he said nothing about a scream." As Rosie turned around, Caitlin did a double take.

"Hang on. How did you get that black eye? Are you alright?"

"Oh, it's nothing. I went to the bathroom during the night and stupidly didn't turn on the light. I walked right into the door; It may have been me screaming, though I can't remember. Sorry if I woke you."

"Are you sure you are okay? It looks nasty."

"No, it's fine. Thanks Caitlin."

"Well, come in and have a cup of coffee, anyway. I'd like to talk to you about some ideas I have for the backyard."

Rosie paused for a second before following Caitlin into her kitchen.

Caitlin expanded on a plan she had just made up for the backyard, hoping that Rosie would open up about her black eye. She talked about shared patios. Fruit trees and flower beds while Rosie sat quietly fiddling alternately with the buttons on her jacket, her watch and her coffee mug, saying nothing.

"It sounds wonderful, Caitlin, but I really must go. Thanks for the coffee."

"Before you go, Rosie, take this." Caitlin handed her a wad of her stickers.

"I work with the women's shelter in this area. If you know anyone at all experiencing domestic violence and needs help, please hand these out."

Rosie took the stickers and looked at them. "Nails?"

"That's just a cover. To protect victims should their abuser find the sticker, it looks perfectly innocent." The two women locked eyes; then Rosie turned away.

"I told you, I walked into the door in the dark. I don't need these—and I don't know anyone else who does." She put the stickers down on the table. "Thanks for the coffee and I appreciate what you're doing, but I'm fine."

Caitlin shrugged her shoulders and said, "well, take them anyway. You never know when you might come across someone who needs my help." She picked up the stickers and put them into Rosie's hand again.

"Okay, if you insist." Rosie walked quickly out of the house.

Caitlin heard the door close and sighed. She stared out at the wilderness behind the house, wondering what she could do to get Rosie to open up to her.

Perhaps she did walk into the door. Maybe I am seeing abuse everywhere. I just don't trust that guy, Brad. But I guess Terri would point out, I don't trust any

Caitlin's Escape Route

man.

Then she thought about George and smiled. *I trust George. I do—yes I do trust him.*

That night Caitlin awoke again to the sounds of screams. This time it was not her dreams and definitely not a dog. A second scream, coming from the unit next door, Rosie's unit. After a brief silence, a man's voice yelling and another scream followed the first one. She got out of bed, listening. Silence. Finally, she called the police. She didn't want to call George at this hour; she knew he was due to go off duty a short while ago and didn't want to risk waking him. Instead, she called 911 and reported the screaming and gave the address. Then she quickly dressed and went downstairs to wait for the police to arrive.

It wasn't long before two squad cars pulled up outside. One police officer started banging on Rosie's door while a second headed towards Caitlin's. She opened the door before he reached it.

"Hi, you're Caitlin Donnelly? You called 911?"

She nodded. "Yes, I heard screaming from next door. I know Rosie and I was worried about her. She had a black eye yesterday."

"You're a friend of George's, right?"

"Yes, that's correct."

"I'm Brian, I work with him."

They turned to see who had finally opened the door. Brad was standing there in boxer shorts and a t-shirt.

"Quick! My girlfriend fell down the stairs. She's unconscious," He yelled.

"Did you call an ambulance?" Brian said.

"No, I only just found her. I was asleep. The banging on the door woke me."

Brian rushed into the house and bent down beside Rosie while his partner called for an ambulance.

"Did you not hear the screams just now?" Caitlin said to Brad.

"What screams? I heard nothing, just the banging on the door."

Caitlin pushed past him and squatted down beside Rosie. "I'm a nurse. Let me look."

"She's dead!" Caitlin gasped. "I think she's broken her neck, and I can't feel any pulse."

She stood up and looked at Brad. "You have a nasty scratch on your arm. It's bleeding."

Caitlin's Escape Route

Brian looked from Brad to Caitlin and was about to say something when the ambulance siren could be heard coming around the corner.

EMS confirmed Rosie was dead and as they drove off with her body in the ambulance, the police told Brad they would need him to come down to the station.

"You are not under arrest; we just need you to come so we can take your statement."

They let him get some clothes on and as they loaded him into one of the squad cars, Caitlin heard him telling one of the cops that Rosie had recently started sleepwalking, that the night before she had even walked into the door. They closed the door of the car on him and drove off. Brian turned to Caitlin.

"We'll need you to come down and give a statement, too."

She nodded. "Yes, I understand. Let me just get my purse and keys." She locked the house and got into the car with Brian.

Caitlin was sitting in one of the interview rooms, waiting to give her statement, when George stuck his head around the door.

"There you are!"

She stood up as he came and put his arms around her.

"I thought you were off duty."

"I was on my way home when I heard it come across the radio. Are you alright?" He studied her face.

The concern on his face gave her a feeling she could never remember experiencing before in her life; she felt safe. Perhaps she had felt it when her mother was alive. She couldn't remember.

"Yes. But poor Rosie!" She couldn't stop the tears from spilling down her face. "I tried to help her. Yesterday she had a black eye, and I explained to her how I could help. She swore she got it by walking into a door." She rested her head against his chest. "I failed to save her."

He held her tighter and said, "it wasn't your fault; you can't save everyone."

She pulled away and sat down. "I know, I know—but I want to. No one should have to put up with being treated like that by the person who should protect them, or at least respect them."

George sat down opposite her. "They've arrested Brad on suspicion. Rosie had blood and skin under her nails and, as you pointed out, Brad had a series of scratches on his arm, so chances are they'll confirm that there was a fight. Along with your testimony as to the screams and the timeline, there's very little doubt that he's responsible, and they'll charge him with murder."

Caitlin shook her head slowly. "I suppose that is something. Poor Rosie." She sighed.

"I'll get someone to take your statement now and then I'll drop you home."

"Thank you."

Two hours later, George walked Caitlin to her door.

"Go home and get some sleep. You must be exhausted."

"Good night, Caitlin. Try to get some sleep, too."

"Thank you again." She put the key in the lock, then turned back to him. Reaching up, she kissed him. Suddenly, his arms wrapped around her as they kissed. He let go and stepped back, breathing heavily.

He hugged her and then waited until she was inside with the door locked.

Caitlin wandered into the kitchen, feeling slightly lightheaded.

Wow, just wow, what just happened?

She sat down at the table and took a few deep breaths. What the hell is happening to me? I thought I had life figured out. I thought I was in control. God, I hope I'm not making another terrible mistake.

She went to bed, thinking about George—and that kiss. She had never felt anything like this before, so perhaps that's a good sign. If everything before was wrong, just maybe this is right. She thought as she dropped off to sleep.

Next morning Caitlin woke to the sound of her phone.

"Hello?" Her mouth moved, but nothing came out. She swallowed and tried again. "Hello?"

"Caitlin, are you alright?" Terri's frantic voice on the other end caused her to fully wake up. "I was just checking on our surveillance and—what the hell was going on over there?"

"Oh Terri. I totally forgot that you could see everything on the video. I should have texted you when I got home. Yes, I'm fine. Poor Rosie is dead. It looked like Brad pushed her down the stairs. She broke her neck." Suddenly, she was crying so hard she couldn't speak for a few minutes. Finally, she took a deep breath. "It was horrible, Terri. I could see that she was having issues. I talked to her and tried to get her to open up. She kept insisting there was nothing wrong. We could have saved her."

"No, we couldn't, Cait. We can only help the ones who want to be helped, or who want to help themselves. Remember Maria? First, they have to accept that what is happening to them is wrong, and not their fault. I know you did your best."

"I did—I tried. At least I was here to make sure the police arrested that bastard, Brad."

"I'll contact Joe to find out what to do about the unit. The rental agreement was with Rosie. Brad has only been around a couple of weeks. He had not moved in. I don't think he has any rights. But we need to figure out what we can do with it, and with the poor girl's property," Terri said.

"Thanks Terri. I didn't even think about that."

"I'll let you know what he says."

Later that day, Caitlin called Terri.

"Hey, I talked to Joe, and he said we need to get in touch with Rosie's next of kin so they can come get her things."

"Okay, we've that information on the rental agreement, besides I'm sure the police have already advised them. Poor people. I'll follow up on that."

Caitlin spent the next hour tracking down Rosie's next of kin. Her brother Peter, living in Wisconsin. Before calling him, she checked with George, who confirmed that yes, they had advised the brother of Rosie's death.

The phone rang for so long Caitlin was about to hang up when someone picked up.

"Hello," a male voice said, somewhat impatiently.

"Hello, is this Peter?"

"Who wants to know?"

"My name's Caitlin Donnelly. Your sister, Rosie, was renting a house from me. I'm so sorry for your loss."

"Oh. Okay—Thank you," Peter said.

"I wondered what you want to do about her belongings?"

There was a pause, and then a cough, before Peter responded, "I hadn't really thought about it. We can't get down there to sort it out, not for the foreseeable future, anyway. I have a family and commitments."

"I understand. If you like, I can pack up everything and send it up to you?"

"Thank you. That would be very helpful." He paused. "Would that cost very much? I mean, is there a lot of stuff?"

"Well, she rented the house furnished, so there isn't any furniture. There'd be things like clothes, pictures, maybe some jewelry. I'd have to go through it all to know what. But I don't mind covering the cost—it's the least I can do."

"That would work then. Do you have my address?"

Caitlin double checked that the address she had was still current and hung up.

I'll make time tomorrow, after the police are done, to clean out next door and send that stuff off to Peter.

CHAPTER SIXTEEN

Caitlin had just finished packing Rosie's belongings when the ER phone pinged. She still had to clean out the bathroom and kitchen. That would have to wait. She answered the phone as usual.

"Hello, Caitlin's Nails."

"Hi Caitlin, this is Ted. Sorry to call on this line, but it is the only number I have for you."

"Ted? Oh, Ted! How are you?"

"Doing really well, thanks. I'm planning to be in Austin next week and was hoping we could meet up. I've a couple of ideas to run by you if you've time."

"Really? Sounds interesting. Let me give you my personal cell phone number. You can call me when you're in town."

Caitlin gave him her number and hung up. She turned back to cleaning out Rosie's things. She decided to just throw away all the food and cleaning items in the kitchen and all the toiletries in the bathroom.

Before she left, she took one last look around.

The place looks like Rosie had never been there. She thought sadly.

Then she loaded the boxes into her car and headed to the post office to mail them off to Wisconsin. As soon as she got home, she called George.

"Hi Caitlin. What's up? Still on for dinner?" George said as soon as he picked up.

"Definitely still on for dinner." She smiled. "I got a call from Ted earlier."

"Ted? Is he okay?"

"He sounded fine. He said he was going to be in Austin and wanted to talk to me. I just want to check if you'd join us. I'm not exactly sure when, but I thought you might like to see him, too. After all, you put him in touch with us."

"Absolutely. I'd love to see him again and find out how he's doing. I'll make sure that I'm available. Just let me know as soon as you hear from him."

"Thanks George, glad I thought to ask you. See you later."

"You're welcome. I'll pick you up in about an hour. We can discuss it over dinner."

Caitlin hung up and headed to the shower. She had enough time to clean up after all the packing and stress before George got there.

Next morning, Caitlin was sitting in the kitchen, on her second cup of coffee, when her phone pinged. When she picked up, she recognized Ted's voice.

"Hi Caitlin. I just got into town. Would you be free sometime today?"

"This afternoon works for me. Say about two? Let me give you my address." Caitlin was glad that she had checked with George on his availability for the rest of the week, so she knew he was free this afternoon.

As soon as she hung up, she texted George to let him know Ted was going to be at her place at two. He responded almost immediately that he would be there at one-thirty.

George arrived promptly at one-thirty as promised and just before two, Caitlin opened the door to Ted. He looked thinner and fitter than the last time she had seen him.

"Come in Ted, great to see you. You're looking well. We're in the kitchen." She led the way, adding, "George is here too."

The two men shook hands before sitting down across the table from each other and made small talk while Caitlin made coffee.

Caitlin placed the coffeepot on the table with three mugs, sugar and cream.

"Help yourselves," she said, putting some cookies on a plate in front of them.

Ted poured himself a mug of coffee, added cream, and took a deep breath.

"Here's the thing, Caitlin. I've decided to move back to Austin, and I thought maybe you could do with some help with your escape route. I feel I should be giving back and helping others as you helped me, and so far, you have only needed to use me one time in Philly to move Grace to New York."

"Why come back to Austin?" George said.

"Well, it's mainly for Bobby, you know? My ex's son?"

"Yes, I remember. You used to take care of him," Caitlin said.

"Right. Apparently, his mother found another live-in boyfriend. This one did fight back. They had knock-down-drag-out fights, many times in front of Bobby." Ted sighed.

Caitlin glanced at George, watching a series of emotions cross his face before he assumed a neutral expression.

"Poor kid," she said to Ted.

"Yeah. Eventually, they ended up really hurting each other, and Bobby did what he does. He took charge and called the police."

"What happened?" Caitlin asked.

"Amy and her boyfriend ended up in the hospital and Child Protective Services were called in to take Bobby. Fortunately, his grandmother has him now. I want to be around to help the poor kid to get past this. I'm not sure what will happen with his mother."

"That's pretty complicated. Do you think his grandmother will let you see him?" George said.

"Oh yes. We've already spoken, and I think she appreciates any help she can get; she and I always had a good relationship."

"We could definitely use your help. I believe it would be easier for male victims to open up to another male, particularly if they know you had similar experiences and understood."

George nodded his agreement.

"I need to talk to Terri first, but I know she'll agree."

"Sure. I can understand that. I'll leave it with you." Ted stood up to go.

George stood up, and they shook hands as Caitlin walked them towards the door.

"Thanks Caitlin. Talk to you later," Ted said as he left.

Caitlin closed the door and looked at George. "What do you think?"

"I think it's a good idea. You could really do with the help and, like I said before, there are male victims out there. Ted might have more chance of connecting with them than you would."

"I'll call Terri and talk to her about it."

"OK. Thanks for letting me sit in. Let me know what you decide on."

"Perhaps I'll cook dinner for you one day next week and we can catch up." Caitlin smiled at him.

"I'm already looking forward to that. Just let me know when and I'll be here. Meanwhile, I need to head to the station."

As George left, Caitlin called Terri and told her about Ted's suggestion.

"You know something, Cait? Ted could move into Rosie's unit. It would be good to have someone next door in case you ever needed help. And I really do like the idea of expanding our reach to help male victims. It's horrifying how much of this goes on behind closed doors."

Caitlin agreed with Terri and said she would call Ted and see what he thought about it.

Ted jumped at the opportunity and two days later, he moved into number two, which was now being referred to as Ted's unit.

"Thanks Caitlin. I'm really excited about getting started on this. Naturally, I'll still keep busy with my rideshare driving, but that'll also be very useful, I'm sure. Whenever necessary, I can help by moving victims down the ER. I do like that name." He grinned at her.

"Yes, it amuses me too. And it'll be great having you help with it."

Caitlin showed him the escape tunnel and the surveillance system. She explained Pat would move into that unit and gave him some background on her situation. She also gave him a cell phone and explained that she had ordered stickers with the number, and 'Ted's Barber Shop' on them. She planned to pick them up the following day.

The next day, Caitlin had several chores to do. The final one was to pick up the stickers and drop them into Ted, who was busy sorting out his stuff and putting the place in order. All signs of Rosie were gone now. She returned to her own unit and wandered over to the back window. She stood looking out at the wilderness that was the shared backyard for the four units. The same backyard she had devised an imaginary plan for when she was trying to get Rosie to open up to her. Perhaps she should put that plan into action in memory of the poor girl. She felt an emptiness inside her, like she would never be fully in control of her own life again. Turning, she picked up her gym bag. She did what she always did when she needed to de-stress; she headed to the kicking bag.

After an hour at the gym, a shower and a solitary dinner, she called Peggy.

"Peggy? It's Caitlin. Do you have a minute to talk?" They talked for some time until finally Caitlin said, "thanks Peggy. That helps a lot. I'll see you in the morning. I'm meeting Pat there." She hung up, turned on the alarm, and went to bed.

CHAPTER SEVENTEEN

Caitlin and Pat arrived at the shelter at the same time and walked in together.

"Hi Pat, Peggy's looking forward to seeing you again."

"I'm excited to see her, too. It's amazing that we never thought about me helping with the kids at the shelter."

"I guess you had to find your feet before that could be a consideration," Caitlin said.

Peggy greeted them at the door. "My word, Pat, you're looking well. I'm thrilled that you are going to be helping us here," Peggy said as they hugged.

"I'm looking forward to repaying all you did for me."

Less than two hours later, Pat said goodbye. They had a schedule prepared for classes to start the following Monday. Pat had met the children and their mothers, and everyone was excited to get started.

"I'll see you this afternoon," Pat said to Caitlin as she left.

Peggy led Caitlin into her private office. She closed the door and pointed to the chair in front of the desk. "Have a seat, Caitlin." The two women sat silently, studying each other.

Finally, Caitlin said, "thanks for your time, Peggy. I didn't know who to turn to, then I remembered you said you were a psychologist and—I realize I need to talk to someone who can help me understand."

With Peggy's gentle questioning, Caitlin started first with her firm belief that all men were potentially abusers. She related her experience with her father, then Mack, who had tried to force himself on her when they were in college. It was after that incident that she had taken up martial arts. She even told her about Paul, the guy who was responsible for the scar on her forehead. He had attacked her after she had beaten him in a Karate competition, hitting her across the head with a metal chair. Finally, Keith's treatment of Terri. And, when they had started working with the victims here, she became more convinced.

"What exactly started you questioning your belief?" Peggy asked.

Caitlin stared at the far corner of the room, not seeing anything. She remained silent for a while before saying, "I think it started with George—no, maybe it was Ted. After I spoke to Ted, I started looking at George differently, and seeing that, in fact, he *is* different."

"Different from who? Or what?"

"Different from the other men in my life up to now, I suppose." Caitlin paused. "To be fair, there have not been many. I have avoided men, for the most part. Except for Jim and Paddy."

"Jim and Paddy?"

Caitlin smiled. "They intervened when Mack was attacking me. They suggested karate, in fact Jim taught it. I felt safe with them because they were gay, I suppose. And because I felt safe, I assumed that gay men were not abusive—then Victor called. Now I don't know what to think."

Peggy studied Caitlin for a few minutes. Then she stood up and came around the desk. "Okay Caitlin. I think it's time for you to meet my assistant, Robby. Follow me." And she hurried out of the office.

Caitlin had to run to catch up with her. "I didn't know you had an assistant," she said.

Peggy didn't answer but marched down the passageway and tapped on a door at the end by the back entrance.

"Come in."

The two women went in, and Peggy closed the door behind them before introducing Caitlin to Robby. Caitlin studied him. He was a tall pale man, mid-forties, with thinning blond hair and gray eyes. He wore blue jeans and a gray t-shirt. A stack of papers littered his desk and an open laptop sat on a side pedestal.

"What's up Peggy?" Robby said.

"I'd like you to tell Caitlin your story—all of it. And how you came to be working here with me."

Robby's eyes widened. "All of it?" he said.

"All of it." Peggy nodded.

"Okay. I trust you know what you're doing." Robby gave a half smile.

Peggy looked at Caitlin. "This may add to your confusion at first, but I hope it'll also help to give you a wider view. Nothing's ever just black or white," she said.

Caitlin nodded, not sure what to expect. She sat down, facing Robby as Peggy left the room.

Sometime later, Caitlin left Robby's office and hurried to her car. She arrived home just as Pat was pulling up outside number four. Caitlin showed her around the unit. She took her through the escape tunnel from number one, her own unit. Explaining that she would likely be up there from time to time. Checking on the surveillance system—and hopefully not escaping, but that it was there for that purpose. As they descended into the garage of number four, she showed Pat how to manipulate the ladder should she ever need to use the tunnel herself.

"Hopefully not!" Pat said. "But I have to admit, it makes me feel a lot safer knowing that's available."

After that, she took her to meet the other tenants. Jeremy and Pete were on their way out for the evening and welcomed Pat to the community, as they called it.

Ted was expecting them and he, Pat and Caitlin sat down to discuss how they could all operate together going forward.

"If we're going to be working together on this, maybe an intercom system would be useful, you know, so we can communicate in a hurry if necessary?" Ted said.

"That's a good idea, Ted. I'll talk to Terri about it," Caitlin said, getting out her phone and making a note.

"What about Jeremy and Pete? Are they also part of the network?" Pat asked.

"No—not at the moment—" Caitlin made another note on her phone. "I think that's something else I need to talk to Terri about, too. It might be a good idea to at least let them know what we do." Caitlin sat back, lost in thought, while Ted and Pat chatted together. Slowly, their conversation leaked into her thoughts. She realized they were exchanging stories about their different experiences with their respective partners. They were completely absorbed in their conversation with each other. She watched them silently for a few minutes until it was apparent that they had completely forgotten she was there.

Eventually, she interrupted them, saying she would leave them to it while she went next door and called Terri. She smiled to herself when they barely nodded and continued talking as she let herself out. *It looks like those two will become firm friends.*

Caitlin called Terri when she returned to her own unit.

She started talking as soon as Terri picked up. "Terri, interesting developments to report and a few items to discuss."

"Hi Cait. How did it go with Pat?"

"Let's see, I have a few notes, so I forget nothing. First, Pat starts teaching at the shelter on Monday. Second—Ted suggested setting up an intercom system between the units. Third—I'm wondering if we should let Jeremy and Pete know about our operation?"

"I think the intercom system is a great idea. Jeremy and Pete—" Caitlin waited while Terri gave this thought. "I think it might be a good idea. I mean—before it was just you and various tenants. But with three units all around them, involved in an operation that could prove dangerous—" Terri paused again. "Yes. I think we should tell them. For their own sake and because it could prove useful to our efforts, too. Who knows? They might offer to help."

Caitlin couldn't help laughing at that suggestion. It was getting to a point where they had more people working on helping victims than there were victims to help. Not a bad thing, but still amusing.

"By the way, when I left them, Ted and Pat were deep in conversation. I thought perhaps I should start a matchmaking business on the side," Caitlin said.

"Well! That would definitely be a one eighty turn for you!"

Caitlin paused before continuing, "Yeah, I'm definitely having to adjust my thinking—still Terri, it's great that they're getting along so well. They'll be working closely." Caitlin glanced at her watch. "Must go, I can still make it to Karate if I hurry. We can talk about the logistics of all this tomorrow."

She wasn't sure why she had not told Terri about her conversations with Peggy and Robby.

"See you tomorrow, Cait."

Caitlin hung up and picked up her sports bag by the front door and headed out.

When Caitlin's class finished up, instead of going home, she sat in her car and called Angela.

"Hi Angela, would it be alright to call over now, or is it too late? I was hoping to have a chat with Aunt May."

"Definitely not too late. Come on over."

"Okay, on my way. I'll see you in about twenty minutes."

CHAPTER EIGHTEEN

Fifteen minutes later, she pulled into Aunt May's driveway. She was happy to see that she no longer needed the crutches; she was still limping but definitely improving. Angela excused herself, saying she had some work to catch up on.

"Hello dear, how nice of you to visit! Sit down and talk to me," Aunt May said.

Caitlin sat and took a deep breath. "I've a problem; I really need your perspective—and experience." She paused; the older woman just nodded. "I remembered you mentioned your two gay friends who helped you to get away—I was also saved by a gay couple. Seems like a long time ago now. I somehow thought that gay men would not be abusers; but—we recently had a gay man contact us. His partner was abusive.

"Previously, I discovered some men are victims, and the female is the abuser. Today I met a man who works at the shelter for battered women. He told me he was once an abuser. In fact, his wife had lived at that same shelter after he beat her badly. That was a number of years ago and he has been attending anger management and psychotherapy—now I'm totally confused." Caitlin stared at Aunt May, who stared back at her for a few minutes.

"And you're hoping that I can make some sense of it for you?"

Caitlin nodded her head, saying nothing.

"People are all different. Being gay is just the same as being straight, well of course it is different, but it doesn't mean any more than having blue or brown eyes. It just is. We're all products of our environment and our upbringing, and of course, our genes. How it affects us depends on how we perceive ourselves and the world around us. For instance, look at you and your sister? You're twins. You grew up with many of the same experiences and influences, yet you see the world very differently. Those experiences impacted you differently." She paused, watching Caitlin, who sat silently staring back at her. "I told you about my first marriage. My second marriage was very different."

"I didn't realize you were married twice," Caitlin said.

"Yes, indeed, I was—to a wonderful man. We were very happy. Oh, he wasn't perfect, but neither am I." She smiled and was silent for a few minutes. "Shortly after we met, he told me he had attended anger management in an effort to save a relationship. It didn't work. That is, the relationship could not be saved, the anger management worked. The lesson he learned was that you're not responsible for how people think and feel, only for your own reactions. He had a temper in the early days, but he never even came close to hitting me." She looked at Caitlin with raised eyebrows, leaning slightly forward.

Caitlin looked back. It seemed they sat staring at each other in silence for a long time. Finally, Caitlin said, "I think I understand what you're saying. It's sort of the same as Terri has been saying for some time. I just didn't get it—I think I get it—perhaps I need psychotherapy," She whispered.

"My dear, it's my opinion that psychotherapy is like dentistry. Everyone needs it regularly."

"Thank you so much, Aunt May. You've given me a lot to think about, and you've definitely opened my eyes to my own stupidity."

"It's not stupidity; it's what we mortals do to try to make sense of a world we can't possibly understand or control."

The two women stood up and Caitlin put her arms around the older woman and hugged her. Aunt May patted her on the shoulder, and they said goodbye.

The following day, Caitlin sat at her desk in the office. She had gone through her email and established that there was nothing there requiring anything more than deletion. She let her mind wander back over the past year. So much had changed and yet so much had stayed the same. She wished Keith would finally be caught and they could stop planning their lives around his possible appearance. Sometimes it felt like they were suspended in time, but at other times she could see how far they had progressed. Particularly when she looked at the list of victims, men and women, they had helped to escape their abusers and make a better life for themselves. She just wished there was a way to stop the batterers; it didn't seem right that they literally lived to fight another day. The ringing phone pulled her back to reality.

"Caitlin's Nails."

"Hi Caitlin, I'm sorry for such late notice, but I need to cancel my appointment with you—this is Mel."

"Okay Mel, thank you for letting me know. I hope everything is alright with you?"

"Oh yes, great thanks. My brother turned up at the door early this morning and I'm on my way home with him now. I'm free."

"Delighted to hear it. Stay safe." She hung up and stared at her phone for a few seconds.

I guess that deserves some sort of report before I head home.

As she turned back to her laptop, her phone rang again.

"Hi Caitlin, this is Maria again. Please don't hang up!"

"Hi Maria, don't worry, I won't hang up. I told you to call me if you decided you needed help." Caitlin smiled to herself. She couldn't imagine a situation where she would hang up on a client. Even one as scatty as poor Maria. "What can I do for you?"

"I was hoping I could come and talk to you."

"Sure, when would suit you?"

"Well—now actually. I'm parked outside your office."

Caitlin slowly shook her head. *This girl really is scatty.* She thought to herself.

"Okay, come on in. I just had a cancellation," she said as she walked towards the front door.

"Oh my God Maria!" she gasped as she opened the door. "What happened to you?"

Maria stood at the door with what looked like a sock held up to the side of her face. It was doing very little to stem the flow of blood. It had soaked into her shirt and down the side of her jeans.

Caitlin led her to the small kitchen area and pulled one of the chairs from the office for her to sit on. She grabbed a towel and started to wipe the girl's face.

"Here, hold this towel to the wound while I go get my first aid kit from the car." She dressed the wound, a long gash running from the corner of her chin up to her cheekbone.

"Okay, I've managed to stop the bleeding, but we need to get you to the hospital for stitches."

"Will I have a scar?" Maria said.

Caitlin paused and looked at her for a second. "You most definitely will have a nasty scar if we don't get stitches. But yes, you will have a scar no matter what. Come on, let's go. I'll drive."

Two hours later, Caitlin pulled up outside Pat's unit. She helped Maria out of the car. Pat opened the door and let them in. As Pat got Maria settled in her spare bedroom, Caitlin went back to her own unit to get some clothes for her. She came back with a pair of sweatpants and a T-shirt. Maria was already asleep.

"That poor girl," Pat said. "What a horrible wound it must be. The bandages cover half her face, and her clothes are ruined!"

"Yeah. She had to have twenty stitches!"

"How awful!"

"Naturally, they called the police, and they interviewed her at the hospital. The last time I saw her I recommended they try couples counseling. He wouldn't go, but she had been seeing a therapist and was beginning to accept that he was being verbally abusive. When she told him what her therapist said, he lost his temper. He threw a cast-iron skillet at her, and it caught her in the face, nasty cut across her cheek."

"Do you need me to transport her somewhere tomorrow?"

"No, that won't be necessary. You remember Susan in San Antonio? She brought Grace to us, and you moved her along the ER towards Bangor, Maine?"

Pat nodded. "Yes, I remember Grace."

"Well, Maria has family in San Antonio. Susan's coming to pick her up in the morning."

"Okay. I'll take care of her until then. Is there anything else you need me to do?"

"Yes, there is. I need you and Ted to get her car and drive it down to San Antonio. She drove herself to the office today, and it's still there. The biggest problem is that she bled all the way from her home to the office and the car's a mess."

"Ted and I will clean it up and then I can drive it to San Antonio. He can follow me and drive me back."

"Perfect! Thank you so much Pat."

"After all you have done for me, Caitlin, it's very little to ask. I'm happy to do it."

Caitlin returned to her own unit. She still had to write up a report on Maria, and on Mel's canceled appointment. At least that was a happy ending. Instead, she called Terri.

"Hi Cait, what's up?"

"What a day! I don't know where to start. I'll send you the written reports tomorrow. Let me tell you about it."

"Go ahead. I'm listening."

Caitlin started by telling her sister that Mel had canceled and made her own plans.

"Oh, that's good news," Terri said. "So, what else happened?" She listened while Caitlin described Maria turning up at the office and the injuries. She occasionally interrupted with a question.

When Caitlin stopped talking, they each sat in silence, thinking about what she had said.

"My God, Cait! It just keeps happening. I don't think you could have done anything more to prevent this. At least she is out of it now."

"I know. I'm so glad that I have both Pat and Ted here right now. In the morning, they'll take care of Maria's car while Susan drives her down to San Antonio. That would have been really difficult to manage without them. I can take a break tomorrow, apart from typing up that report."

They chatted some more and as soon as she hung up, Caitlin headed to bed.

CHAPTER NINETEEN

Caitlin had just finished her shower and was thinking about bed when her ER phone pinged.

"Caitlin's Nails," she said as she picked up.

"Hi, is this Caitlin?" A woman's voice whispered.

"Yes, what can I do for you? Did you want to make an appointment?"

"Would you be able to see me tomorrow morning?"

"Certainly. Would ten work for you?"

"That would be perfect, thanks."

"Okay, let me give you directions."

Caitlin hung up and texted Ted to see if he was available the following morning. She had seen him return from San Antonio, so she knew he was home. He responded immediately, confirming he was free and would be happy to join her.

Caitlin went to bed. She spent some time thinking about how best to incorporate Ted into the process. This was going to be something new. She didn't want to intimidate the victims by having a man present. She drifted off to sleep before she came up with a plan of action.

Next morning, she still wasn't sure how to approach it when Ted texted her. She suggested he come and have coffee with her, and they could discuss how best to work together.

She need not have worried.

"I've been thinking about how to do this. I'm worried that a female victim might not be comfortable with a man in the room," Ted said as soon as he sat down with his coffee. "How about we start with me giving her an account of how you helped me? Perhaps if she sees me as another victim and hears how you helped me, it might make her feel safer and help her open up."

"That's a great idea. I was worrying about what approach to take. That solves so many issues at once."

They finished their coffee and headed to the office in separate cars. There was a possibility one of them would need to transport the victim to her next stop if she took the ER option.

Ted arrived just ahead of Caitlin.

"I didn't realize how weird it would feel to be here again. It's like a flashback," Ted said, looking around.

They settled down to wait for Geraldine. She arrived just a few minutes after ten. When Caitlin opened the door, she explained she had another victim with her to answer any questions she might have.

Geraldine was tall and athletic looking, with short strawberry blond hair and pale blue eyes. Tiny freckles covered her face and made her look almost childlike, though she was probably in her thirties. She looked surprised when she saw Ted, but said nothing as she sat down in the chair beside him.

Ted immediately started talking. He had been practicing what he would say on the drive over and he launched into his speech. He told her how he had been victimized and that the police had given him Caitlin's sticker and how it had changed his life.

"But why are you still here? I thought the idea was to get as far away as possible?" Geraldine said.

Ted explained that was exactly what he had done, and why he had returned. Caitlin remained quiet, watching, and waiting to speak if she felt it was necessary. So far, Ted was doing great, and Geraldine was visibly relaxing as she listened.

"And now I've the honor of helping Caitlin to rescue other victims." He finished with a satisfied smile.

Geraldine needed no further prompting; she started into her own story. She had lived with Dave for three years in Northern Michigan before they got married and moved to Austin. That was when he started getting violent. Before that, the worst he had been was a little moody from time to time. At first, his moodiness became more frequent and then he became verbally abusive.

"It's almost like—" Her voice trailed off as she tried to find the words.

"Like once you no longer had family or friends around, he became more controlling?" Caitlin asked.

"Exactly! At first, I thought he was feeling homesick, but then I began to realize that it was because I didn't have any support—apart from him. Eventually he started hitting me."

"Anything more than that?" Ted asked.

"Oh, he progressed. I suppose when he found he could get away with the occasional slap, he tried punching. After that, sometimes he would choke me, or pick me up by my neck and throw me across the room or into furniture."

"Did you fight back? I mean, you look like you could take care of yourself," Caitlin said.

"No, I was terrified of doing anything that might make him worse. He's a big guy, and strong. When he gets into a temper, it's like he literally sees red. Like a wild dog. I think—I think he wanted me to fight back, like there was a pent-up anger he was still not releasing. If I fought back, it would allow him to—I don't know, I just didn't want to find out."

"We come across that more often than we would like," Caitlin said.

"Really? I thought it was my fault. He said it was." Geraldine looked down at her hands, then back at Caitlin. "I used to love him," she said as her eyes filled up with tears.

She looks so totally miserable, poor girl.

Ted handed Geraldine a tissue, and they sat in silence while she tried to stem the tears.

Caitlin took a deep breath and went through the standard questions she asked all her clients. She was still trying to stop thinking of them as victims and referring to them as clients in her head and in her conversations.

Geraldine confirmed she had no children. She had a miscarriage shortly after Dave started getting more violent. And yes, she was definitely ready to disappear. She wanted to go home to Traverse City and her family and friends. If he followed her home, at least she would have family to protect her and she would start divorce proceedings as soon as she got there.

Ted looked at Caitlin and she nodded.

"Here's what we'll do, Geraldine. I'll drive you to Dallas. We'll meet up with someone there who'll give you a room for the night, and a small bag with all you'll need for the few days it'll take to get you home. Tomorrow, she'll move you along our escape route, passing you over to one of our other operatives. This'll continue until you get to Traverse City and home." He looked at her expectantly. "Are you up for this?"

"You can call me Gerry. And yes, I can't believe you are doing this for me." Her eyes widened as she looked from Ted to Caitlin. "Right now?"

"Absolutely Gerry. This is what we do, and it has to be right now. We do not want Dave to figure out you've left until you are well away and safe." Caitlin assured her.

"I can't thank you enough. If I can be of any help to you in the future, please let me know."

Caitlin smiled at her as they stood up. "We just might do that; we don't have a presence in Michigan yet. Meanwhile, just take care of yourself."

"I will, and I'll let you know when I'm safely home."

"I'll know as soon as you do," Caitlin said. She turned to Ted. "Are you ready to go now?"

He nodded. "Yes, I anticipated this and have an overnight bag in my car. The tank is full. I've everything I need."

Caitlin smiled. *Having Ted here is going to make the process so much smoother.* "Thanks Ted, drive carefully and be sure to rest before the return drive. We need you here safe and sound."

"You bet. Please let Pat know where I've gone in case she wonders why I suddenly disappeared." He grinned at Caitlin as they left the building.

Caitlin said she would do that, and she watched as Gerry and Ted left in his car, then she went back inside and got her own vehicle out of the garage and headed home.

***

As the sun went down, Keith steered the jet ski back to the marina.

Damn it. This is the second Friday I have wasted, and she hasn't turned up. I could buy a bloody jet ski with all the money I'm spending on renting one. I need to rethink this. He thought as he docked and went to change out of the wet suit.

He realized, although he'd seen Caitlin on the lake on Friday a few times, she did not keep to a regular schedule. As he drove back to his motel room, he decided he'd have to find a way to watch Caitlin's house without her noticing or becoming suspicious.

For the next two days, Keith visited every pawn shop he could find, finally finding almost exactly what he wanted. He bought an old theodolite in one and a tripod in another. The theodolite didn't fit the tripod exactly, but with the help of a roll of duct tape, he could make it work. While he was looking for the duct tape, he also bought a packet of small red flags, chalk, a hard hat, and a yellow safety vest. He was fairly sure that no one took any notice of a surveyor; or if they saw one, they assumed they were on city business and paid no further attention. Certainly, he knew he would not look suspicious. With these items, he believed he could become virtually invisible.

The following Friday afternoon, he parked his motorbike. Tucking it in behind the shrubbery surrounding the trash cans to the side of Caitlin's building. He used the hard hat over a bandanna to conceal his hair. His beard was now full and bushy. A pair of sunglasses and the yellow vest completed his disguise. He spent a couple of hours alternating between peering through the theodolite and sticking little red flags in random spots. Occasionally, he drew chalk marks on the sidewalk.

He watched as a car pulled up and a man got out and knocked on Caitlin's door. A few minutes later, she came out, and they both climbed into his car. He was fairly sure she would not be going to the lake that evening. Waiting until the two of them drove away before packing up and heading back to his motel room.

The following morning, Saturday, he repeated the process. He was just in time to see Caitlin's garage door open. He watched her drive out. By the time she had reached the corner and was waiting for the light to change, he had thrown his disguise into the shrubbery and was on his bike, ready to follow. When he was certain she was heading to the lake, he accelerated and sped past her.

Reaching the marina well ahead of Caitlin, he was sitting on the idling jet ski a few hundred yards up the lake, watching the lockup garage where she parked her car. He finally spotted her pull into the garage. He waited until he saw her boat ease out of the slip and head up the lake.

He took off in the same direction, up the lake and around the first bend ahead of her. Then he turned and motored down the lake, past

Caitlin's boat. Almost immediately, he turned again and went back up the lake, passing her boat as she went around the bend. He pulled into an empty dock on the South shore and watched as she continued up towards the next bend. As soon as she was out of sight, he followed more slowly. He was just in time to see her pull into a slip with a tent covering. She moored the boat and as she walked off the dock the tent came down completely hiding the boat from view.

No wonder I didn't spot it! Got you now, bitches!

He waited until Caitlin disappeared into the line of trees surrounding the house, just visible from the shoreline. He pulled up against the dock, remaining out of sight of the house, pulled his phone out from the inside pocket of his wet suit and enabled GPS. It didn't take him long to pinpoint exactly where the house was located. He headed down the lake, back towards the marina, unable to keep the smirk off his face.

He dropped the jet ski back to the rental slip, changed out of the wet suit and headed back to town.

CHAPTER TWENTY

Caitlin and Terri sat on the balcony sipping wine and watching the sun go down over the lake.

"I'll never tire of this view," Terri said.

"I know. It reminds me so much of when we were kids on the garage roof back in Connemara," Caitlin said. "Did you see that guy on the jet ski?"

"Yeah, those machines are so irritating."

"Fool came very close to me as I came up the lake, caused quite a wake."

"Enough chitchat, Caitlin. Tell me about George?" Terri watched Caitlin blush and smiled.

Caitlin looked at her for a few minutes in silence.

"First, I need to tell you something else," Caitlin said.

Terri studied her sister but said nothing.

"After talking to Victor and then Margo, I was feeling—" Caitlin paused, searching for the right words, "I guess confused is not the right word, but it'll have to do. I talked to Peggy—you remember she told us she was a psychologist?" Terri nodded and Caitlin continued. "She was great. She sat and listened to me for ages. Then she introduced me to her assistant, Robby. She told him to tell me his story. It was obvious he didn't want to, but he did." Caitlin was quiet for a long time.

"And?" Terri prompted her gently.

"And—the short version is, he told me he was married to a wonderful girl. That he beat her regularly and eventually she left him.

Caitlin's Escape Route

She stayed at Peggy's shelter for a while before finally going home to her parents. He tracked her to the shelter after she had left, and he and Peggy talked. Peggy convinced him to seek help. He attended anger management classes and therapy. He's still attending therapy, and that was three years ago. He has been working with Peggy ever since."

Terri's eyes got wider as Caitlin talked. When she had finished, they sat in silence, looking at each other.

"I've decided that I'm going to find a psychologist," Caitlin said.

"I believe that is a tremendous step in the right direction, Caitlin, and I think I will, too. It stands to reason that what Dad did to us, especially after we had just lost Mom, must have had an impact. We need to understand that before we can get past it."

"Exactly! And Terri—I'm frightened. I think I'm in love with George, and it scares the hell out of me. I want to get rid of that fear. What if he's just like the others, if what Dad did to us turned us into victims?"

"Don't be silly, Cait. I'm absolutely certain you would not love him if he wasn't trustworthy. I know you! And with therapy, you'll get to know you, too. There is no way you would have let him get past your armor if he were not to be trusted."

"I know. You're right. I hope so because I'm going to go with my gut and give it a chance."

"He's a lovely guy, Cait. Why don't you bring him out here for a weekend?"

Caitlin snorted loudly. "A weekend! We are not nearly at that stage yet."

"Well, I suggest you get a move on, then. He's too good to risk losing."

Caitlin started to shake her head and then nodded slowly. "You're right, of course," she said.

"Come on, let's go in. The sun is gone for the day." Terri picked up their glasses and led the way while Caitlin locked the door behind them.

"You know something, Cait? I almost wish that Keith would find me, and we can get this over with. The creeping around and constantly looking over my shoulder is wearing me down."

"I know what you mean, but be careful what you wish for."

Next morning Caitlin headed back to fourplex. She had invited George to dinner that evening and wanted plenty of time to clean up, shop and cook before he got there.

Later that day, grocery shopping was done, dinner was on, and she had showered and taken extra care doing her hair, which was getting long. She had even applied a little makeup. Something she almost never did because she felt she looked more nondescript without it, and she definitely didn't need to stand out. The less attention she drew to herself, the happier she was. Except tonight. Settling for a deep blue, knee length dress. She knew it made her eyes look good. Her mother told her many times that blue was her color. She slipped her feet into a pair of leather dress shoes with low heels and studied herself in the full-length mirror.

She went downstairs to check on dinner and set the table. For the first time, she wished she had a dining room set up. The kitchen would just have to do. She jumped when the doorbell rang. *Why do I feel so nervous?* She shook her head as she went to answer the door.

George stood on the doorstep. A bunch of orange roses in one hand and a bottle of wine in the other, an expression on his face that made him look like a high school kid going to his first prom. Their eyes locked for a moment and they both smiled shyly.

"Come in," she said, opening the door wider.

He stepped in and handed her the roses.

"These are for you—obviously." They both laughed, and she took the flowers from him.

"How did you know orange roses are my favorite?"

"I want to say I guessed, but actually I asked Terri."

Then he stepped closer and wrapped his arms around her, being careful not to crush the flowers or drop the wine. He hugged her gently and then stepped back, held the bottle up to her.

"How about a glass of wine?"

Caitlin turned into the kitchen. She found a vase for the roses while George picked up the corkscrew from beside the stove. He opened the bottle, pouring it into the two glasses on the table and handed her a glass.

He raised his glass to her and said, "thank you for trusting me. I promise you I'll never, ever let you down."

Caitlin swallowed hard and blinked a few times before raising her glass to his. "I believe you George. Thank you for—for everything."

George broke the silence. "Dinner smells good."

"Let's eat." She smiled and started serving.

"This tastes even better than it smells. You're quite the cook,

Caitlin." George raised his glass to her.

"Thank you. When we were growing up, back in Ireland, our housekeeper taught Terri and me to cook. She had been a chef at one of the best restaurants in Galway." Caitlin smiled as she remembered Lily. She topped up her glass and when she went to fill George's, he put his hand over it.

"I'm driving. Better not have a second glass," he said, glancing down.

Caitlin paused with the bottle still held over his hand. She eased his hand out of the way. "You don't have to drive tonight."

He moved his hand as though the glass was suddenly on fire and looked at her.

"Are you sure?"

She nodded. "I'm certain." Blushing, but holding his gaze for a moment before looking back at the glass while she topped it up.

Next morning Caitlin woke early and looked at George sleeping beside her.

Holy God! I hope I did the right thing. It sure felt right.

He opened his eyes and turned to see her looking at him. He leaned across and kissed her gently.

"Wonderful food, great company and an amazing night. I must get moving as I'm on duty at ten." He got up and showered. Coming back into the bedroom with just a towel around his waist, he said, "could I borrow a razor? I didn't have the nerve to bring my own."

"Of course, there are a bunch of disposable razors in the right-hand drawer and shaving foam in the shower. Help yourself." She grinned up at him. "There are also a couple of those free toothbrush and toothpaste packs the dentist hands out in the drawer with the razors."

While George was shaving, Caitlin went down to the kitchen and made coffee. She had already established that he also didn't eat breakfast. Over coffee, he told her he would be on duty until late. They agreed to have dinner the following day.

"Let me cook dinner for you tomorrow," George said as he got ready to leave.

"I'll look forward to that."

"Reserve judgment until you've tasted my cooking," he said, kissing her before closing the door after himself.

Caitlin's Escape Route

Sitting in the kitchen, lost in thought. Caitlin couldn't decide whether to dance around the house or pack her bags and run away. Last night was so perfect. In her heart she knew she could trust him, but the old Caitlin didn't want to be silenced. Her phone pinged abruptly, bringing her back to reality. It was a text from Ted.

Just saw something suspicious. Are you free to talk?

She immediately called him back.

"What's up Ted?"

"Hi Caitlin, sorry for bothering you. I'm not sure if you know I used to be a Survey Technician for the City."

"No—I didn't know that." Caitlin wondered what Ted was talking about.

"Did you notice the guy outside yesterday, you know—in a hard hat?"

"No—I didn't notice anyone—why?"

"Well, if he was a surveyor, I'm a jackass. Nothing he was doing made sense. The chalk marks on the sidewalk might be something new since I did that job, but I don't think so. They might as well have been hopscotch."

"You mean, you think he was watching one of us? Let me go check on the surveillance video…and thanks for warning me."

***

From behind the theodolite set up among the trees on the side of the road, Keith watched with interest as George drove off. This time, he was not there to follow Caitlin. Now that he knew where Terri was living, he just needed to be sure she was alone when he confronted her. He wanted to confirm that Caitlin was not going to the lake today. The fewer witnesses, the better. He planned to make sure the victim was not around to be a witness.

He waited for another thirty minutes to make sure that Caitlin was not leaving. Then he wheeled his bike out of the bushes. Looking around to make sure no one was watching, he pulled the hard hat and bandanna off his head. He replaced it with the helmet that had been hanging from the handlebars. Then, climbing on the bike, he freewheeled down the street before starting up the motor.

***

Caitlin's Escape Route

Caitlin sat, staring at the monitor. Her eyes widened as she saw the man emerge from the bushes pushing a motorbike.

Jeeze! I swear that looks like Keith!

She watched as he got on the bike and rolled down the street, and then fired up the motor and took off.

What the hell!

She picked up her phone and called Terri.

"Terri? Quick, look at the video history for my place for this morning."

"Hi Cait. Hang on. Looking now."

Caitlin waited.

"Ah-ha! I see him. So, did George call around for an early cup of coffee, or did he stay over?" Terri said.

"No! Not that. Keep watching."

"Shit! Shit! That's Keith! He has a beard, and his hair is long, but it's definitely him. Oh, dear mother of God. He's here in Texas, and outside your house!"

"Ted noticed him over the past few days, disguised as a surveyor. I didn't pay any attention to him, but looking back over the video, he has been there almost every day this week. I think he's the guy I saw before we put up the monitoring system. I swear he has been following me. A guy on a motorbike was behind me when I drove to the lake a few days ago. If he has been following me since then, he may well have found out where you are. We can't take a chance on it. We have to assume he has. I'm leaving now and heading over to you."

Caitlin rushed downstairs, grabbed her purse and almost ran into the garage. Minutes later, she was heading towards the marina. It was still the quickest way to get to the lake house. As she drove, Caitlin called George.

"Hi Darling!" His Texas drawl almost made her forget what she was calling about. "You alright?" He added quickly.

"Hi George. I'm on my way to Terri's place. We've discovered that Keith is in Austin and I believe he has been following me. He was watching the house this morning when you left."

"What!? Are you sure?"

"Certain. We—Terri did too—saw him on the camera. No doubt."

"I'll call Terri's local station and head that way myself immediately. Be careful!"

Caitlin's hands-free unit shut down as George hung up. She concentrated on getting to the boat as quickly and safely as she could.

CHAPTER TWENTY-ONE

Terri sat down in front of her monitor and made sure the system was working, both audio and video. As she stared out at the lake, she decided. She was tired of hiding and sneaking around. She would wait in the open for him to turn up.

I'm fed up with all this uncertainty. If he really has found out where I am, let him come. We can finish this one way or the other.

Sitting on the balcony, she alternated between the monitoring app on her phone and watching the lake for any sign of Caitlin. Finally, she spotted the boat coming around the bend, moving fast toward the dock. She watched her pull into the slip.

As the tent descended to hide the boat, Terri's phone vibrated. She looked at the screen and took a deep breath. A motorbike was pulling up in front of the house. She quickly texted Caitlin to warn her that Keith had arrived and that she should stay out of sight. Then she waited.

Terri watched Keith on her phone. He pulled his motorbike into the trees and approached the house on foot. She watched until the camera lost him as he crept around to the back, then she leaned over the balcony and watched him peer through the windows.

"What the fuck are you doing here, Keith?" she yelled down at him, having the satisfaction of seeing him literally jump as he looked up.

"Oh Terri, I'm so glad that I found you and you're okay."

"Huh. No thanks to you!"

"Let me in. We need to talk. After all, you're still my wife."

"Go around to the front door and I'll meet you there," Terri said. She didn't want him to see Caitlin, who was still at the dock, staying out of sight.

Terri went down to the front door and waited until Keith was right outside. She wanted to be sure that they captured any conversation on the audio, and she didn't trust him to not try to drag her away from the house.

When she opened the door, she stood back, and he walked in.

"Nice place you have here," he said. "Rental, of course."

"How do you know that?"

"How do you think I found you? I had to wait until you purchased a house. Then it was easy. I'd have been here sooner if you'd bought this one instead of renting."

"What do you want from me?" Terri asked.

"Like I said, you're my wife."

"I've already filed for divorce. After what you did to me, you surely don't think I'll remain your wife?"

"What I did to you?" he said. "You did that to yourself!"

"Don't be stupid Keith. I couldn't kick myself unconscious and then lock the bedroom door and set fire to the house."

"Maybe not, but your behavior pushed me to do it. Fooling around and then threatening to leave me."

"I know you won't believe me, but I never fooled around on you. The only reason I was leaving was because you were abusive."

"You know it was your fault, Terri. The only reason I hit you was because you forced me to do it. You kept pushing my buttons."

"Why did you set fire to the house!?" Terri held her breath, hoping he would say something to confirm that's what he did.

"I hadn't planned to do that; it was a last-minute stroke of genius, and it would have worked if your neighbor hadn't poked his nose in and called the fire department. I was going out of the garage and knocked over the gas container. It was a spur of the moment decision. Opportunity presented itself. I drove the car out to the road, then came back and just as the garage door was closing, I set fire to an oily rag and threw it at the pool of gas—I knew you would get out."

"How would I get out? Not only was I unconscious, but you also locked me in! You prick!"

"Well, you got out. Didn't you? Here you are none the worse for it. Except, hopefully, you learned your lesson."

"You realize the police are looking for you? You're wanted for attempted murder and arson." Terri took a step back as Keith's fists clenched and he took a step towards her. A sound like a growl escaped from him.

"In order to convict me, they have to find me, and they need a witness."

"Look at me! I'm here. I'm a witness."

Keith grabbed her by the arm. "You have to be alive in order to be a witness," he said as he dragged her out of the house. "Let's go swimming."

***

Caitlin had been watching the video on her phone, crouched behind the dock. She called George and let him know she had just arrived at the lake house and that Keith was there as well. He confirmed he was about twenty minutes away.

Caitlin crouched beside the dock. She kept one eye on her phone app with the camera view, until she saw Keith come around the side of the house, dragging Terri by her arm, heading towards the lake. She texted George.

"Where are you guys? He's taking her down to the lake. I don't like the look of this. I'm going to try to stop him."

As she put her phone away, it pinged, but she ignored it because Keith was dragging Terri towards a kayak that was pulled up on the shore.

"Get in the front seat," he yelled at her, picking up the paddle. As she sat down, he pushed the kayak towards the water.

Oh my god, he is going to drown her. Where the hell are the cops? I have got to do something!

For a second she felt paralyzed, unable to move or think. Then she moved fast. Leaping from the dock, she landed almost on top of Keith just as he pushed the kayak into the lake and was about to climb in himself. He spun around and swung at her with the paddle, aiming for her head. She sidestepped, and the paddle grazed her shoulder. She almost lost her balance. As he swung again, she moved towards him and to one side. Grabbing his forearm and, at the same time, turning and dropping her weight just enough to throw him completely off balance. She twisted as he lost his balance and gripped his hand, bending it backwards to immobilize him. One look told her that was unnecessary, as he had hit his head on a rock when he landed and was out cold. She dropped to her knees, breathing heavily, trying to control her heaving stomach. Shaking her head, she took a few deep breaths and then stood up shakily. She made it back to the boat and grabbed a length of rope out of it and minutes later, Keith's arms and legs were bound tight.

Suddenly, she heard her name and looked around. She hadn't noticed that the kayak was floating out into the lake with Terri on board, and the paddle was on the ground beside Keith. Although she had no way of getting back to shore or steering the small craft, she was desperately trying to use her hand as a paddle.

"Hang on Terri, I'm coming!" Caitlin yelled, as she once again returned to the boat to head out to rescue her sister. She heard the police sirens and quickly texted George to let him know what she was doing, and that she had hogtied Keith on the shore. Probably needing some medical attention. Then she turned the boat toward the kayak, now almost out in the middle of the lake.

She could hear the noise of vehicles and voices coming from the shore, but concentrated on maneuvering the boat alongside the kayak. Once she was within shouting distance, she tied a rope to the ladder at the back of the boat and yelled to Terri.

"I'm going to come alongside and throw the rope to you. Once you have it, I'll hold position while you pull yourself towards me. I tied the rope to the ladder. You should be able to climb aboard from there." She paused. "Did you hear that, Terri?"

"Yes. Got it. I'm ready."

It took three attempts before Terri actually caught the rope. Then Caitlin concentrated on holding the boat steady while watching Terri slowly haul herself towards the ladder. As she reached forward to take hold of it, she almost lost her balance, but on the second try, she managed to pull herself out of the kayak and climb aboard. She sat in a heap on the deck and buried her face in her hands.

Caitlin ran over to her. "Are you alright? Did he hurt you?"

Terri looked up; her face covered in tears. "Thank you, Cait. I can't believe that I once loved that man. I'm okay, a bit shaken up, but thanks to you, I'm okay."

Caitlin steered back to the dock. By the time the two women docked and tied up the boat, George and the local police had arrived. Keith was regaining consciousness but couldn't move. George looked from the dazed and bleeding man to the two women.

"This is the second time I've seen a man incapacitated at your feet," he said to Caitlin. "You can explain it to me later." He continued, as he helped the local cops to untie and cuff Keith.

"I've already contacted SF and they are waiting for confirmation of his capture before sending someone to pick him up."

Terri looked at Caitlin for a second before bursting into tears again and hugging her.

"I can't believe this is almost over," she said between sobs.

"It's over Terri. It's over—for us," Caitlin said, tears streaming down her face.

Terri wiped her eyes with her sleeve and nodded.

The police led Keith up to the house, where they loaded him into the car.

"He'll spend the night in hospital tonight," George said. "Assuming the hospital discharges him, they'll lock him up until SF sends someone to pick him up. He'll be their problem then."

"I've an audio and videotape of him admitting to locking me in the house and setting the fire. I'll get that ready for you to give them when they come get him," Terri said.

The three of them followed the police up to the house.

"I'll accompany them to the hospital and then come back here—if that's okay?" George looked from Terri to Caitlin.

"Absolutely!" Terri nodded before Caitlin could say anything. "We'll wait here till you come back. Right Cait?"

"Okay. Guess I'll have to wait to test your cooking, George. We'll have dinner ready when you get back."

Terri watched as George kissed Caitlin before hurrying to his car and driving off after the police car. Then they linked arms and walked back to the house together.

Terri got out some glasses and put them on the table. "Hang on a minute," she said as Caitlin reached for the bottle of wine on the kitchen counter. She headed out to the garage and came back with a bottle of champagne.

"I was saving this in the refrigerator in the garage for exactly this occasion. I must admit, I didn't believe it would ever happen."

They toasted each other and sat in their usual seats out on the balcony. It was too early yet for sunset, but it was good to be alive.

"I just can't believe it is over," Terri said.

"Well, our trauma is finally over. We still have all of those other women out there who need our help," Caitlin said.

"And men, don't forget the men."

"And men, I won't forget them, Terri."

"Now. Tell me about George!"

Caitlin brought her sister up to date on her dinner and breakfast with George.

"That definitely deserves another toast." Terri filled their glasses.

By the time George got back, dinner was ready, and the two sisters were back on the balcony. This time, the sun was going down. He joined them and Terri poured him a glass of wine.

"Before you ask George," Caitlin said. "I have a brown belt in karate and a brown belt in aikido. That is how I could protect myself against Malcolm and Keith. I wasn't hiding it; the subject just didn't come up."

George raised his glass to her. "I've got to say that makes me feel a lot better about your safety."

They had dinner and George refused a second glass of wine. He suggested he would drive Caitlin home that night and they could pick up her car from the lockup in the morning. Terri agreed.

"You're definitely not fit to drive a boat or car this evening, and there's no longer any need to go through the subterfuge of taking the boat here."

"I'll cancel the lockup and the marina slip in the morning, too," Caitlin said. "That'll be a saving, not to mention a great relief."

After they'd cleared up the dinner things and loaded the dishwasher. George and Caitlin headed back to Austin.

"I'll talk to you in the morning, Terri. Sleep well."

"You can count on it! Talk to you tomorrow."

George dropped Caitlin at her home. He had paperwork to do, and they agreed he would come around in the morning for coffee and then drive her to take care of her car and cancel the lockup and marina rentals.

"Tomorrow, I'll cook you dinner. Okay?" he said as they kissed goodnight.

"I'm looking forward to that," she said as she got out of the car. She turned and waved to him before locking the door and setting the alarm.

CHAPTER TWENTY-TWO

George arrived early and as soon as they had coffee, he drove Caitlin to pick up her car.

"I have a meeting later this morning. Are you okay for now?"

"Thanks George. I'm fine. I'll see you this evening."

"I'm looking forward to that. See you at about seven" George kissed her. She got out of the car and turned at the marina office and waved, watching him driving off.

An hour later, Caitlin headed home. When she got there, she called Terri.

"How are you doing, Terri?"

"I can't tell you how good I feel, Cait. I didn't realize what an enormous weight was on my shoulders until it was lifted. I feel amazing."

"I know. It's amazing. I've canceled the slip at the marina and the lockup. Now we can concentrate on our ER."

"Have you given any thought to what we do now? I mean, apart from the ER. We need to figure out our living arrangements."

"I have to admit, I didn't give that a thought. There's the fact that we're now both involved in relationships. Each having our own place seems like a good idea."

They both giggled at that.

"Let's just let it ride for a few weeks while we get used to not having to worry about Keith, and then we can figure it out," Terri said.

"Yeah, probably a good idea."

"Were you planning to come over here tonight?"

"Not tonight. I'm having dinner with George—he's going to cook."

"That works out well, because Joe invited me out for dinner. Tell George I said hi."

"Say hi to Joe for me." Caitlin hung up and headed for the bathroom. Time to soak in a bubble bath and think about their future plans.

Caitlin knocked on George's door at exactly seven. He opened it almost immediately.

"Come on in," he said, holding the door open for her. It was her first time there. The outside of the house was unremarkable. It was clearly an older home, on a street of similar small single-family homes. It was probably once in the suburbs. Before Austin grew so big that the street was now almost on the edge of the industrial area surrounding downtown and the huge university campus.

He led the way through a small, neatly arranged, spotless kitchen and into the backyard. A grill stood in one corner of the patio. The smell of burning charcoal wafted from it. A small table with two chairs sat under a garden umbrella on the other side of the patio, with a bottle of wine and two glasses on the table. A flowering creeper covered the privacy fence. Trimmed shrubs and well kept flowerbeds surrounded a small patch of grass.

George put his arms around her and kissed her before pulling out a chair and pouring her a glass of wine.

"We're having grilled steak, baked potatoes and salad. A Texas dinner."

"Sounds, and smells, delicious!" She looked around. "What a beautiful yard. I'm guessing you enjoy gardening."

"I do, when I can get the time." He raised his glass to her. "Sorry, I started without you—a glass of wine is an integral part of my cooking process."

She smiled up at him and raised her glass. She relaxed into her chair and watched as he finished cooking. As he served, a large marmalade cat appeared from the bushes and headed over to her. He rubbed against her legs and then jumped into her lap and settled down, purring loudly.

"Is this your cat?" she asked.

George glanced up from serving. "Oh yes, I'm sorry. I hope you like cats. Apparently Mr. T likes you."

Caitlin stroked the soft coat and Mr. T rewarded her with an increase in the purring volume. "I love cats. I never owned one, but I do love them." She continued to stroke him.

When he had finished serving their meal, George put some food in a dish on the ground and Mr. T jumped down and headed to it. Over dinner, he told Caitlin that he had a meeting with Joe and Phil the following week to discuss working for them.

"You don't mind leaving the police force?"

"No, I joined because it was the first available opportunity once I graduated, and I needed to work. I would probably be happier if I made detective with the force, but what I really want to do is start my own private detective agency. This job with Joe would definitely be a step in that direction."

"You'll have to buy some more clothes." She teased him.

George laughed. "I guess I will. I'll have to get used to wearing a suit and tie, too."

"At least you can go casual sometimes when you are undercover." They both laughed.

They cleared off the table and carried the dishes into the kitchen and loaded the dishwasher.

George turned to Caitlin. "You'll stay here tonight?"

"Yes, I will, but if we're going to make a habit of this, perhaps I should bring a few things and leave them here?

"You can pack all your things and bring them, as far as I'm concerned. Stay with me forever." George wrapped his arms around her.

Caitlin relaxed against him and sighed.

I never thought I could be this happy spending time with a man...or feel this safe.

The following day, Caitlin drove out to the lake. It felt strange to not have to go through the subterfuge of the boat, but it was also an immense relief. As she entered the kitchen, Terri put two mugs of coffee on the table, and they sat down and looked at each other in silence for a few seconds.

"It feels so strange, Cait. Like we have moved out of a bad dream into a whole new life."

"I know exactly what you mean. I was thinking the same thing."

"So, what now?"

"I think we continue as we've been doing, without the addition of the boat." Caitlin paused for a moment before continuing. "What's the one thing I say most to all our victims?"

"Have you got any children?" Terri said immediately.

Caitlin smiled. "Probably, but I was thinking of something else. 'Batterers usually just move on to another victim within six months'."

"Okay—"

"Last week I started thinking about that. We are just accepting it as though there is nothing we can do to fix it. Just keep moving each new victim out of the area but knowing there'll always be more."

"What can we do? Do you have some bright idea?"

"I have an idea; not sure how bright it is. But now that I've started looking at things from this angle, I can't stop thinking we have to do something. Remember, I told you about Robby—doing anger management and how it's working for him?"

Terri nodded. "Go on. I'm listening."

"Well, we're in the ideal position to, at the very least, give these abusers the information that might just turn them towards doing what Robby did. Also, Margo and Roger are working through their problems. I know that there are those like Keith, who're just plain bad and will never even consider it. But maybe someone like—say Malcolm—would think about it, if it meant saving their relationship, they might." Caitlin waited for Terri to respond.

"It kind of makes sense, Cait. As you say, we know who the abusers are. We even know where they live. What did you have in mind?"

"I was thinking. Perhaps a leaflet listing the advantages of anger management. With the names and contact information of professionals who specialize in it. I had even thought that maybe Robby would be interested in being an initial contact. For anyone who decided to investigate the possibility. Sort of 'speak to someone who has been through it'. Just anything that might tip the balance and reduce the possibility of continuing abuse."

"It could work. I like that idea," Terri said.

"I think I'll talk to Robby and Peggy about it. If they agree, we can put together a draft for a leaflet. If it just works for one abuser in ten—hell, one in twenty—it's still going to be worth it."

They chatted some more about the various possibilities before Caitlin headed back to Austin, promising to call Terri after she spoke

Caitlin's Escape Route

to Peggy.

CHAPTER TWENTY-THREE

Caitlin arrived at the shelter earlier than usual. She knocked on the door to Peggy's office.

"Come in."

"Hi Peggy, is now a good time to talk, or should I come back later?"

"Hello Caitlin." Peggy glanced at the clock on the wall beside her. "Oh, it's your day to be here. You're early, but yes, I've time now. What's up?"

Caitlin sat down and told Peggy what she and Terri had discussed the day before. Peggy listened quietly, nodding occasionally.

"Let me pull Robby into this discussion," Peggy said as Caitlin finished, she left the office and returned a few minutes later with Robby.

"Hi Caitlin," Robby said. "I'm sorry if I freaked you out the last time we spoke. You can blame Peggy for that."

Caitlin smiled at him. "I admit I was a bit freaked out, but it also gave me a whole new perspective. It's what started the germ of the idea we're talking about now."

As Robby sat down in the chair beside Caitlin, Peggy told him what they had been discussing.

"This's a terrific idea!" Robby said. "I don't know why we didn't think of it before now. The percentage of batterers who respond well to anger management is very small. Most have more than just an inability to control their temper, many are sadists or otherwise mentally disturbed. It would still be worth it."

Caitlin's Escape Route

"I know that anger management is usually part of conditions for parole when an abuser appears in court. I just think that's a bit too late. If we could get their attention before it came to that, perhaps they'd be more inclined. At least some of them," Caitlin said. Then she told Peggy and Robby about Margo and Roger and what they'd been through.

"So, Robby, would you be prepared to front such an operation?" Peggy said. "I mean, talk to the abusers and tell them of your experience and what it has meant to you?"

Robby nodded. "I'd be so happy to feel I could make a difference; somehow stop the cycle for others."

"Okay Caitlin. I'll talk to the therapists we have a relationship with and put together a list of those willing to take part in this. Together with the list Margo gave you, we should have quite a choice."

"Thank you both. Oh, and also, Margo did offer to be of assistance to us and I think this might just be something she could really help with. Could you contact her Robby and talk to her about it?"

Robby nodded. "Will do." He made a note on a pad balanced on his knee.

"Great! I'll start designing a leaflet and once we have all the data, we can meet again and review it before I get it printed up," Caitlin said as she stood up.

The following day, Caitlin and Terri sat side by side at Terri's computer, working on designing their anger management leaflet. Peggy had emailed them a list of therapists willing to take part along with their contact details. They both agreed that the central idea should be based around Robby being a success story and, for more information, contact him. The list of therapists could be included on the back in case any abusers wanted to be more anonymous. The most difficult part was getting the wording just right.

"We can't put that, Caitlin; it sounds way too angry. You have to get past your own personal feelings and look at it from the abuser's point of view."

Caitlin stared at her sister for a long time, thinking about that. "You know, I never even tried to do that. But—how could I? Can you? I mean, can you look at what Keith did to you and feel anything but anger?"

"Okay—when you put it that way—let me think," Terri said. "Let's start from when I first met him. I fell in love with him because he was so kind and attentive, and took charge of situations, without seeming to be controlling. When we moved to the Bay Area, he became controlling and very suspicious, and finally violent. Can we glean something from that to use?"

Slowly and painfully, they tried to analyze each of the abusers, and what they knew of their pattern until they finally put together an opening paragraph.

"Now what we need to do is show that to Robby and get him to 'fix it', using what he understands about how it all works. I'll bring it over to the shelter tomorrow," Caitlin said.

Terri looked at her watch, "why not go now? I'll go with you. I would really like to meet Robby and get his point of view; see how far off base we are."

Caitlin knocked on the door to Peggy's office and waited. Peggy opened the door.

"This is a surprise. I wasn't expecting you today, Caitlin—and Terri, too. How nice to see you again! Come in."

"We are really sorry to interrupt you, Peggy. We have a draft of the leaflet we were talking about and hoped that Robby could take a look," Caitlin said.

"Of course, that was fast. I'll get him."

A few minutes later, the four of them sat around Peggy's desk, studying the pages Terri had spread out.

"We actually created four different versions. To be honest, it was not as easy as we expected."

After some discussion, they settled on one of the drafts with a lot of changes made by Robby.

"I suggest we ask one of the therapists we work with to review this and give us feedback before we complete it," Peggy said.

"That's a great idea. Once you have their feedback, let me know and we can arrange to get it printed," Caitlin said.

That evening, over dinner, Caitlin told George her idea about expanding into the anger management side of domestic violence. He thought it was a great idea.

"You could give the police the leaflets to hand out when they respond to DV calls."

"Good idea. Our plan is to send them to the abusers of our victims, but even better, if the police hand them out, it is one step before the ER."

As they were cleaning up after dinner, George reminded Caitlin that he was going to speak to Phil and Joe about working with them the following morning.

"It'll be great if that pans out. You won't have to put in so many crazy hours and you can start on the next steps towards having your own business."

"I'm excited about it."

George stepped out of the elevator and approached the young woman seated behind the glass table.

"My name's George Little," he said. "I've an appointment with Joe Trainor." He glanced at his watch and added. "I'm afraid I'm a little early."

"No problem. Mr. Little, Joe's expecting you. I'll let him know you're here. Please take a seat."

George sat down and pulled out his phone. He didn't have time to unlock it before Joe came out of the office behind the reception desk.

"Thanks for coming in, George." They shook hands. "Follow me." Joe led him down a corridor. "We'll meet in Phil's office," he said, knocking on the door and, at the same time, opening it. "After you." He held the door open.

Phil stood up and came around his desk and offered his hand. "Good to meet you, George," he said, walking towards a coffee table in front of a couch. He directed them to the armchairs on either side.

All three men sat down as the receptionist came in with a tray containing coffee and placed it on the table in front of them. Phil thanked her.

As Lucy closed the door he continued, "I won't lie to you George, we could consider some of the work we do kind of sleazy. Things like catching a cheating spouse in the act." He paused to take a sip of his coffee. "Sometimes we end up proving that there's been no cheating, though in my opinion, it's a doomed marriage if there's such a lack of trust or communication. But I'm not a marriage counselor. I'm a divorce lawyer, so we keep our opinions to ourselves." He grinned.

George just nodded and smiled while Joe continued, "my requirements are usually less sleazy than Phil's. Identifying and questioning witnesses, following up on alibis. That sort of thing. I could also use help when questioning potential clients. A second opinion is always valuable. That'd be where your expertise and experience would be very useful. Of course, there's always a lot of paperwork to do."

"So, George, what do you think?" Phil looked at George with his eyebrows raised and his mug halfway to his mouth.

George nodded slowly. "I'm definitely interested. What sort of compensation, benefits etc., are we talking about?"

The three men discussed the details, and Phil and Joe answered George's questions.

"So, what do you think?" Phil repeated.

"Where do I sign and when can I start?" George answered with a wide grin.

"I assume you'll need to give two weeks' notice to the police force, so let's say two weeks from Monday?" They all shook hands.

***

George and Caitlin got to the restaurant a little early. They sat at the bar and ordered drinks. They were halfway through their drinks when Joe and Terri arrived, and the four of them followed the hostess to a table.

"Congratulations on the new job, George," Terri said.

"And congratulations Joe, on your new hire," Caitlin said.

"Thank you.," George and Joe said, almost at the same time.

"Seriously, I'm looking forward to starting." George raised his glass to Joe.

"So, what's next for your ER, Caitlin?" Joe asked as they finished up their meal.

"Ted and Pat are taking over most of DV side. I'm going to be working with Peggy and Robby on the AM—Anger Management."

"And how is that going?" Joe said.

"We have only just started distributing leaflets, but I'm guessing it will not be easy. I'm applying for UT's PhD in Psychology program. That should equip me to be better able to help there."

As they were leaving the restaurant, Joe wished Caitlin good luck getting into UT.

"Thanks, I should hear in the next couple of weeks," she said, crossing her fingers.

George was in the backyard when Caitlin came out to join him.

"Hi Darling. How was your day?" He put his arms around her and kissed her.

"Hi George, hi Mr. T," she said, bending down and stroking the cat who was rubbing against her legs. Then she smiled up at George. "My day was magic! I heard from UT. I have been accepted."

"That is great news! Congratulations." George hugged her again. "This calls for a toast. Hang on and I will get a bottle and a couple of glasses. We can have one before I start cooking."

Caitlin sat down with a satisfied sigh and smiled as he disappeared into the kitchen, returning with a bottle and two glasses.

"I do love this yard," Caitlin said as she sipped on her wine.

"Why don't you move in with me? Now that I'm no longer working for the force, my hours are more civilized. There's no reason not to?"

Caitlin said nothing, studying his face.

"What? You do love me? Why not move in?"

"Yes, I do love you. I'm not saying no. I'm just not sure if I'm ready."

"Well, think about it. After all, you are here most of the time anyway, and you could sit out here and study."

That made her smile. "I'll think about it."

CHAPTER TWENTY-FOUR

The library was almost empty and, as always, quiet. A few desk lights scattered around among the bookshelves broke the dim lighting. Caitlin pushed her hair out of her eyes and kept on reading. Two minutes later, her hair had fallen across her face again. She rooted around in her pocket for a hair tie and pulled her hair back in a ponytail. For the next two hours, she continued working through the books piled up on the desk in front of her, making notes as she went. Finally, she packed up her bag, turned off the desk lamp, and made her way quietly out of the building.

She sat in the car for a few minutes before pulling out her phone and calling Terri.

"Hi Cait, how's the studying going?"

"Good, thanks. It's a lot of work—and reading—but it's so fascinating, I'm really enjoying it."

"Are you heading this way?"

"Yes, I'll see you in about an hour."

Caitlin hung up and headed towards the lake. Joe and George were away at a conference, and the sisters were having a rare evening together.

Terri was sitting on the balcony with a bottle of wine and two empty glasses when Caitlin arrived.

"How are things going since you moved in with George? Not regretting it, I hope?"

Caitlin smiled. "Absolutely no regrets. It only took me a few weeks to realize it was the right decision. It's wonderful."

"I'm glad to hear it. I don't know why you took so long to decide."

"Gosh, it seems such a long time since we did this," Caitlin said, pouring wine for both of them.

"Well, to be fair, it has been almost six months. This is the first evening we've had together without the guys since you started working on your PhD. How are things going with the ER and the new effort?"

"Pat and Ted are taking care of the ER. I rarely have anything to do with it now. They keep moving victims through, or at least giving them the option. The network keeps growing. Almost every victim released into their new life has become an active member, helping others."

"And the AM?" Terri asked.

"Not really doing much. I mean, Robby, Peggy and I meet regularly to talk about it. Robby has actually spoken to a couple of guys who showed an interest. One of them is currently attending group meetings. But—"

"But what?"

"The more I read, the more I realize it isn't just anger. By the time it's full-blown abuse, almost the only way to stop it is to change the laws. Letting abusers out on bail and expecting them to observe a restraining order is unrealistic. It's archaic. It's giving the abuser more rights than the victim. I think so anyway. I think dealing with the problem way earlier would work better. Playground bullies probably turn into domestic abusers. It's that same mentality. Anger management can really only help those few who aren't sadists—or mentally disturbed, as Robby pointed out; those who don't believe they've a right to control others. It's too late for the rest of them. At least that's what my dissertation is going to deal with."

The sisters sipped their wine in silence for a few minutes.

"Don't get me wrong, I still think it is worth pursuing the AM route. At least it's better than doing nothing at all. It worked for Robby, after all—and for Aunt May's husband. But while the law's not actively protecting victims, and so many victims cannot turn their backs on their abusers, for whatever reason, it'll continue," Caitlin said, shaking her head slowly. "Can you see anger management making any difference to Keith?"

"No, you're right there. He might agree to do it, as a means to stay free, but he has such a warped view of life at this stage, it wouldn't change him one bit," Terri said. "Oh, and by the way, they've postponed his trial."

"Oh, for heaven's sake! What a pain. I'm sure you just want to get that over with by now. But at least he remains locked up while waiting for it. If he hadn't set fire to the house, I'm sure he would be out on bail too."

"Yeah. As soon as they set a new date, Joe and I will spend a couple of weeks in San Francisco. Hopefully, the trial won't take that long, and we can get a bit of a vacation as well. Anyway, let's eat!" Terri served dinner.

Next morning Caitlin headed back to Austin.

***

When Joe and George returned from their conference, the four of them met up for dinner. George suggested they take a cab, as he felt like relaxing and having a few drinks.

"Wow, this place is swanky," Caitlin said as they went in.

"Joe's choice. He says it's the best he has ever tried. I agree, it's a bit on the high-end side," George replied, grinning.

The manager led them to the table where Joe and Terri sat waiting. A table in the far corner of the restaurant, close to the servers' station. A bottle of wine, four glasses, and four menus were already on the table. They took their time reading through the menu and ordering.

"This is a beautiful restaurant, and from the fact that there are no prices on the menu, I'm guessing it's expensive! What's the occasion, Joe?" Caitlin said.

Joe grinned at them for a few seconds before answering. "Terri has some exciting news that I believe is worth celebrating." He turned to her and raised his eyebrows.

Terri looked around the table, enjoying the suspense.

"Come on Terri, what?" Caitlin said.

"I'm officially divorced. Phil called me earlier."

"This calls for champagne, I believe." Joe signaled the restaurant manager, who was hovering expectantly nearby. Minutes later, he appeared at the table with a bottle of pink champagne and four glasses on a tray. He placed the tray on an empty table to one side, opened the bottle and poured the bubbling liquid into the glasses.

"To us," George said, and they all raised their glasses. "And now to our news."

"What?" Terri said as he paused.

"Since you have purchased the lake house, we've been looking for something close by. We put an offer on a house on the North Shore, literally ten minutes' drive from your house."

"I know you two are going to be living in the tunnel unit while your reno is in progress, so we won't be neighbors for a while, but at least we'll still have a deck overlooking the lake to sit on and drink wine," Caitlin said.

"That's brilliant news!" Terri said. "Now all we need is for the trial to be over with and Keith locked up."

***

Two months later, Terri and Joe flew to San Francisco for Keith's trial. It lasted a week. The jury found him guilty of arson, assault, and attempted manslaughter. Terri's testimony was uneventful. She confirmed Keith had attacked her when she said she was leaving, and it was not the first time he had been violent. The audio and video from the lake house, showing Keith not just admitting to setting the fire, but explaining how he did it. That sealed his fate. The jury took only two hours to come back with the verdict and the judge set sentencing for the following month. Luckily, Terri would not have to testify at the sentencing. Her recorded testimony was sufficient.

Before returning to Texas, Terri and Joe had dinner with the neighbor responsible for saving her life, Damian and his wife.

"I never got the opportunity to thank you properly, Damian."

"No thanks needed, Terri. I was very glad I was there, and that I got you out in time."

"Not as glad as I was," Terri said, smiling at him.

"You'll be welcome to visit us anytime in Texas," Joe said to Damian as they were leaving.

***

Keith slowly opened his eyes. He tried to sit up but couldn't move his arms and he couldn't see what was holding him down.

Where the hell am I?

Then he remembered. The police van taking him from the

courthouse to the prison to serve his sentence had skidded off the road. The last thing he recalled was his head banging against something, and his body jerking against his seatbelt as the van rolled over and over.

How long have I been unconscious?

He noticed the dust was still settling around the wreck. Not long.

As his eyes adjusted to the half-light, he could see that the van was on its side. The body of the cop who was in the back with him was on top of him, pinning him down. There was no sound from the front of the van where the driver and another cop were.

He slowly eased his body out from under the cop. It was obvious he was dead. After some awkward fumbling through the dead man's pockets, with his cuffed hands, he located the keys. With some difficulty, he released himself from the cuffs on his wrists. The chain on his ankle was easier to dispose of. It took him a lot longer to remove the broken glass from the window at the back of the van; and somehow, he squeezed out of the opening, landing in a heap in the rocky dirt.

He looked around. All he could see were trees. Above him were sounds of the highway and people shouting, but he could see only thick overgrowth. He saw where the van had torn its way through the grove. The pathway it made had filled back in somewhat with broken branches and rocks that were now precariously balanced. The slope continued on down through thick forest. That was his way out.

Keith got to his feet, carefully checking for any major injury. He didn't feel any broken bones. He was sore all over. There were cuts and grazes on both of his hands, no doubt on his face too. He moved slowly and cautiously towards the front of the van, where one of the wing mirrors was dangling; he wiped the mirror with his sleeve and peered at himself. There was blood all over his face.

He checked in the front cab. Both cops were dead, or at least unconscious. He went through their pockets, removing anything he thought would be useful. Pocket knives, money and, of course, guns and ammunition. He checked the glove box and pulled out a small first aid kit and some maps. Finally, he discovered a backpack on the floor in front of the passenger seat. It contained some paperwork, a pack of cigarettes, a lighter, a couple of bottles of water and some protein bars. He dumped out the paperwork and put all the stuff he had gathered into the bag, which he strapped tightly onto his back. He wadded up some of the paper. Set fire to it and dropped it into the pool of liquid leaking out of the gas tank. Then he turned and, slipping and sliding, he made it down the slope and disappeared into the trees as the van burst into flames.

CHAPTER TWENTY-FIVE

Terri dug in her purse and pulled out her phone.

"Hello—Yes, this is Terri Donnelly—" She sat down hard on the chair. "What? Are you sure? Yes, sorry, of course you know what you are talking about. Do you need me to do anything?" She took a deep breath as she listened to the voice on the other end. "Okay, okay. Thanks for letting me know." She hung up and started shaking. Dropping her head between her knees, she took a few deep breaths. Then she turned back to her phone and hit speed dial.

"Pick up Caitlin!" she shouted as she listened. She hung up when her sister's voicemail picked up, immediately redialing.

"Hello, Cait? Thank goodness."

"Sorry Terri, I couldn't find my phone. What's up?"

"I just got a call from the SF police. Keith escaped!"

"What? No! How?"

"Apparently, the van taking him to prison after sentencing ran off the road. They didn't give me any details, except to say he was free and on the run. They were calling to warn me just in case he headed this way."

"Not again! We really don't need to go through all that again."

"I'm sure he won't come back here. He'll most likely try to get back to Ireland."

"Don't be too sure Terri, I don't see how he could. If he was on his way to prison, he didn't have any of his documentation with him. There's no way he could get out of the country. This is awful!"

"I know. I'll talk to Joe as soon as he gets home and see what he thinks we should do."

"Yeah. I'll ask George to talk to his contacts at your local police station. Just to be safe. Meanwhile, make sure you keep the alarm set and don't forget the escape tunnel."

Terri laughed despite her stress. "Good point! I hope I don't have to use it." As she put her phone away, she thought about the elaborate escape system Caitlin had built into the roof space in the fourplex. Caitlin had actually used the tunnel, on at least one occasion, to hide from angry partners of victims she had helped to escape to a new life.

Now I may end up using that to escape my abusive ex-husband. She thought as she returned to the kitchen and continued preparing dinner.

When she heard the front door open, she hurried into the hall.

"Oh, Joe!" she said, throwing her arms around him as soon as he closed the door behind him. "Thank God you're home."

"George told me. Caitlin called him at work. I left as soon as I heard. Are you okay?" He held her at arm's length and studied her face.

She smiled. "Yes, I was a bit shaken, but I really don't believe he'll try to come here again. He'll want to get as far away from the US authorities. I didn't call you because I didn't want you to worry."

"I think you're right. From what I know of him, he's no genius, but I don't think he's that stupid. Still, we should be vigilant, just in case."

"Caitlin reminded me of the escape tunnel. And I'll take her advice and keep the alarm set. That just makes sense."

Joe nodded. "Absolutely, I agree. George's going to call his old colleagues at our local station, and also the cops out at the lake who captured Keith; if he's looking for you, that's where he'll go. He won't know you're no longer living there. George'll let them know to be on the watch for him. I'm guessing the authorities in SF already warned the police here, but we can't be too careful."

"I guess I should tell Ted and Pat, too. Just so they are aware, if he should show up here, it's as well they are on the lookout."

They were clearing the table after dinner when Terri's phone rang.

"It's Cait," she said as she picked up. "Hey—Okay, great thanks—talk to you soon." She turned to Joe. "George called his contacts at the station, and they confirmed they already knew. They assured him they would watch out for me."

"Good. That's about all we can do at this point."

"I'm still convinced he won't come near Texas. But I'll take extra care," Terri smiled. "I've got a meeting first thing in the morning, but as soon as that's done, I'll talk to Ted and Pat and let them know. After all, if I had to use the escape tunnel, it comes out in their garage. They would need to know. I'll probably let the tenants in the other two units know, too. Just in case."

Next morning, as soon as Joe had left for work, Terri headed to the spare room that she had set up as her home office and spent an hour at an online meeting. When the meeting ended, she peered through the window to make sure the street outside was clear. No sign of Keith or anyone else. She grabbed her keys and phone and headed out to the unit at the other end of the fourplex and knocked on the door.

"Hi Terri," Pat said as she opened the door. "Come on in."

"Sorry to bother you. Is Ted here?"

"In the kitchen."

"Great, I need to talk to you both." Terri followed Pat.

"What's up?" Pat looked worried.

Terri explained to them about Keith.

"I'm sure there's nothing to worry about. I can't imagine he'd be so stupid as to show up here again, but I thought you should know, just in case. If by some chance he does, I might have to use the escape tunnel. Wouldn't want to turn up in your garage without warning." They all laughed at that.

"Still, thanks for letting us know. I'll keep an eye out. Let me know if you need anything at all," Ted said.

"Thanks, the ER and the Shelter keep you and Pat busy, so hopefully you won't have to get involved. How're things going?"

"Sadly, we've been busy. Domestic violence is something that can't seem to be controlled. Even with Caitlin's efforts on the anger management side, we've a steady stream of victims. I just wish more of them would take advantage of the escape we offer them. So many are just convinced they can fix their abuser, or worse, are afraid to leave."

Terri nodded sympathetically. "Anyway, I need to get back to my work. Hopefully, the police will catch Keith quickly and we can relax."

Terri hurried back to her own unit. She spent the rest of the day working at her computer. She had a deadline approaching. It was the only downside of working from home. She felt more pressure to meet deadlines than she would if she were in the office. She was afraid if she missed a deadline, it would look like she was not putting in the hours. At least when you're in an office, they can see you are working.

The only time she took a break was to make a fresh pot of coffee. As she waited for it to brew, she allowed herself to think about Keith, not just the Keith who may or may not be coming to get her. The Keith she had fallen in love with back when they were both students in Dublin. They did everything together. She was sure she had found the perfect man. She looked forward to having a fairy tale marriage and living happily ever after. After they married and moved back to California, life was so perfect until it wasn't.

Terri poured a mug of fresh coffee, slowly shaking her head, her lips pursed and her eyebrows drawn together.

I just know he won't come looking for me this time. There is no reason to. Last time I was a witness, now he's a convicted felon. He won't risk getting caught again—surely?

She headed back to her office, determined to get another few hours of coding done before Joe got home.

***

Keith watched from his perch in a tree some distance from the river. A long line of exhausted looking people, men, women and children, headed to the water's edge, and started wading across. As it got deeper towards the center, the men lifted the smaller children onto their shoulders. As soon as they reached the other side and climbed up the steep bank, police with guns herded them into pens like cattle.

Shit, I'll never get across here without being seen. I need to come up with another plan.

He quietly climbed down from the tree and headed back along the riverbank. They had told him to go downriver, and he would find a raft. They assured him he could safely cross on that. He didn't understand all they had said, but he got the gist of it.

Two hours later, he stumbled across a wooden pallet half in the water but caught on a tree root. He got it loose and dragged it further up the bank, out of the water. Surely this wasn't the raft they were talking about, he wondered as he stared across the fast-flowing river. He couldn't imagine making it to the other side of this river, on that chunk of wood. As he looked more closely, he saw a rope threaded through a plastic pipe, which appeared to be fixed to the center of the pallet. Pulling on the rope, he realized it spanned the river and was firmly anchored on both sides. He located where it was wrapped securely around a large tree a few feet from the water's edge. A second rope was knotted around one of the slats and this was also tied to the opposite bank.

They weren't kidding. This is ingenious.

Keith stripped down to his boxer shorts, stuffed his clothes into his backpack, which was lined with a heavy plastic bag. He climbed onto the makeshift raft and pulled on the rope. It slipped down the muddy bank into the water. Hauling on the rope was hard work and as he neared the center, the current got stronger and he had a fight to keep moving forward, but the rope through the pipe held it steady against the pull of the river. Exhausted, he finally made it to the US shore. He dragged himself off the raft and onto land, a steep rocky bank. Lying among the rushes and tree roots, he waited for his heaving lungs to return to normal. He struggled to get up the bank; once there, he got dressed and headed into the undergrowth, making his way north to El Paso.

It didn't take him long to find the address. A small junk shop down a side street in what he guessed was not the best area in the city. As instructed, he found the back door, knocked and waited. A middle-aged man opened the door a crack.

"What do you want?" he said.

"Carlos asked me to deliver a package to Juan."

The man opened the door wider and checked the street before inviting him in and shutting the door.

"Wait here," he said, disappearing through another door.

A few minutes later, a younger man came out. "I'm Juan. You've a package for me?"

Keith handed over the package, and the man nodded. "Wait here."

Another five minutes and Juan returned with a different package, wrapped in green plastic.

"Give this to Carlos and tell him I said thanks." Juan opened the door to the street and almost pushed Keith out.

Not bloody likely.

Keith stuffed the package into his backpack and headed back the way he had come.

CHAPTER TWENTY-SIX

Caitlin opened the door as soon as she heard Joe's car pull into the driveway. They joined George on the deck, where he was busy grilling.

"How're you doing, Terri?" he said, looking up from turning the burgers.

"I'm fine. Really, I think Caitlin's making too much out of this. I know Keith's dumb, but even he wouldn't be so stupid as to risk being caught again. I'm sure he's long gone. Besides, last time he hadn't been tried and convicted. If he's caught, they'll add escaping to the other charges. He was trying to silence me so I couldn't testify. Now there's no reason for him to try anything."

"I hope you're right," Caitlin said, pouring wine into glasses and passing them around. "I still think it would be a good idea for you to move in here with us for a while. He's just nasty enough to want revenge."

"I don't think that's necessary. I think Terri's right. He won't risk it," Joe said, sipping on his wine.

"Well, how about turning on the surveillance at the lake house? If he does show up, that is where he'll go. As far as he knows, you're still living there."

"Okay, I'll do that the next time I'm out there," Terri sighed.

"And be sure to keep a check of the video at the fourplex, too. Just in case."

Before they left, Terri agreed to meet up with Caitlin the following week to go check on the lake house and switch on the surveillance there.

***

Terri was busy preparing dinner when she heard a noise outside the back door. She paused what she was doing to listen. There was someone out there. It sounded like they were creeping around the back of the unit. She grabbed her phone and headed into the hall, triggering the hidden entrance to the ladder up to the roof space. She closed the door behind her before climbing up the ladder.

She knew there was no need for her to avoid making noise. They had made sure they soundproofed it well. But it was instinctive to move as quietly as she could. She sat in front of the computer that managed the surveillance system. As she studied the view of the back of the unit, she could distinctly see a figure. It looked like a man. He was trying to peer through the window. Then he continued along the back of the house, stopping at each window. Until he got to the end unit, Pat and Ted's unit. Suddenly he jumped back as the lights came on, the door opened and Ted came out. She could see them talking for a few minutes and then they walked around to the front.

Ted stood watching from his front door as the man walked off down the street. As soon as he turned the corner and was out of sight, Terri went back downstairs. She checked through the front window before turning off the alarm and opening the door. She hurried to Ted and Pat's. Ted opened the door at the first knock.

"Hi Ted, that guy who was prowling around out back. What did he want?"

"Hi Terri. He said he was looking to rent accommodation, but I suspect he was looking for someplace to squat. I sent him packing. Why?"

"I'm just a little nervous, I guess. I was afraid it might have been Keith."

"Oh right. Sorry, I should have thought of that. Definitely wasn't Keith. He was too old, must have been in his fifties."

"That's a relief. Thanks."

"No problem, Terri. If I catch anyone like that again, I'll let you know."

"Thanks."

She returned to her own unit, setting the alarm before continuing

Caitlin's Escape Route

with her dinner preparations.

When she heard Joe's car pull into the garage, she switched off the alarm and went to greet him. As he stepped into the hallway, she threw her arms around him.

"What's up? You are shaking like a leaf! Is everything okay?"

"Sorry. I'm just being silly. I got a bit of a scare earlier. Just so glad you're home."

"What happened?" His forehead creased with worry.

"Nothing really. There was someone prowling around out back, and I had a panic attack. For a second, I thought it was Keith. I went up into the escape tunnel and couldn't see much on the video, then Ted came out and chased him off."

"Who was it? Not Keith?"

"No, no. Not Keith. Ted reckoned it was a homeless guy looking for somewhere to squat. He sent him packing."

"You poor thing. I'm not surprised you got a fright. After what that man did to you." He wrapped his arms around her, and they went into the kitchen.

"Like I said, I'm being silly. Let's eat."

***

Keith was out on the lake on a rented wave runner heading for the house where he last saw Terri. So far, his plan had come together. He couldn't believe how much money was in that package from Juan. He hadn't spent much of it either. The car he bought in El Paso was cheap, but it got him to Austin and was still running.

Slowing down and pulling into the shore, he neared the dock where they had arrested him almost a year ago. He tied the wave runner to a dock some distance from Terri's and made his way along the shore, keeping out of sight from the house. Fortunately, there was a line of trees running from close to the lake right up to the house. He could get within feet of it without risking being spotted. However, once he was close enough to see the house, he realized Terri was not living there. The house was undergoing a major renovation. Scaffolding covered two sides and there was a pile of construction material in the backyard, with a crew of men working both inside and outside.

Damn it! I hope Caitlin's in the same place still. If she is, I can trace Terri through her.

He headed back to the lake. Returned the wave runner and drove back to his trailer. Well, it wasn't his trailer. He'd found it abandoned at the back of a trailer park in the hills overlooking the lake. No one seemed to notice when he moved in. It was the perfect location until he discovered Terri was no longer living in the lake house. It was still a suitable location for his plan.

Next morning, he drove to the fourplex in Northwest Austin where Caitlin had lived. He parked as far away as possible but could still see her front door. Then he tried to make himself invisible, sitting hunched down in the passenger seat, with his cap pulled low over his face. He hoped if anyone saw him, they would assume he was waiting for the driver to come back from somewhere. He started to nod off when a car pulled up in front of the unit. Watching, he saw Caitlin walk up to the front door and was surprised to see her knock on it. Even more surprised when Terri answered the door. He watched as the door closed behind the two sisters.

Well, that was unexpected! Terri must be living there. Weird.

He waited to see if one or both of them came out. Another hour went by before the door opened again, and Caitlin came out. As her car pulled away, he moved into the driver's seat and followed her. It wasn't long before he guessed they were heading for the lake. Forty minutes later, Caitlin pulled into the driveway of a large house just a few streets away from where Terri had lived. He headed back to his trailer to rethink his plans.

CHAPTER TWENTY-SEVEN

Terri was heading to the lake house to do her weekly inspection of the renovations. Caitlin had suggested that she call to her first, and they would go together. She guessed that her sister was not so much interested in seeing the progress as afraid to let Terri go anywhere alone.

As she pulled into the driveway, Caitlin opened the door and came out.

"Come on, I'll drive," she said.

As they drove off, neither of them noticed the beat-up car parked on the other side of the road. Ten minutes later, they pulled into the lake house driveway.

"It seems to be taking ages, doesn't it?"

"I guess so, but they're doing a huge amount. I mean, the extension is quite big, that took time. Then they had to replace the roof. And there was a delay waiting for the windows to be delivered."

"Well, at least they're done with the outside now. Let's go look. And you can turn on the surveillance."

Thirty minutes later, they were ready to leave.

"Are you sure you got enough photos?" Caitlin laughed.

"I know, but I want to be sure Joe sees what they've done. He just doesn't have time to get out here himself. He says that's fine because he'll enjoy the transformation all the more for not seeing it half done. Also, it's fun to have a record of the progress."

"Of course, it is. I'm only teasing you. It's going to look great. Have

Caitlin's Escape Route

you time to come in?"

"No, I better head home. Thanks Cait. See you next week."

"You'll have to do next week's inspection on your own, I'm afraid. I've a meeting with the anger management group. I doubt I'll be back in time."

"Okay, I'll share my photos with you then." They hugged and Terri drove off.

***

From behind the neighbor's shed, Keith watched Terri leave. He had heard most of their conversation and couldn't believe his luck. Finally, he could get Terri on her own. Things were going his way. He had a week to put his plan in place.

The following day, he rented a wave runner and spent some time on the lake. When he returned it, he inquired about renting a canoe. They didn't have any, but they gave him the name of someone who had kayaks and canoes to rent.

For the next three days, he kept busy. He bought camping equipment, food and water, and a few other bits and pieces. Rented a canoe for a week and found a quiet location to tie it up out of sight.

Finally, two days before Terri was due to do her lake house inspection, he loaded up the canoe with all of his supplies and headed out onto the lake. When he returned, he tied the empty canoe back in the same cove, close to Terri's house.

When Terri arrived at the lake house the next day, Keith was already hidden among the trees, waiting. He watched her as she disappeared into the house. She had parked the car just a few feet away, under the shade of the trees. He had counted on that. Although the weather had cooled, the sun could still overheat a parked car. While he waited for her to return to the car, he stretched and did a few squats to loosen up his muscles, then he moved closer to the car, stopping behind a tree just feet from the driver's door.

Thirty minutes passed before she emerged from the house. The contractors appeared to all be working inside, as Keith had seen none of them since he arrived. As Terri approached the car, he prepared himself. The second she opened the driver's door, he pounced. One arm pinning her arms to her sides and the other holding his hand across her mouth. He dragged her into the trees. Slamming her hard against the nearest tree trunk, he lowered her limp body to the ground and quickly gagged her and tied her hands and feet. The car keys were still in her hand. Grabbing them, he popped the trunk of her car. He peered at the house again to make sure no one was in sight before lifting her and dumping her in the trunk. Closing it quietly, he climbed into the driver's seat and headed down to the lake.

Terri started to stir and moan as he placed her in the front of the canoe. He had removed the seat to make more space; he put her on the floor out of sight. Climbing in behind her as soon as he had untied it, using the paddle, he pushed against the dock and headed out onto the lake. As he paddled, moving through the water, Terri's moaning grew louder. He didn't care because although sound carried a long distance over water, there was no one on the lake and they were far enough away from the shore that it wouldn't matter. If anyone heard her, they wouldn't know what it was or where it came from.

Forty minutes later, Keith pulled the canoe up onto the shore. He untied Terri's feet and half dragged, half carried her towards a clump of shrubbery. Once there, he sat her down and stared into her eyes.

"You listen to me. I'm going to take your gag off and it won't make a damn bit of difference if you yell yourself silly. No one'll hear you. We're in an isolated area. There's no one for miles. Understand?" He shook her by the shoulders to emphasize his words.

She nodded, and he removed the gag.

"What the fuck do you think you're doing, Keith? You won't get away with this!"

"Ah, but I already did. Here you are."

"What the hell are you doing this for?"

"You owe me some money, remember? We were married. I believe that means when you divorced me, you should've given me half of your money. I intend to get it."

"It isn't my money. It's a trust fund. Caitlin and mine. You tried to kill me, you set fire to our house—it was deliberate, so no insurance payout there! You cleaned out our bank account. You're not entitled to anything!"

"We'll see about that. I'll tell them where you are only when Caitlin breaks that trust and gives me my share."

"You're stupid. She can't break the trust without my signature!"

Keith raised his hand and slapped Terri hard across the face. "Don't call me stupid!"

He pulled a chain out of his backpack and wrapped it around Terri's waist, locking it there with a padlock. Then he walked towards a tree stump about ten feet away, pulling the chain with him. He padlocked the other end around the tree roots.

"You've all you need here. At least for another two weeks. Longer if you're careful."

"What do you mean? You're not going to leave me here!"

"That is exactly what I'm going to do. There's a tent here." He moved one of the bushes to expose the entrance to a small tent. "A sleeping bag, water and food, plus the means to light a fire. You'll find enough wood behind the tent to last you two weeks—if you are careful, like I said."

"Keith! You can't do this to me!"

"Says who? Just watch me. As soon as I get the money from Caitlin, I'll tell her where you are. So, you better pray she does it fast." Keith turned and walked back to the canoe without another word.

***

"Keith! Keith!" Terri screamed after him as he climbed into the canoe and pushed off into the lake.

Terri dropped to her knees and cried until she could cry no more. She lay down on the rocky earth, but as soon as her head touched the ground, the pain in her head forced her to sit up again. Touching her head gently, she could feel a sticky matting in her hair. That bang against the tree had done some damage. Dragging herself to her feet, she headed to the tent to see if she could find something to clean the wound with.

Inside the tent, there were cases of water bottles stacked up in a corner. Cardboard boxes filled with canned foods, mainly soup and beans, plus a few cans of sardines. Some packets of crackers and cookies. A sleeping bag and a box with fire kindling and a couple of lighters. Nothing else. She decided it was best to leave the wound as it was and hope it would heal without infection. Right now, that was the least of her worries. The important thing was to survive for as long as possible. She needed to escape, but how? She would think about that tomorrow. Crawling into the sleeping bag, she fell into a restless sleep almost immediately.

When she woke up, it was pitch dark. She couldn't see her hand in front of her face. For a moment, she thought she had gone blind. Then it all came back to her.

Oh, dear God. What am I going to do? This can't be happening.

It was cold, but there was no way she could light a fire. She couldn't see to find the tent flap, let alone the wood. She buried herself in the sleeping bag, waiting for daylight.

CHAPTER TWENTY-EIGHT

Caitlin looked at her phone.

What is Joe doing calling me at this hour?

"Hello, Joe? Is everything alright?"

"I don't know! Is Terri with you?"

"No! I haven't seen her today. I had a meeting. She was going to check on the construction on her own. Is she not home yet?" Caitlin jumped to her feet.

"No. And she's not answering her phone. I've been calling for ages."

"We'll go over to the lake house right now and see if she's still there. I'll call you right back."

She turned to George. She felt the same lead weight in her chest that she experienced when she heard Terri was in hospital; after Keith almost killed her. Her legs were shaking.

George got to his feet. "What's up? You're as white as a ghost!" he said with a frown, stepping close and putting an arm around her shoulders.

"Terri! She didn't come home, and she isn't answering her phone. We need to go check the lake house."

George nodded, grabbing his keys. "Let's go!"

He headed for the door. Caitlin ran after him.

They pulled up by the trees in front of the lake house a few minutes later. It was dark and there was no activity. The contractors had obviously left for the day. Caitlin got out of the car and stood staring

Caitlin's Escape Route

at the house, not knowing what to do.

"Let's go in and see if any of the contractors are still here," George said.

The house was locked up, and there was no one around. They walked to the back, but it was too dark to see anything. Their phone flashlights provided inadequate light to be helpful.

As they returned to their car, Caitlin heard a phone ring. She pulled her cell phone out. She looked at it and then turned to George.

"Is that your phone ringing?"

"No, not me."

He started looking around and traced the sound into the trees. He turned on his flashlight and immediately spotted a cellphone in the dirt. Picking it up, he looked at Caitlin.

"It's Terri's."

"Oh, my God. What's happened to her—Keith! I knew it!"

She pulled her phone out again and called Joe.

"Joe. There's no one at the lake house, but we found Terri's phone under the trees. It's too dark to see if there is anything else, but she's not here—yes, okay, see you shortly."

"He's coming over here?" George asked.

"Yes—well, to our house. We can decide what to do then."

"Okay, let's get back there. I'll call the station and let the guys know. They probably won't do anything until tomorrow, but with Keith on the loose, they might get moving sooner."

By the time Joe arrived, George had already called the local police. Local to the lake house. That was where they assumed Terri had been abducted.

"Are they going to do anything, or do they have to wait?" Joe asked as he paced up and down the kitchen.

"In theory, they have to wait twenty-four hours, but the officer I spoke to was one of those that arrested Keith and he remembered him. Because of that, and because there is an APB out for Keith, he is going to start the investigation immediately."

"Thank goodness you know these guys. It helps a lot that you used to be a cop." Joe ran his hand over his shaved scalp before pulling off his tie and sitting down. "Thanks man."

"Absolutely, we'll get her back," George said, putting his arm around Caitlin and squeezing her gently. "I promise."

She stared at him like a frightened cat. Making a superhuman effort, she took a deep breath.

I won't let Keith get the better of us!

"Meanwhile, there is a lot we can do ourselves," Caitlin said, suddenly ready for action, aware that it is the only way to fight the feeling of panic. Anything to avoid feeling helpless.

"Like what?" Joe asked.

"We need to check the surveillance tapes from the fourplex. We have to assume that he was there. Also, we can check our own tapes from our doorbell. And we turned on the surveillance at the lake house! I totally forgot we did that." She picked up her phone and pulled up the app that Terri had installed for her. "Look! The light isn't great, but you can see Terri walking to her car and a man jumping out of the trees. It has to be Keith! He grabbed her—hang on! He pulled her back behind the trees—no, wait! There he is! He put her in the trunk and drove off!"

Her commentary was unnecessary, as both Joe and George were peering over her shoulders.

"It looks like she is bound and gagged. We need to get this to the police and check the other videos," George said, getting out his own phone. "We should go back a couple of weeks at least, in case the asshole was lurking around like he did before. Remember? He pretended to be a surveyor?"

"I guess I should go home and check the video there," Joe said, standing up.

"No, no need to do that, Joe," Caitlin said, waving her phone at him. "When Terri set up the surveillance, she set it so that we could both watch both the lake house and the fourplex. It was originally to protect me from angry abusers, after one of them broke in."

George's mouth twitched. "I remember that! You kicked him down the stairs."

"It was self defense!" Caitlin said, as she switched the app to the fourplex video history.

"While you're going through that, I'll send a copy of the video from the lake house to the police." George got up and headed to the next room, Caitlin's office.

Caitlin and Joe followed him in. It was as though they didn't want to be out of sight of each other.

George prepared the video clip, called his contact at the police station to get an email address, and then sent it off. Meanwhile, Caitlin was still scrolling through endless video history for both the fourplex and her own house.

Joe leaned over her shoulder. "Anything?"

"No, the only thing I see that might be a clue, is a battered up old car that was parked cross from the fourplex, and what looks like the same car, parked outside our house here a different day. Here, see if you think it's the same car." She handed the phone to Joe.

George came over and watched as Joe flipped from one view to the other. "Let's put it up on the computer. We can get a bigger view and enhance it."

After some playing around with the images, they all agreed it was the same car. However, they couldn't make out the license plate.

"I'll send these to the police, too. They have better technology than we do and may be able to identify the car."

"Joe, why don't you stay here tonight? It is way too late to be driving home. We can continue our own detective work in the morning," Caitlin said, stifling a yawn.

"I feel it is wrong to even think of going to sleep when we have no idea where Terri is, or if she is okay." Joe's face was a picture of the misery Caitlin also felt.

"I know, but we can't do anything tonight, and we won't be any use to her if we are exhausted. I made up the bed in the guest room while we were waiting for you. You know where it is."

It was very early the next morning when George's phone rang. They were already gathered in the kitchen drinking coffee.

Joe and Caitlin watched George as he answered.

"Hello—Yeah, hi Jim. Any news?" He stood up and started pacing back and forth. "Yeah, really? Okay, that's good news, right? Sure. Thanks a lot." As he hung up, he said, "the cops found Terri's car on one of the roads that lead down to the marina. Close to the lake house. They have fingerprinted it and towed it back to the station."

"He must've taken her somewhere by boat—" Caitlin said, suddenly remembering the last time Keith tried to take Terri in a kayak. That time he was planning to drown her so that she couldn't testify.

Jeez, I hope she is alive. There would be no reason for him to kill her now, she already testified. They convicted him.

She glanced at Joe, not wanting to give him any more to worry

Caitlin's Escape Route

about than he already had.

"Also," George continued. "They're going to have a photo of that beat-up car on the news this morning, asking for anyone with information to come forward. They're working on getting the license number."

Caitlin got up and turned on the TV. The news hadn't started yet.

"I'll go pick up the mail while we are waiting. I have got to do something."

Five minutes later, Caitlin came crashing into the kitchen, junk mail scattered all over the floor. Gasping for breath, she waved an envelope at George.

The two men jumped to their feet, not sure what to do.

"Look—in the mail—"

George took the letter from her and pulled out a single sheet of paper and read aloud.

Caitlin,

By now, you will have noticed that Terri is missing. Yes, that's right, I have her. That is to say, she is somewhere you will never find her. And don't even waste your time trying to find me. By the time you read this, I will be long gone.

You have exactly two weeks to deposit one million dollars in the bank account listed below. Once I see that money in my account, I will tell you where to find your sister.

I know you have way more than that in your trust and as Terri's husband, I am entitled to at least that much.

I can't guarantee that Terri will survive beyond two weeks, so hurry up!

Keith.

They stared at one another; the color drained from Caitlin's face. "Oh, dear God. I can't break the trust without Terri's signature. I will get in touch with our lawyers in Dublin, but I know what they will say. What are we going to do?"

Joe sat with his head in his hands.

"At least we know she is still alive," George said. "That is a good start—hang on, the news is starting."

They stared at the TV, waiting. The picture that was shown of the car was a lot better than the ones they had sent to the police, clearly they had managed to enhance it quite a bit. Hopefully, that would bring in some information. When the broadcast ended, Joe stood up.

"I need to call the office and tell Lucy to cancel all my appointments for the next two weeks—I'll tell her you'll be out too, George. We need to give all of our attention to finding Terri. And even if we can't do anything useful there, I can't concentrate on work right now."

"Absolutely agree Joe. Thanks."

CHAPTER TWENTY-NINE

As the sun rose. Terri struggled to untangle herself from the sleeping bag. She was stiff and cold and desperately needed to go to the toilet. Of course, that was not something Keith gave a damn about. She moved deeper into the shrubbery around the tent. Behind the tent, she found a large mound of wood. Looking around, this seemed to be the most private place she could reach, given the length of the chain. Of course, there was no one out on the lake this late in the year, anyway. She squatted down and relieved herself, using a tissue she had in her pocket.

I better go through the supplies Keith left. I sure hope he left me some toilet paper!

She made her way back into the tent and went through the cardboard boxes and found a pack of two toilet rolls. There was also a small trowel.

Very thoughtful, the asshole! At least I can bury my waste.

Looking at the food, she realized it would only last two weeks if she was very careful.

I am going to have to make it last longer than that, just in case.

She fought hard to squash the feeling of panic rising from somewhere deep inside. Looking around her, she felt like a caged animal; she had an urge to run, but even if she wasn't tethered by a fifteen-foot chain, she had no idea where she could run to.

She inspected the padlocks on each end of the chain. She decided that her first task had got to be breaking at least one, if not both of these. The padlock at the tree was going to be easier for sure, because the other one was on her waist. She doubted she could do anything with that. At least she could hammer at the other one with a rock. With the padlock off, she could get down to the lake's edge. If any boats came by, she had more chance of waving them down. Or even venture into the wilderness Keith had mentioned was all around her. If she could just get rid of the chain, she could at least try to make her way to civilization. After all, why else would he put the chain on her in the first place.

She sat down just inside the entrance of the tent, out of the breeze that was blowing across from the water, staring out across the lake.

This must be what Robinson Crusoe felt like. Wait, didn't he put a message in the sand with stones? I wonder, would that work for me? I know there are lots of small aircraft that fly up and down the lake, giving flying lessons. They might see a message!

She set off to see how close she could get to the shore with the chain. Not nearly close enough.

I hope it doesn't start raining and bring the lake up. It could easily swamp the tent. This section of the shore is so flat.

Another thing to worry about. Definitely, her first priority was to break that padlock. She went over to the tree stump and studied what Keith had done. It was one of the many trees they had cut down before damming the river to create the lake. Like most of them, the stump was about two feet high, with a number of roots stretching out like arms. He had wound the chain around two of these roots. The padlock didn't look all that solid, and was flat on the ground, so that was one good thing.

She decided she would first try to smash the padlock. The ground beneath it was solid rock. All she needed was to find a rock, heavy enough to smash it, but not so heavy she couldn't yield it like a hammer. If that didn't work, perhaps she could break the roots and release the chain that way. She fetched the trowel from the tent and started jabbing at the smaller of the two roots. It was immediately obvious that wasn't going to work. The wood had almost become petrified from soaking in water and then baking in the Texas sun. Another indication that this area would get swamped if the lake level were to rise.

I wonder if I could set fire to it. Would it burn?

She had a vision of the chain turning a scorching red from the fire and decided that would not be such a good idea. Not without an anvil and hammer, and probably way more strength than she could muster, even fully fit. But with her head throbbing and hunger eating away at her, no way. The thought of her hunger made her turn to her food supplies. She would need to eat something. It was almost twenty-four hours since she had last eaten. There was no can opener in any of the boxes, then she realized that all the cans had pull tabs.

Huh, probably worried I could use the can opener to escape. And yet, he left a trowel. Perhaps that was an accident, probably he used it to clear around the tree roots.

She opened a can of beans and ate half of them, using a plastic spoon she found in the bottom of the box. She would have to be careful with that spoon. It seemed to be the only utensil. Half a bottle of water was all she allowed herself. She didn't want to run out of food and water before they rescued her.

If they rescue me—they will! They have to!

As she searched for a rock to start hammering at the padlock with, she realized most of the likely rocks were at the water's edge. Taking the trowel, she started digging to see if she could find any hidden in the sparse dirt around the shrubbery. Thirty minutes later, she unearthed one that might just work. It was heavy, but not so heavy that she couldn't lift it. She carried it over to the tree stump and started bashing the padlock. After the first few blows made no impact, she climbed onto the stump, held the rock as high as she could, then dropped it. It hit the padlock squarely but made only a small impression. However, the rock bounced and hit the chain some distance from the padlock.

Jumping down, Terri studied the damage done to the chain and realized it might be easier to break.

If I am going to break the chain, I might as well do that as close to me as possible.

Sitting cross-legged, she got as close to the flat rock as she could. Placing the chain on it, she started to hammer.

Two hours later, her nails broken and dirty and her knuckles grazed, but one of the links looked like it was about to give. She tugged at it; it held fast. She realized that it would soon be dark; she needed to get this done before it became impossible to see, and she needed to light a fire. With all her strength, and the desperation of her situation giving her incentive, she lifted the rock one more time and dropped it on the chain. It bounced off and hit her square in the knee, slicing the skin and bringing tears to her eyes. She wiped away the tears and inspected the gash on her knee.

More precious water will be needed to clean that out.

She staggered to her feet, and the chain dangled against her injured knee, adding to the pain. Suddenly, she realized the chain was swinging back and forth against her leg. It had broken. One minor victory!

She built a small fire a few feet from the tent. And before it became too dark to see, she finished the beans she had opened earlier and washed out the can in the lake. She half filled it with water from the bottle she had opened earlier and, by the light of the fire, managed to clean out her knee, using the hem of her T-shirt. Sipping on the rest of the bottle of water, she sat staring into the flames, wondering what was going to happen to her. She had to keep positive. Had to believe they would rescue her, and she had to keep busy trying to help that effort. She finished the last of the water and crawled into her sleeping bag.

Next morning, Terri had difficulty getting out of her sleeping bag. She realized that the wound on her knee had stuck to the inside of the bag. Reaching across, she got hold of a bottle of water. More precious water was used to damp down the fabric to release her.

I am going to have to figure out a way to bandage that knee.

Without a knife or scissors, it would be impossible to cut a bandage and she was fairly sure she could not tear her T-shirt. She tried pulling at the hem with her teeth, but that just hurt her and made her head throb again. Taking one mouthful from the bottle, she screwed the cap back on, placing it carefully to one side.

With some difficulty, she hobbled down to the shoreline. It was early morning and there was not a soul on the lake. Although the weather was no longer the baking hot Texas summer, it was still reasonably mild. She stripped off, leaving her clothes in a neat pile on a rock, and stepped into the water. At least she could attempt to keep herself clean, and it was very refreshing. She stared across the lake at the high canyon walls opposite. Houses peeked out from trees along the top of the cliff. She wondered if the people in those houses could see as far as this. She knew that lots of people along the lake had telescopes; they seemed to have a fascination with studying the opposite shore. She remembered her idea of putting a message on the shore.

If I build a message with rocks along the shore, they might just see it.

As soon as that thought occurred to her, she climbed out of the water. Looking around, she realized she hadn't considered how she would dry herself. Grabbing her T-shirt, she got halfway dry and then she got dressed. The T-shirt would dry on the bushes. Her knee was bleeding again, so she took one of her socks. Pulling the string from the hood of her sweatshirt, she tied the sock around her knee. She could put the sock back on once the wound had dried up. At least this way, it won't stick to the sleeping bag.

She spent the rest of the day gathering rocks and building the word HELP! As big as the space along the shore would allow, taking care to have it facing towards the canyon across the lake.

As the sun went down, she dragged herself back to the tent. Too tired and too miserable to bother lighting a fire or getting something to eat, she climbed into her sleeping bag and cried herself to sleep.

CHAPTER THIRTY

Caitlin turned on the TV to catch the evening news. They had spent most of the day at the lake house, questioning the contractors who said they saw nothing. Searching in the wooded area for any clues and down at the marina questioning anyone there. No one had seen anything suspicious. One man told Joe that he had seen a canoe tied up to his dock two nights ago, but it was gone the next day.

"Kids think they can do whatever they like," he said.

They sat in front of the TV with their Chinese delivery. None of them had time or interest to cook. Once again, there was a report on Terri's disappearance, the fact that there were no new developments, and they showed the photo of the car again, asking for any information. George had been in touch with the police and they confirmed that no one had come forward yet.

"You know what?" Caitlin said. "We should offer a reward for any information that leads us to the car."

"You'll have all sorts of cranks coming out of the woodwork if you do that," George said.

"But if just one of those cranks has information that would help, it would be worth all the trouble of sifting through them."

"It's worth a try," Joe said. "I'm prepared to try anything at this stage. However distressed I am, I keep thinking about poor Terri…" His voice trailed off as his eyes filled with tears. He stood up quickly, putting his plate in the kitchen.

"How much were you thinking to offer? And what conditions?"

George asked.

"Let's say—$200 for information that proves to be valid and helpful. With an extra $2,000 if it leads to capturing Keith or freeing Terri."

"Okay, that might work. I'll give Jim a call." George pulled out his phone.

When he hung up, he said, "they are going to announce a reward at tomorrow's update, but we will have to go through all the tips. He assured me there would be hundreds and they don't have the resources to follow up on all of them. He wants us to do the sorting and then pass any possibilities to them."

"That works for me. It'll give us something concrete to do, instead of sitting here doing nothing," Caitlin said, and Joe nodded his agreement.

"They'll give a phone number to report to. A hot-line if you will, they'll gather all the tips and email them to me," George said.

Next morning, Caitlin was up early, ready to go through anything that might come in on the tip line. She had set up the dining room table as their control center. Three legal pads and a bunch of pens set out with two water bottles and a glass by each of the pads.

George took one look and shook his head, trying not to smile. "That's my Caitlin. Organized and on the job." He hugged her. "We'll find her, I promise."

Caitlin sniffed and blinked hard. "We will."

For the rest of the day, the three of them sat around the table sifting through hundreds of tips; claimed sightings of the car, some were worth following up, but most were of no use. *Spotted driving south on I-35* could have been true, but not useful, especially when it was followed up with—*on Friday or Saturday of last week.*

Whenever a tip appeared to be in any way helpful, they spent time on the phone talking to the people to gather as much information as they could.

"This one looks worth following up on." Joe held up a sheet of paper. "Someone reported seeing the car parked at their neighbor's private boat launch. Later, they saw a canoe tied up to the same neighbor's dock. Apparently, the neighbor is only there on weekends."

"Definitely, that sounds promising," George agreed.

"There is one here that might be useful," Caitlin said. "The security at a sports and outdoors store reported that the car showed up on their video. They sent a screen shot. Looks like the same car to me." She passed the picture over to George, who nodded his agreement.

"We should go talk to them. I'll add them to our list for tomorrow," Joe said, making a note on his pad. He already had a note to follow up with a major supermarket. One woman had reported seeing a man load two large cartons of canned foods into the trunk of that car. She noticed him because as he lifted one of the cartons out of the cart, it started moving across the car park. The woman had stopped the cart and held it for him as he emptied it. She noticed he had two cases of bottled water in the trunk of his car as well. They had an appointment to look at the store's video records.

"Here's another one worth adding to the list," George said. "Wood—firewood, to be exact. This guy was selling firewood on the side of the road. A man in a similar car bought all of his wood, filled the trunk and the back seat with it."

George kept in touch with Jim, his contact at the local police station, giving him details of the tips they felt were worth following up on. They arranged to meet the following afternoon to discuss next steps.

After spending another morning going through a fresh list of tips, Joe stood up and stretched.

"I have to head home and get some fresh clothes. Is it okay with you guys if I come back here till we get Terri back?"

"Of course, that just makes sense," Caitlin said, and George nodded his agreement.

"I'll drop into the office too and make sure nothing needs our immediate attention," he said to George.

"Do you need me to come into the office?"

"No, I need you here working with the police. Thank goodness you used to be a cop and they trust you to work with them! I'll let Phil know what we're doing and that, unless he absolutely needs one or both of us, we are off the grid until further notice. I'm sure he and Alex can handle anything that comes up."

"Thanks, man," George said.

"See you this evening." Joe headed for the front door.

Caitlin and George grabbed a sandwich before heading to the police station to meet with Jim. They waited in a small conference room and as soon as he joined them, the three of them went through the list of tips they had decided were worth following up on.

They agreed there was no more information to be had from the firewood seller. But both the stores were good leads, if they had video that showed details, and if any of their associates could remember serving Keith. Jim told George to go ahead and follow up with them.

CHAPTER THIRTY-ONE

The first place they called to was the sports and outdoors. It was a huge store, in a sprawling outdoor shopping mall. Jim had called ahead and told the manager to expect them. As soon as they arrived, he came out to meet them. Shaking hands and expressing his sympathy for their problems.

"I really hope we can be of some help. Follow me." He led them to the section of the store where all the camping gear was.

"This is Sandra. She remembers serving the man we saw driving that car. You can give her the reward."

Sandra was a tiny girl, mid-twenties with long blonde hair in a loose ponytail.

"Hi Sandra. What can you remember about him?" George asked.

"Well, for one thing he looked like he might be homeless, you know? Very scruffy and not very clean. He bought a tent, a sleeping bag and a fifteen-foot chain and two padlocks. What was unusual was that he paid for it with cash. It was a lot of money and he had a huge wad." She smiled. "That was hard to forget. Most people pay with plastic for stuff that expensive."

"Anything else?"

"I asked him if he was planning to go camping—I mean, he must have been, but I was just trying to make pleasant conversation. He just grunted and didn't answer. So I didn't say anything else."

"Thanks Sandra." George handed over $200.

Sandra thanked him and tucked the cash into the back pocket of her jeans.

Their next stop was the grocery store. It was a massive discount place fairly close to the first store. Once again, Jim had prepared the ground for them and the manager brought them into his office. They all sat down around his desk while he played the videotape. They could clearly see the car. It was definitely the same one that they had seen on their own tape. As they watched, a man wheeled a large cart piled high with cartons.

"That's Keith!" Caitlin gasped under her breath. "He definitely looks scruffy and dirty, but it's him."

George squeezed her hand. They continued to watch. As he started loading the cartons into his trunk, the cart began to roll away from him. A woman ran forward and caught the cart and pulled it back to him. He finished loading the trunk, took the cart and pushed it into a bay beside his car, climbed in and drove off.

"Does anyone remember serving him?" George asked. "I mean, someone might remember him buying so many cans?"

"Yes, actually, I will get Heather in here." He left the office and returned a few minutes later with a plump, middle-aged woman.

"Hi Heather." George stood up. "I understand you remember serving that guy." He nodded towards the screen. The manager rewound and paused at the shot of Keith loading the car.

"Yes, I do remember. He had two large cardboard boxes filled with cans of soup, beans and sardines—and some boxes of crackers. He had to replace some of the cans of soup because they were not pull-tab. He said he didn't want to be bothered with a can opener. He also bought two large cases of bottles of water."

"Thanks Heather. That is very helpful."

Although the tip didn't come from her originally, but from the woman who had stopped the cart from rolling, Caitlin gave her $200 for the information. She thanked them and left the office, looking very pleased with herself.

They thanked the manager and headed out of the store. They would make sure the original tipster got her payment, too.

That evening, over another take out dinner, George and Caitlin told Joe what they had found out so far.

"I think it is obvious he was setting up camp somewhere and stocking up for a long stay. Was that for himself, or Terri, or both?

Caitlin's Escape Route

After all, he said in his letter that he would be long gone, but perhaps that was just to confuse the issue," Joe said.

"No, I believe he stashed Terri somewhere with all those supplies, but how could he be sure she wouldn't escape? And where? I know there are quite a few isolated spots around here, up in the hills, but he couldn't be sure someone wouldn't stumble across her. Or hear her if she yelled," George said.

Caitlin was quiet, her face was creased with worry. She couldn't shift the leaden weight pressing against her chest. George looked at her. "What do you think, Cait?"

She took a deep breath. "I've no idea—I believe he's gone. It's the sort of thing he'd do. He thinks I can get the money, and he knows I would if I could. I would do anything to keep Terri safe. I'm worried about the padlocks and chain. It's terrifying to imagine what he wanted them for. And how's she managing in all this rain?"

"Well, we know he bought a tent and a sleeping bag, so presumably she has some cover," George said. "And we all know that she's tough and resourceful."

"Yes—but she's on her own! Totally alone!"

"Do we have any other tips to follow up on? I feel I've left all the legwork to you two today," Joe said. "Let's keep working towards finding her. We can't give up."

Caitlin stared at him for a moment, then she took another deep breath. "You're right, of course, Joe. Sorry."

"It's okay Caitlin. I understand." Joe leaned across and squeezed her hand.

"I haven't looked since this morning. Let me check." George headed to the computer, the other two followed him. He logged in and opened up his email, spending a few minutes scrolling through it. "Not much worth following up on here—wait a minute. This looks interesting!"

"What is it?" Joe stepped forward, peering over his shoulder.

Caitlin watched them from the armchair she had collapsed into.

"Some guy in El Paso. Apparently, he sold that car to Keith last month, and he spotted him in El Paso today!" George grabbed his phone.

"Hey Jim! I think we might have a solid lead to Keith's whereabouts—Yeah, El Paso. Someone spotted him there today—Great, thanks."

"Jim's going to alert the police in El Paso. But looks like you were right, Cait. He did leave. Stupid fool obviously has no idea how trust funds work. Apart from the fact that he's no way entitled to any of it."

George turned back to the computer with more enthusiasm and continued going through the reported tips.

"This one might be worth following up."

"What is it?" Joe asked.

"Someone reported seeing a man pitch a tent on a piece of private property. The land has been for sale for some time."

"Let's go look at that tomorrow. It's too late now. We wouldn't be able to see anything," Caitlin said.

As soon as they had breakfast the following morning, they headed to the location the two young men who had called in the tip had given them. They said the land had been for sale for some time and they had been fishing along the shoreline when they spotted a man pitching a tent among the trees.

They parked the car up on the grass verge and made their way across the rough, overgrown ground to the lake shore. Once there, they walked along the shore towards a clump of trees. Immediately, Caitlin spotted something blue.

"Look, there." She pointed. "Looks like a blue tent."

It wasn't possible to hurry across to it; the ground was uneven and littered with rocks and chunks of wood. When they got closer, it was obvious that it wasn't a tent; it was a tarpaulin, draped from a branch. There had been no attempt made to make it a shelter of any sort. Perhaps it had originally been set up as a tent, but there was nothing tying it down and the wind had blown it almost off the branch.

As they stood there looking at it, a couple of men approached them from the road.

"Can we help you?" the older one said.

George introduced himself and explained who they were and what they were doing there.

"Someone's pulling a fast one on you. We chased a couple of young guys off here yesterday. My guess is they came back later and hung that tarp up. Trying to make a fast buck, no doubt."

"I'm afraid you are right. That's always the problem when a reward is offered. We knew it would be an issue. Sorry, didn't mean to trespass."

"No worries, sorry you wasted your time."

CHAPTER THIRTY-TWO

Terri decided that she would start walking along the shore. Perhaps she could find a roadway and make her way to civilization. Keith had said she was in a very isolated area, perhaps it was a large ranch, or one of those huge areas that used to be ranch land and was now waiting for developers to purchase it. Either way, it must be possible to find a way out of it.

With no way to carry food, she decided to just bring two bottles of water. If she walked slowly and rationed the water, it should last her a couple of days. Surely that would be enough time to make it to somewhere near people.

At one point, the opposite shore was so close she thought she could almost throw a stone and hit the steep, rocky wall. There was a narrow strip of land jutting out into the lake from below the cliff. Then the shore curved sharply to the right, and continued to do so for about twenty minutes.

It must be some sort of peninsula. He stuck me at the very end.

She continued walking, following the water's edge as it once again curved to the right. She had been walking for at least forty minutes when it dawned on her.

It's an island! There's my sign on the shore up ahead. It must be one of those islands that appears when the lake level drops.

She dropped to her knees and let out a yelp as her wounded knee hit a rock. Then she lay down on the rocky ground. For what seemed like a very long time, she sobbed with complete abandon. It was just

Caitlin's Escape Route

too much to deal with.

She felt too weak to even move, and not caring what happened to her, a movement close to her face caused her to sit up and focus. A large spider was heading directly to where her face had been a few seconds earlier. The fright was enough to give her the energy to jump to her feet.

Dammit, I won't give in. I won't let Keith win! Caitlin and Joe are looking for me. I have to do something to help them.

She attempted to run to the tent, but the injury to her knee made that impossible. Instead, she hobbled as fast as she could. She started carrying wood from the pile behind the tent down to the shore. Building another, bigger HELP out of the wood. By the time she had completed it, she needed to go to the toilet. She hurried back to the tent, grabbed the trowel and a roll of toilet paper and found a spot behind the tent where she could dig a hole in the ground. As she was digging, she hit something metal. Scratching around, she uncovered a rusty old pocket knife. Putting it to one side, she completed her rudimentary toilet, filled in the hole and carried the toilet paper, trowel and the pocket knife back to the tent. Nothing she did would get the pocket knife to open, so she took it down to the lake and washed it, getting rid of a lot of the dirt and grit. Still, she couldn't shift the blades.

Back at the tent, she opened a can of sardines and poured some of the oil over the knife, working it into the cracks with a twig. Every so often, she tapped it against a rock, and more dirt and rust fell off. Finally, she forced one of the blades open. Another drop of sardine oil and more massaging with twigs, and she had a second, smaller blade open plus two small screwdrivers. As she admired her find, not yet sure what use it would be, she realized that daylight was fading and hurried down to light her help sign.

Once the wood was blazing, she headed back to the tent, sitting outside watching it, eating the sardines she had opened for the oil, with a couple of crackers and half a bottle of water. A flash of lightning over the lake, followed by a loud clap of thunder, caused her to jump up and move into the tent. Almost immediately the rain started, at first just a few drops and then a downpour.

No! This can't be happening.

The feeling of panic rose inside her as she watched the fire turning into bellowing smoke and finally even the smoke washed away. She crawled into her sleeping bag and cried herself to sleep.

When she woke up, it was already light. She lay still, thinking about the dream she had. She and Caitlin were children again, back on the garage roof. Watching the sun go down over the Atlantic Ocean, on the wild west coast of Ireland.

"I will not let Keith destroy me!" She shouted out loud as she struggled out of her sleeping bag. The rain was still beating down, she could hear it hammering on the tent. Luckily, it wasn't coming through. She opened the flap and the first thing she noticed was that the lake was rising. It had risen enough to almost cover the rocks she had used to write her message of help. She sighed.

I will not let Keith destroy me. He won't win.

With nothing else to do, she turned her attention to the pocket knife.

I wonder if I can use it to open the padlock on my waist.

She pulled at the padlock; the chain was not tight around her, there was just enough play to see the lock if she held it at a certain angle. Setting to work, she started poking the smaller of the two screwdrivers into the keyhole. She knew nothing about picking locks, but she had all day to learn and was determined not to give up. Every time she felt frustration or panic rise, she repeated her mantra.

I will not let Keith destroy me.

She worked on the padlock for the rest of the day, stopping briefly to eat a can of sardines, some crackers, and drink half a bottle of water. The rain continued to pour, and she was sure she could see the lake rising and getting closer to the tent. She was poking at the padlock without paying much attention, when it suddenly clicked and popped open. The rain eased, slowly reducing to a light mist. At last, something good was happening. Pulling the chain off her waist, she headed down to the lake edge to inspect her message. It was under a few inches of water already. Looking around, she found a piece of wood about two feet long. Using a rock, she hammered that into the ground at the water's edge. That would give her an idea of how fast the lake was rising. She knew it wasn't her imagination.

Then she gathered up the soaking wet remains of her fire and stacked that wood behind the tent, rebuilding her wooden HELP with dry wood from under the tarp. Setting the fire, she sat in the tent watching it burn. At least now it was growing dark. Perhaps it would attract more attention. Just so long as the rain held off.

Next morning the wood was just ashes moving around the shore in the breeze. There was no way to know if anyone had seen it.

Terri walked down to the water's edge to see if the lake had risen any during the night. Although the rain had held off, she knew run off would continue to seep into the lake. And it was obvious that it had. The post she had stuck in the ground had at least half an inch of water lapping around it. As she inspected it, she heard a motor in the distance. She looked up and spotted a worker barge heading up the lake. Taking off her sweatshirt, she stood on a rock, watching as the boat got closer. She started waving her shirt over her head frantically, yelling "Help". She was fairly sure they couldn't hear her over the motor. It was very noisy, but there was no way she was not going to yell. As the boat got closer, one of the men onboard waved back at her. But they kept moving forward without paying her any further attention.

She jumped down from the rock, put her sweatshirt back on, fighting the feeling of panic once again rising inside her chest.

I will not let Keith destroy me.

She repeated over and over again as she headed back to the tent.

CHAPTER THIRTY-THREE

The following morning, they plowed through another round of tips. Once again, most of them were useless.

"Look at this one!" The excitement in George's voice gives Caitlin a moment of hope.

"What is it?" she said.

"Two kids sent in a photo. The car is in the background. It's definitely the same car. They say it was parked at the back of their trailer park."

"Let's go over there right now and check on it." Joe stood up. "I can't just sit here another day going through these tips. If I don't do something, I'll go mad."

"I agree. I feel the same." Caitlin stood up, too.

George grabbed his keys. "It's only a few miles from here. Let's go."

They pulled off the main road, on to a dirt road leading up the gently sloping hillside. There was what looked like an office just inside the entrance. They parked beside it and George knocked on the door. There was no answer, so they started walking deeper into the park. There were probably about a hundred homes spread across the hillside, but most were tucked into clumps of cedar, so not visible from the road, nor from each other; giving an illusion of privacy.

At some point, an area in the middle of the park had been cleared to create a rough recreation area with a basketball hoop. A few teenagers were shooting hoops there. George headed for them, with

Caitlin and Joe at his heels.

"Hi guys, I'm looking for Kyle," George said.

One kid stepped forward. "I'm Kyle. What do you want?"

"Hey Kyle." George stuck out his hand. "I wanted to talk to you about the tip you called in to the TV station."

"Oh, with the reward?" Kyle said with a wide grin, shaking George's hand.

"That's the one. We were hoping you could answer some questions."

"Where's the money?"

"We have it, and we'll give it to you if you can answer our questions. The reward was offered for tips that are helpful. Yours sounds like it's going to be very helpful, but we need some more information."

"Okay, what do you want to know?"

"How long has the car been parked around here, and can you show us exactly where?"

"Sure, follow me." Kyle turned and headed up the hill. "It was there for about a week, on and off," he said, pointing to a trailer that was clearly abandoned. "Beside that old trailer, we saw him go in and out a few times, so we know he was squatting there."

"Who owns it?"

"No one. It's been empty for years. When we were kids, we used to use it as a clubhouse."

"So, it's not locked?"

"Oh no, anyone can go in." Kyle pulled open the door of the trailer.

George and Joe stepped inside. Caitlin stood at the doorway, her nose wrinkled up at the stench.

"Ugh," she said. "It stinks!"

Kyle laughed. "That's the toilet. It doesn't work anymore. I guess that guy was using it, anyway."

"Well, I guess we owe you $200, Kyle. Thanks for phoning in the tip."

"What about the $2000?"

We'll pay that if any of the tips lead us to the man who was here.

Kyle's face turned red. "Well, actually, I checked in there already—after the TV report—I found this." He handed over a cell phone. "It was on the floor in the bedroom."

"Man, that is very useful! Thank you! That puts you at the top of the list for that big reward." George managed to hide his irritation.

Caitlin counted out $200 into Kyle's outstretched hand. "We'll be back with the big prize if this tip pans out. Thanks so much."

"Thank you, ma'am," Kyle responded, looking pleased with himself.

As soon as they were back in the car, Joe said, "the little shit was going to keep that phone and say nothing! Good call there George."

"Let's get this phone to Jim. This could be the breakthrough we were looking for. They can track Keith's movements via the GPS. It's a pity any fingerprints have been compromised, but we already know it was Keith who abducted Terri from the letter, so no harm there."

"You think they can figure out where she is from GPS?" Caitlin was so excited her voice came out as a squeak.

"Absolutely, they can. If he had the phone on him when he took her."

As they hurried into the police station, Jim got up from his desk behind the counter and came forward.

"Hi George. Y'all look excited—something good?"

"I think so." George handed over the phone. "We got a tip that Keith was using an abandoned trailer at the Hillview Trailer Park. When we followed up on it just now, the kid who called it in said he found this phone in the trailer after Keith had left."

"No kidding! That's maybe the breakthrough we need." Jim took the phone, stuck it in an evidence bag and labeled it.

"I'll get this off to forensics and as soon as we hear back I'll let you know."

By the time they got home, Caitlin started to come down from the high she was feeling. She let out a long sigh as she climbed out of the car.

"What's up sweetie?" George asked.

"I'm not sure. I've been so stressed out since Terri went missing, suddenly that phone seemed like something huge. But she's still missing. Now I just feel deflated."

"It's great news Caitlin, really it is," Joe said. "I know exactly what you mean, but it's the first real clue we've got, and it's a big one. That phone's as good as a treasure map with a big X in the middle. We will find her."

"Joe's right. Remember, Keith said we had two weeks to find her. The food and water he bought at that supermarket was enough to last one person two weeks. We know he's not with her because someone reported seeing him in El Paso. We will find her!" George put his arms around her and hugged her. "And one good thing is that he's not with her. At least that is something to be glad about. Come on, let's clean up and go out to eat. We should be celebrating."

Dinner wasn't exactly a celebration. They were all still worried about Terri. George managed to lighten the atmosphere by getting them talking about next steps.

"Okay," he said. "We believe that the phone's going to be the lead we need to point us to where Terri's being held. But we can't just sit back and wait. We need to keep looking ourselves. We will continue to follow up on any tips, but let's figure out a plan of action. If only to keep us from going crazy."

"I agree. Let's do it," Joe said.

Caitlin nodded. She didn't feel like talking; she felt like screaming and breaking something. It was all she could do to sit quietly and listen. But she knew that George was right. They had to keep moving and stay positive.

"Cait, you knew Keith. Think about what you know of him. What do you think he would have done with Terri?"

"Nothing I know about him would help. He is book smart. He did well at college, but he's stupid. I guess he's just very self-centered. Everything's always about him. But he doesn't really plan ahead. So whatever he does, it's sort of spur of the moment."

"Let's approach it from another angle," Joe suggested. "We know he rented a canoe for a week but returned it after five days. We know he bought cans of food, bottles of water, a tent and a sleeping bag. Presumably the canoe was to transport all this stuff somewhere, so we can be fairly confident it is on the lake—I wonder why he wouldn't rent a boat rather than a canoe?"

"Easier to hide a canoe?" George suggested.

"Yeah, that's a good reason. And also, it's easy to transport a canoe overland if he needed to, I suppose."

Caitlin listened as the two men tried to figure out what happened. All she could think of was poor Terri, alone in some isolated wild spot, not knowing what was going on.

As they drove home, the weather forecast on the car radio reported heavy thunderstorms for their area, starting overnight or early the following morning.

"Oh, my God! That's all we need!" Caitlin said. "I can't believe this is happening."

They drove the rest of the way in silence.

"George," Caitlin called from the kitchen. "Your phone's ringing." She picked up the phone and met him at the door as he came running in.

"Hello. Hey Jim, tell me something good…Okay. Hang on, let me put you on speaker phone…Okay, go ahead."

"First, the El Paso police reported that they have located the car, abandoned down by the river. They found a man's body in the trunk. He had been bound and gagged and shot in the head, execution style." The dispassionate voice came out of the phone.

Caitlin's knees went weak, and she sat down on the nearest chair, staring at the phone with her mouth open and her hand to her neck.

"Was it Keith?" George said, as he sat down beside Caitlin, grasping her hand.

"They think so, but they are in touch with the SF police to verify fingerprints. We should know fairly soon for sure. Second, we have the GPS tracking information back on the phone."

"Okay, hopefully that's better news?"

"We can be confident that the phone belonged to the suspect. It was located at both the supermarket and the sports and outdoors store where he was known to have been. It also shows the canoe rental and the location where the canoe was reportedly tied up."

"Anything else?" George held his breath.

"Something odd. It looks like he spent two days out in the middle of the lake."

"On the lake? That's definitely odd."

"We have the co-ordinates and Texas Parks and Wildlife are going to follow up on it first thing in the morning. We should have more information once they report back."

"Thanks Jim, that is the most promising news we have had since Terri disappeared. Talk to you tomorrow!"

"Just one thing George."

"What's that?"

"There is a major storm forecast for the area. If it rolls in by morning, we'll have to wait till it passes before we can do any investigation on the lake."

Caitlin buried her face in her hands.

"Understood. Thanks, Jim." George disconnected the call with a sigh.

A loud crash woke Caitlin. She sat up in bed as the room lit up and another crash.

Damn it! I hope that storm rolls over fast!

It didn't. By morning, the rain was pouring down, and the wind was howling. To make matters worse, if that were possible, there was a Tornado Watch for the area. There would be no one on the lake today, not even the police.

Joe and George spent most of the day either on conference calls with the office or on their computers, attempting to get some work done. Caitlin tried to take care of housework, but she kept wandering to the window to stare out at the lake, willing the storm to pass. Eventually, she went into the kitchen and made a salad for lunch. Just as they sat down to eat, George's phone rang.

"Hi Jim—Yeah, we assumed nothing could be done today—Okay, good to know, thanks…Talk to you tomorrow."

"Anything?" Caitlin asked.

"Just confirming that the body was Keith's, as we assumed."

"Well, at least the asshole is dead, but that is not necessarily good, I suppose. Right now, he's the only person who knew for sure where Terri is. I hope they find her tomorrow!" Caitlin didn't feel hungry, but she picked at her salad, staring out the window at the rain.

The storm raged for the rest of the day. Thankfully, the Tornado Watch expired with no further expectations. Caitlin didn't even want to think about Terri somewhere out there, with only a tent for protection against the storm. The idea of a tornado was more than she could bear. When they went to bed that night, the rain was still coming down.

Caitlin was up early. The first thing she did was open the shades to see what the weather was doing. It had stopped raining. Although it was still dark, she could see stars, which meant the storm had passed. The gloom had lifted. Yesterday, it seemed to have not just filled the entire world, but it felt like it had seeped into her body and taken over her mind.

George came into the kitchen as she was about to pour the coffee.

"The storm has passed. They'll be on the lake as soon as it's light. They'll find her." He put his arms around her and held her close.

"Oh, I do hope so. I can't stand another day of this. Poor Joe, too. I know it must be killing him not knowing where, or how, she is." She poured them both coffee. "How are things at the office?"

"All quiet, we caught up with a few things yesterday and had a quick call with Phil last night. He told us to just concentrate on getting Terri back. He's taking care of work, with help from Alex. Thankfully, business is slow at the moment."

The morning dragged on. They drank coffee and stared out at the lake or at George's phone, almost willing it to ring. Suddenly, Caitlin jumped to her feet and ran to the back window.

"What's up?" George said.

"Shh—I hear a boat."

The two men joined her at the window.

"There. It's the Game Warden!" She pointed to the gray boat as it sped past, a large wake washing towards the shore behind it. "We should hear soon!" She felt a swelling inside her, as though her heart was trying to burst out of her chest and chase after the boat. "Oh, I can't stand this waiting. I am going to go have a shower." She ran out of the kitchen, leaving the two men still watching as the boat disappeared around a bend.

George picked up his phone again and set the volume to its highest level. He didn't want to miss Jim's call.

CHAPTER THIRTY-FOUR

Terri sat just inside the tent and watched the rain pour down.

I used to love watching storms. I doubt I ever will again—if I survive this.

From where she was sitting, she could see the stick that she had used to mark the water's edge. The lake was already lapping around it. She wasn't sure how fast the lake could fill, nor how quickly this tiny island could disappear. All she could do was sit and wait.

No! I refuse to give up. I won't let Keith win!

As soon as the rain eased, she went around to the woodpile and started sorting the wood. All the longer thin pieces she could find, she carried around and stacked in front of the tent. She stood there studying them for a few seconds, before ducking into the tent and pulling the chain out of the box she had dumped it into when she had opened the padlock. It was fairly short, definitely not long enough for her purposes. She headed over to the tree stump and, grabbing the rock she had used to break the chain before. She started hammering on the end closest to the battered but still closed padlock. It didn't take as long this time to break it. Dragging it back to the tent, she placed it beside the wood. Then she sat down again and stared at the wood and two pieces of chain, moving them around like pieces of a jigsaw puzzle.

Lining up the strips of wood, she started wrapping the chain around each piece, attempting to tie them together to form a raft. The problem was there was no way to hold the chain in place. If only she had a rope, it would be easier. Standing up, she studied the guyline ropes. Perhaps they would work, but then she wouldn't have a tent. But if she could make a raft that worked, she wouldn't need a tent. As she sat back down, she spotted the laces in her sneakers; they were high-tops, so the laces were long. That might work! As she untied her shoes, she noticed the stack of empty water bottles at the back of the tent.

The rain started again, and a bolt of lightning flashed almost overhead, causing her to drag her project into the tent. For the next hour, as the storm raged around her, she worked to tie the chains in place using her laces, placing the plastic water bottles between the wood for extra flotation. When she finally felt satisfied that she had done her best, darkness had already fallen, and the rain continued to pour. Assuming the rain stopped by morning, she would drag the raft down to the water and test if it would float. It was small, but big enough for her to sit on—if it floated.

Terri stared at the sunrise. The one good thing about thunderstorms is that when they pass, the sky was always beautiful. The rain had stopped, and the lake level was still rising. She dragged her raft down to the water and slowly edged it into the lake. She definitely didn't want to let go, and risk losing it, but she also didn't want to end up being dragged out into deeper water until she was sure it would not sink. Once she felt confident it would float, she planned to drag it to the section of the island closest to the shore. She definitely didn't want to spend any longer on it than necessary. Besides, she doubted she could cover much distance before she ran out of strength to paddle, especially given she didn't actually have a paddle and would have to use a piece of wood. She had found a piece that was thin at one end and widened at the other, more like a cricket bat than a paddle, but hopefully it would work.

Pulling her jeans off, she waded out up to her waist; the water was definitely much colder than it had been a few days earlier, but the raft did float. Dragging it alongside her, she moved a little way along the shoreline, then she pulled it onto dry land. Her next task was going to be difficult. Dragging it all the way to the other side of the island. She headed back to her tent to get something to eat and drink, and ponder on how best to achieve that feat.

As she ate, she studied the guylines holding the tent in place. If she was going to leave the island on her raft, she wouldn't need the tent anymore. She got out the rusty old pocket knife, found a flat rock, and started sharpening the larger blade. Stopping every few minutes to test it, she was finally satisfied. And it did actually cut the first guyline, albeit with some difficulty. The second one took even longer, but it was going to be worth it. She could tie one to the raft and pull it through the water while she walked along the shore. That would definitely make it easier. With the second line, she planned to tie the paddle to the raft. The last thing she needed was to lose the paddle halfway across the lake. And now that she had cut the guylines and the tent was partially collapsed, she had no choice. She was totally committed to attempting her escape.

I hope I don't drown in the attempt. But I just can't stay here doing nothing!

Dragging the raft was a lot harder than she expected, partly because, without the laces in her sneakers, walking on the rocky shoreline was not easy. She stopped frequently to take a sip of water from one of the two bottles she had brought and look back to see how much ground she had covered.

At this rate, it will be dark before I get there!

The thought gave her the surge of determination she needed, and she started pulling harder. Just as she approached the curve of the shoreline that she knew would bring her closest to the opposite shore, she heard a boat engine. She got so excited she almost dropped the rope. Quickly, she tied it around her ankle and took off her sweatshirt, waving it frantically in the air, yelling as loud as she could.

"Over here! HELP!"

Of course the sound of the engine drowned out her yells, but she couldn't not try. The sound got closer and eventually she could make out the sign on the side of the boat: Texas Game Warden. She could feel her heart beating faster.

Surely they are here looking for me! Oh, please let them see me!

She started waving more frantically and jumping up and down, screaming as loudly as she could. The boat kept coming closer until she could see the uniformed men on board. One of them had binoculars and appeared to be looking straight at her through them.

Then he lowered his binoculars and waved at her. The engine noise suddenly stopped.

"Hello! Are you Terri Donnelly?" He yelled.

"Yes. Yes! Please save me!" She continued to jump up and down and wave her shirt. Even though they could clearly see her and were pulling into the shore, she couldn't stop. She was afraid if she stopped, they would disappear like a mirage.

As the boat came to a stop a few feet away from her, her knees gave way and she dropped to the ground, sobbing and gasping. One of the men jumped off the boat and came towards her. He had a blanket over his shoulder. He bent down and gently lifted her to her feet. Keeping an arm around her waist to support her, he wrapped the blanket around her.

"You are safe now. We are going to take you home," he said.

She took a deep breath, attempting to speak, but all that came out was a squeak.

"It's okay. Just relax. Don't try to speak."

"I have to untie the raft," she managed to say, pointing to the rope tied to her ankle.

The man grinned and, bending down, he untied the rope and pulled the raft out of the water.

"Did you make this?"

She nodded.

"That's amazing!" He pulled out his phone and took a photo of it before leading her towards the boat.

His partner lent over the ladder and pulled her on board. As soon as they were all seated, one of the men got on the radio and reported that they had located the victim alive, with what appear to be only minor injuries. They were heading back to the dock and requested an ambulance.

"What do you need an ambulance for?" Terri asked them.

"It is pretty standard procedure. You have a head injury, and while you appear to have taken care of the knee, it looks quite nasty. Both should be checked out."

As they pulled into the dock, Terri thanked the men yet again for saving her.

CHAPTER THIRTY-FIVE

Although all three of them had been waiting anxiously for George's phone to ring, as soon as it did, they all jumped. George nearly knocked the phone off the table as he grabbed at it.

As he answered, he hit speaker phone. "Jim? Tell me it's good news!" he said, as they all stood up.

Caitlin grabbed Joe's arm.

"The best news! The guys found Terri alive on a tiny island on the lake. You know, one of those islands that appears when the water level drops. She is in an ambulance heading for Seton Hospital."

"Hospital? Is she hurt?" Caitlin said.

"She has a couple of minor injuries, nothing serious. Just the standard precaution. I'll meet you there."

"Thanks, Jim. We're on our way."

As George and Caitlin got into George's car, Joe headed for his own.

"Why not all go in mine?" George said.

"I plan to stay there until they discharge her. I'm not letting her out of my sight again," Joe said.

"I guess I can understand that," George said, as they drove off behind Joe, who had practically squealed out of the driveway, wheels spinning.

When they got to the hospital, Terri was being admitted. They asked Caitlin to fill in paperwork as next of kin, Jim came looking for George and they huddled in one corner, while Joe walked up and down, every so often sticking his head out to see if anyone was coming to get them. Caitlin finished the paperwork and got up just as the nurse came in to get them.

"She can have two visitors," she said, looking from one to the other.

"You two go ahead," George said.

"Please follow me."

Joe and Caitlin followed her down the corridor and into a private room. Caitlin stood at the end of the bed and started crying while Joe rushed over to Terri and threw his arms around her.

"I thought I would never see you again," he said, wiping his eyes, sitting on the edge of the bed, looking at her. "They said minor injuries—where are you hurt? What did he do to you?"

"My head. He slammed me against a tree and knocked me out. The other injury is a cut on my knee. I did that one myself." She looked at Caitlin. "Cait, stop crying. I'm fine, really."

Caitlin wiped her eyes and took a deep breath. "I'm just so happy to see you. I've been holding those tears in for so long I couldn't stop them. Thank God you're okay!" She rushed over to the other side of the bed and hugged her sister.

"I'm just sorry I didn't listen to you. You were right, of course. He came looking for me. He was hiding in the trees when I came out of the lake house."

"Well, he won't ever hurt you again."

"What do you mean?"

"They didn't tell you?"

"Who?"

"The police."

"The only police I have spoken to were the guys on the boat who rescued me. I guess I've to give a statement to the local police. They're sending someone to take it."

Joe caught Caitlin's eye, and she nodded.

He took Terri's hands in his. "Keith's dead, Terri. After he left you on that island, he sent a ransom note to Caitlin and then drove to El Paso. The police there found his body in the trunk of his car. Gunshot to the head."

Terri looked at him, her eyes big and her mouth opened and closed a few times, but she made no sound. She shook her head as though her brain had stopped functioning and she needed to kick start it.

"Dead—gunshot—" She lay back on the pillow for a moment and

stared at the ceiling.

Caitlin watched her silently.

Then she sat up and said, "I'm trying to feel sorry for him, but I can't. I'm just glad I never have to see him again."

Just then, George stuck his head around the door.

"I thought only two visitors were allowed?" Caitlin said.

"I am here on official business." George grinned. "Well, not really, just coming to tell you that your time is up. Jim needs to get a statement from Terri, then you can come back in after that."

Joe kissed Terri. "I'll be right outside and will be back as soon as Jim's done."

Caitlin nodded.

As Jim came in, they followed George back to the waiting room.

It was almost dinner time when George and Caitlin left the hospital. Joe refused to budge. He insisted he was going to sleep in the chair beside Terri's bed. There was some discussion between him, the nurses, and Jim. Terri said she wouldn't stay without him. They agreed he could stay. She was so glad he did.

Within an hour of dropping off to sleep, Terri woke with a nightmare. She was back on the island and the water was rising. After the third time, Joe lay down on the bed beside her and she slept quietly for the rest of the night, wrapped in his arms.

Just as Terri and Joe were finishing breakfast, Caitlin arrived with a backpack.

"How're you feeling this morning?" she asked her sister, as she put the bag into the closet. "I brought you clean clothes and some toiletries." She nodded towards the closet.

"Thanks! That's great. Did you think of shoes?"

"Everything you might need is in there. I'm assuming they'll send you home today. You two should come over to us at least till tomorrow. Joe has been staying with us since—you went missing, so will have to pick up his things, anyway."

Terri grinned. "Absolutely. We can have a celebratory dinner together. The nurse said that the doctor would be by to see me soon. He's doing his rounds. She expected him to say I could go."

"Great, I'll hang on till he gets here. Then I've to go give that Kyle kid his $2000 for finding the phone and not keeping it."

"He earned it. We would never have been able to locate her without

Caitlin's Escape Route

it," Joe said.

"I was just about to attempt to cross to the mainland on my raft when the cops arrived. It might have worked. Now, we'll never know."

"I'm glad you didn't have to find out, considering you can't swim."

"I know. I was terrified at the thought, but more terrified of being stuck on that island with the lake rising."

Just then, the doctor came in, Joe and Caitlin left to get some coffee while he examined Terri, and he was gone by the time they returned.

"Well?" Caitlin said.

"All good. I'm free to go."

"Terrific. I'll see you guys back at the house. By the way, George said to tell you he has gone into the office for a few hours."

"Good for him. We'll get back to normal next week," Joe said.

Dinner was a very happy celebration. Caitlin kept looking at her sister as though she expected her to disappear at any moment. She couldn't believe she was back and safe. Better yet, they didn't have to worry about Keith ever again bothering them.

Joe and George cleared the table, and the two sisters sat together on the couch.

"Let's see if they mention you on the news," Caitlin said, switching on the TV.

As the two men joined them, the news anchor announced the rescue of kidnapped Terry Donnelly. Then a video of the island came on. The lake level had risen in the last three days and almost reached the tent. Terri watched as though they were playing a video of her nightmare. Then the camera panned out to show the distance to the opposite lake shore. There on the point jutting out from the cliff, the point Terri was going to attempt to reach, the raft was half out of the water, resting on the rocky shore.

"Look!" Terri jumped to her feet. "My raft! It made it across the lake! It worked!"

Then, they interviewed the game warden who had rescued her. He showed the photo he had taken of the raft and explained that she had built it out of firewood, the chain that had originally tied her to a tree stump, empty water bottles, and her shoelaces.

"No doubt the TV station will look to interview you next, Terri," Caitlin said. "Will you talk to them?"

"Absolutely not. I'll write a book!"

Caitlin's Escape Route

* * *

ABOUT THE AUTHOR

Aideen was born in Dublin, Ireland. In 1994 she emigrated to America, having won a green card in the lottery. She now lives just outside Austin, Texas.
She worked as a Software Quality Assurance Engineering Manager until her retirement in May 2021.
Her first book, Peeling The Onion, a memoir, was published in 2013. Caitlin's Escape Route is her first novel, and she is currently working on the second novel in the series.
When she is not writing, she enjoys fishing or boating on Lake Travis.

Printed in Great Britain
by Amazon